HEIRS of

Oksana

by Susan K. Downs

and Susan May Warren

Oksana

ISBN 1-59310-349-2

Scripture quotations are taken from the King James Version of the Bible.

Scripture quotations are also taken from the HOLY BIBLE, NEW INTERNATIONAL VERSION®. NIV®. Copyright © 1973, 1978, 1984 by International Bible Society. Used by permission of Zondervan. All rights reserved.

For more information about Susan K. Downs and Susan May Warren, please access the authors' Web sites at the following Internet addresses:
www.susankdowns.com
www.susanmaywarren.com

Acquisitions and Editorial Director: Rebecca Germany
Editorial Consultant: Becky Durost Fish
Art Director: Jason Rovenstine
Layout Design: Anita Cook
Cover design by THE DESIGNWORKS GROUP

Published by Barbour Publishing, Inc., P.O. Box 719, Uhrichsville, Ohio 44683, www.barbourbooks.com

Our mission is to publish and distribute inspirational products offering exceptional value and biblical encouragement to the masses.

Member of the
Evangelical Christian
Publishers Association

Printed in the United States of America.
5 4 3 2 1

SUSAN K. DOWNS

God sets the lonely in families.
PSALM 68:6 NIV

Dedication:

To my nephews and niece, Robbie and Ryan Rohr and Barrett and Grace Guynn, who started out life as Sergei and Dimitry, Alexander and Natalia. I thank God for His magnificent Providence, which brought each one of you from such faraway places as the village of Pechory, in the Russian province of Pskov, and grafted you into our family tree. Though you are as American as they come now, never forget your roots. When you are old enough to read the "Heirs of Anton" series, I hope it instills a sense of pride in your heritage and inspires you to learn all you can about your birth country.

And, to my mother, Betty Classen Williams, who from my earliest memories relayed our Classen family history through pictures, heirlooms, and personal accounts. Thanks, Mom, for piquing my curiosity about the pioneer adventures of the real-life Anton—the namesake for this series' patriarch. More important than an appreciation for my ancestral roots, you showed me the way to the Father and introduced me to the Son. I'm forever grateful. No one could ask for a richer legacy!

SUSAN MAY WARREN

Dedication:
For your glory, Lord.

Acknowledgements:
How I long to have the faith of Abraham, or David, believing in God's promises and his sufficiency! But I can be such a fickle lamb, forgetting the care and leading of my shepherd, baaing in fear or even despair when the skies overhead turn dark. Such was the situation when I wrote *Oksana*. Overwhelmed by deadlines and the awesome task of writing this story—a story of faith and courage, a story about a man and a woman who began three generations of faith—I stared at the blinking cursor of the computer and baaed. Thankfully, God is not fickle or afraid. He is sufficient and has the right words for every writer. As I pulled my laptop onto my lap and began tapping, one verse hung in my mind: "You are my witnesses," declares the Lord, "any my servant who I have chosen, so that you may know and believe me and understand that I am he" (Isaiah 43:10 NIV). God *is* who He says He is—my provider, my sustainer, my encourager. And, as *Oksana* poured out onto the page, I saw this verse come alive in my life. Never had a story emerged with such passion from my heart as this one did. Never had I sensed God's hand in writing more than in the birth of *Oksana*. Never did my faith grow as it did when I flung myself into God's hands and lived out Anton and Oksana's story—a story of trusting God, one step at a time, believing in his faithfulness to all generations (or, all chapters, as the case may be!).

I wish I could see ahead to my children's lives, to know

that they will walk in faith and that their lives will be fruitful for the Lord. But I can't—I can only put them into God's hands and walk faithfully today. Oksana and Anton's story has encouraged me that God is at work in this generation and the next. His faithfulness in my life has included the following people who have encouraged me on this journey:

Susan K. Downs, thank you for participating in this journey for me and for being an instrument God uses to remind me of His faithfulness and blessings! I will forever be grateful for your friendship and the privilege of writing this series with you.

Rebecca Germany and Barbour Publishers, for taking an idea that seemed a little outlandish and believing in it. For making the heirs of Anton come to life and for believing in two writers with a heart for Russia. I am honored and blessed to work with you.

Tracey Bateman, for walking this journey of faith with me and praying for me, and for being friend and encourager. God blessed me so much with your friendship.

My children, David, Sarah, Peter, and Noah, who prayed with me and supported me. I am so proud to be your mother and watch you grow into children who love God.

My sweet husband Andrew, who shows me every day what true courage is and what it means to love sacrificially. You are my hero and my prince. *"Grow old with me. . .the best is yet to be!"*

For the LORD is good
and his love endures forever;
his faithfulness continues
through all generations.
PSALM 100:5 NIV

ALEXANDER PALACE, TSARSKOE SELO,
SOUTH OF PETROGRAD, RUSSIA
27 FEBRUARY 1917

From the outside looking in, she lived the fairy tale—a peasant caught up in a princess life. But regardless of what the revolutionaries and dissidents thought about those who served the royal family, Oksana Nikolaevna Terekhova had endured her fair share of suffering in her twenty-plus years. She possessed no immunity from heartbreak, no royal dispensation of never-ending bliss. From the inside looking out, the fairy tale was fast turning into a tragedy before her very eyes.

Starting with her hair.

She still couldn't bear to look in the mirror. True, the pinned damask drapes allowed in only the barest of light, but she could trace her appearance in her thoughts. Crude, barren. Oksana ran her fingertips along her now-naked scalp, stripped of its crowning glory. A bad case of the measles had caused her hair to fall out in clumps, and the mantle of sores that covered her had made it necessary for Yulia to shave Oksana's head to keep the gooey discharge from caking what little of her hair remained. In the grand scheme of things, her humiliation should be of no consequence, she knew. She was just an orphan, raised to serve the needs of Romanov royalty. But she couldn't help but think she'd die of embarrassment before her hair returned.

If the measles or the revolutionists didn't kill her first.

Revolutionists.

This morning's news from Petrograd brought the bleak report that the capital city had fallen into rebel hands. The insurgent horde that fought to bring down the monarchy had already seized control of the village of Tsarskoe Selo. They now pushed toward the Alexander Palace grounds, intent on attacking the tsar's residence. Had anyone bothered to tell the revolutionaries that Tsar Nikolai wasn't at home?

As if the threat of an imminent hostile coup wasn't stress enough to bear, an outbreak of measles had erupted among the tsar's children and confined them to bed. For over a week now, Oksana, too, had suffered from the disease, quarantined from all human contact save that of Yulia Petrovna, her fellow servant and best friend.

If she closed her eyes, she could pretend away the humiliation and instead find herself cruising the Gulf of Finland on summer holiday.

The gentle scent of lilacs and lilies surrounded Oksana. She opened her eyes.

The tsarina's candle glowed in the chamber.

Terror balled in her throat. A midnight visitation from Her Royal Majesty Tsarina Alexandra herself did not portend good news.

Oksana's eyes ached at the unaccustomed brightness. She swiped at her tears and struggled to rise.

"Don't get up, child. I know you're ill." The tsarina spoke in English, her voice as soft as the candle's radiance. "Poor thing. You look just like my girls."

Both her choice of language and her tone added fresh credence to Oksana's fears. What the tsarina had to say she must not want to have overheard and understood by a passing guard. However, that Oksana's misery held such esteemed company served to ease her embarrassment at her wretched appearance. She eased back on her pillow.

Dressed in her invariable Red Cross uniform, the tsarina looked more apparition than human—pallid in color, cadaverous in form. She set her candle on the nightstand, then perched herself on the bedside chair. "I regret having to disturb you when you're so sick."

Oksana recoiled beneath the royal's scrutiny. Her fever welled in her chest. Why was Her Majesty staring at her? No, not at her. Through her.

The tsarina shook off her trance and reclaimed her thought. "But our present circumstance dictates that I speak with you." She sighed and looked away. "I'll try to be brief." The flickering candlelight sent the tsarina's silhouette on a nightmarish dance across the ceiling and ornate plaster walls. "We all pray this season of rebellion is soon suppressed and order restored to our land, but in the event such is not ordained. . ."

Oksana's pulse roared in her ears. She swallowed hard. Did the tsarina truly believe this rebellion, this affront to everything noble and just, might overtake, even overthrow so many centuries of holy rule?

Tsarina Aleksandra's gaze fixed on her hands. She smoothed and picked at the folds of her uniform. "As you know, the tsar is a thorough and deliberate man, and although he, as do I, places his full trust in our troops' strength and abilities to protect us, he feels we should prepare for any eventuality. I'm certain, as always, I can trust in your discretion concerning any matter we discuss."

"Of course, Your Majesty." Oksana's reply came out wobbly and weak. She cleared her throat and started to reiterate. "I—"

The tsarina spoke over her. "Child, I've come to extend an offer to release you from service to our family." All remaining color drained from the royal mother's face, save the deep burgundy circles that ringed her eyes. "You must flee to safety while the opportunity for such action still exists."

"No—" Oksana's protest barely made it past her lips.

The tsarina silenced her with a stay of her hand. "Hear me out." Empress Aleksandra patted Oksana's quilt-covered arm.

Tingles radiated from the spot the tsarina touched. She had seen the tsarina extend such tenderness time and again to the soldiers she nursed in her hospital work.

"You've served us well and faithfully from the first day the nuns brought you to us as a child," the tsarina said. "You have fulfilled all we've asked of you. Our girls see you more as another sister than a subservient. However, in your position of personal service to the grand duchesses, you've been made privy to information which, if it should fall into the wrong hands, would bring disaster to the crown."

Nausea forced Oksana's eyes closed. Fall into the wrong hands?

"I fear a day is fast approaching—is, in fact, now upon

us—when a decision of loyalty to the crown will put your life at grave risk. Think about my offer before you respond. Weigh the gravity of your decision. Already, other servants have chosen to leave. I bear them no malice. On the contrary, I understand their fear. But I believe I know you well enough to surmise you will insist on staying with us, both due to your station as an orphan and your adherence to that which is noble."

Oksana nodded in agreement, looking to the tsarina to affirm her loyalty.

The tsarina shook her head, her lips pinched. "I need to warn you, Oksana Nikolaevna, if you choose to remain here, you will likely face whatever sentence is imposed on the nobility. The result may include imprisonment or, God forbid, death." The tsarina's speech faltered. She gave a quick shake of her head. "I need to know, should you make your choice to remain loyal to our cause, are you willing to accept whatever direction your sovereign deems best?"

To live outside the circle of the only family she'd ever known, such would be a fate worse than death. Oksana didn't need to deliberate. She had but one answer to give. "Your Majesty, now, as always, whatever you require, I will do."

CHAPTER ONE

3 MARCH 1917

The whole of Russia had gone mad. And if Anton Klassen didn't get off this stalled passenger train soon, he feared he would join his comrades in their race toward insanity. He had lost all feeling in his right arm long ago, pinned by a sleeping soldier's bobbing head of greasy black hair. He nudged his elbow into the side of the snoring, vodka-reeking man who'd made a pillow of Anton's shoulder, but he failed to dislodge the parasite. At least his seatmate couldn't ask questions while he slept.

He always hated the questions.

The inevitable questions.

Just once he hoped for an answer that might satisfy even himself.

A force stronger than Anton's personal resolve pulled his gaze, once again, to the gauze bandage that swaddled the end of the soldier's right arm.

Anton instinctively fisted then fanned all ten of his fingers across his pant legs. He didn't know which disgusted him more—the void beneath the corporal's frayed uniform sleeve or the accusing outline of his own whole and healthy hands.

In the month's time he'd been back in the Molotschna Colony on business for the family's harness factory, all the news reports and gossip in the streets of his quiet village claimed that a reign of chaos now stormed Petrograd, threatening to overtake all of Russia. He had hoped to return to his flat in the capital city of Petrograd and find the rumors untrue. Instead, the frosted windows of the halted railroad car confined him in a microcosm of Russia's lunacy.

In the aisle next to him, a babushka clutched a chicken in one arm, a prized goat in the other. The combined misery of the two farm animals was enough to make him want to tug his mink *shopka* over his ears. Peasants and gypsies and militia all wrestled to occupy a nonexistent extra inch or two. No matter how much he'd been willing to pay, he'd gotten only a laugh when he tried to buy a berth in a private car when he left his Ukrainian village. And the smell of traveling for two days and sitting for one more probably had the power to lay waste to all of Kaiser Wilhelm's army.

Anton looked out into the night. Through the rimed window, the world seemed more hallucination than reality. Thick frost sent moonlight spearing across a barren potato field and into the front lines of the forest beyond.

A constellation of lanterns dotted a path alongside the tracks. Within their misty spotlights, vendors from a nearby village peddled their harvest of foodstuffs to the rail passengers, despite the wee morning hour. Steam rose from the carts and makeshift stands laden with belly-warming fares such as *chebiriki*, *peroshke*, boiled eggs, potatoes, or borscht. Anton's stomach growled. He'd finished off the last of the food his father's wife had packed for him several hours ago, fully expecting to be in Petrograd by the dinner hour.

Was it only last evening that, without announcement or fanfare, their train had chugged to a stop in the middle of the Pskov countryside? Not even the conductors gave indication of why, although delays were more the norm than anomaly on Russia's rails. Tonight, however, the interminable length of time it usually took to remove run-of-the-mill impediments such as dead cows or snowdrifts had long passed. And the ever-accommodating natives grew more restless as the night dragged on. It didn't help matters that the toilets had been locked as a matter of procedure when the train first ground to a stop.

Anton weighed his hunger and other urges of nature against the discomfort he knew he would face if he were to disembark. He'd been lucky to get this seat. He knew full well his small square of bench space would be swallowed up by this human sea as soon as he stood.

Still, the thought of a warm peroshke made his mouth water. What good would a seat do him if he starved in it?

Propping the sleeping soldier upright with one hand, Anton hauled his outerwear and rucksack up from their resting place between his feet. Ever so slowly, he rose.

The babushka, her barnyard creatures still in tow, melted into his vacant space with a nod and a "*Spaceebah.*" A smile washed over the sleeping soldier's lips as he nestled into his new seatmate's amply padded shoulder.

Anton wedged his way through the human clog until he stood on the platform between the cars. He paused at the top of the steps, sucked in a gulp of subfreezing air. It iced his throat and pricked at his lungs, but he welcomed the jar to his senses. Coal dust, axle grease, and roasted potatoes combined to give off an oddly comforting scent. Anton shrugged into his coat, slipped on his gloves, and left the train, walking toward the first food cart.

Dark, tired eyes stared out from layers of woolen scarves and skirts and sweaters and coats. The muffled voice, with a tinge of femininity, named her price for the vegetable-filled dumplings over which she kept guard.

Anton bit off his right glove and held it between his teeth while he fished his pocket for kopecks. Taking the *vareniky* wrapped in a roll of newsprint, he walked toward the forest edge in search of a quiet spot. He tried to stay close enough to make it back on board should the locomotive bellow to life, yet sufficiently secluded from the train's thousand bored and curious eyes as to eat his midnight snack in peace and to smell the fresh night air—a sort of reprieve before his return to the asphyxiation of the train.

Why couldn't his father simply allow him to run the business from Petrograd without the bimonthly reports in person? One would think a man who had been trying to ignore his only child for nearly three decades might be happy to have him a few thousand versts to the north.

But that would assume Johann Klassen trusted Anton or, at the least, respected him. According to him, how could he find anything to appreciate about the unwanted child who had destroyed his life?

Using his rucksack as a cushion, Anton wedged himself into a comfortable spot in the V of a two-trunked birch tree, then peeled back the wrapper and picked out the dumplings one by one. Between bites, he stared into the black woods, listening to the pops and cracks of the forest floor. This woodland world held a universe all its own. He wondered what secrets these trees guarded.

Ever so briefly, a light flickered in the forest bowels. Then it vanished.

At first, Anton thought he'd imagined it. Just his tired eyes playing tricks on him.

But there, he caught sight of it again.

He trained his gaze to follow the pale beam. Back and forth. Slow. Fast. Slow again. This way, then that. Careening. Dancing. Playing tag among the trees. In and out—a wild zigzag pattern akin to the summer lightning bug's trail.

The more Anton stared, the more certain he became. The light came from a lantern. Someone was out there.

In all likelihood, some drunk from the train had wandered off to relieve himself in the woods and gotten lost. Anton looked back over his shoulder at his railcar and debated reembarking. Still, his gaze couldn't escape the mesmerizing pull of the undulating glow.

What if a woman or child carried the lamp—a little girl, perhaps, lost and panicked to the point of terror, desperate in her attempt to find the way out of what must seem a haunted forest? What kind of gentleman, what kind of Christian would he be to turn and walk away without so much as a look-see? Anton cast another glance toward the train, then eased himself away from the tree. Dangling his rucksack over his right arm, he stealthed his way, one slow step at a time, in the direction of the light.

When he got within twelve meters or so, Anton hugged the shadow side of a tree and looked out at the small, illuminated clearing.

The lantern bearer proved to be neither woman nor child but a man. A man, rather small in stature and in military dress.

From this distance, and owing to the fact that Anton had never served in any branch of the service, he wasn't certain what rank the man held. He didn't appear to be drunk, however, for he paced the small clearing in a straight line, his posture erect. The man was talking to himself, or perhaps praying. Anton couldn't make out his words.

Judging by the way the man paused and scrubbed his hand over his face, then combed his fingers through his hair, it was obvious he was embroiled in intense spiritual hand-to-hand combat. At last, the man collapsed to his knees. Nesting his lantern on the loam of the forest floor, he cradled his head in his hands.

Anton felt a wash of shame for his voyeurism. He himself had such quarrels with the Almighty. And he had no desire to share those conversations with anyone. He turned, intending to leave, and snapped a twig beneath his footfall.

The stranger looked up. "*Zdrastvootya.* Show yourself!"

Anton winced but stepped forward into the light at the command.

"Sir, I'm sorry to disturb you," Anton said. "I saw you pacing, and I was. . .concerned. I'm sorry. I'll leave you—"

"Stay." The stranger genuflected and moved to rise. He brushed away the dried leaves that clung to the knees of his trousers, yanked on the tail of his coat, and pulled himself up straight.

Even in the pale light, something about the man's full russet beard and moustache, his piercing gaze, struck Anton as being very familiar. An off-center row of buttons traveled down the left side of his uniform's long belted coat. Gold ropes and braid adorned the epaulets, and a red crest breast badge decorated his left chest. Anton guessed he would stand a good head and shoulders above this man, but despite a rather diminutive physique, the officer commanded an air of authority that went beyond his military uniform.

A grand and horrifying recognition seized Anton and drove him to a deep bow. "Your Imperial Highness! Begging your pardon. . . I'm sorry to disturb. . . I would never. . . Had I known, I. . ." He fell silent, every cognizant thought having left him save a desperate plea for the forest floor to open up and swallow him whole. How could he have eavesdropped on the sovereign ruler of all Russia? He felt more ill than he had on the train.

"Save the protocol, young man. Tonight, we are just two of Father Russia's fellow partisans."

Anton dared to raise his head.

Tsar Nikolai Alexandrovich Romanov offered him a nod before shifting his gaze to scan the clearing's perimeter. Certainly, beyond the scope of light, sentries guarded the head of all of Russia. Why hadn't they stopped him?

"Fear not. You are in no danger." Tsar Nikolai's voice seemed to assure both of them despite the incongruity of that thought. Anton nodded, as if agreeing, and noticed the worry that cut deep valleys into the monarch's forehead. "Pardon my lack of courtesy," Tsar Nikolai continued. "You obviously know who I am, but I have yet to make your acquaintance. Might I learn your name?"

"Anton, Your Majesty. Anton Johannovich Klassen." He offered the Russian version of his name in his best Russian accent. With another fleeting glance at the tsar, he dropped his gaze. He wasn't at all sure where he should train his eyes. He had never studied the proper protocol for conversing with royalty, had never been in the position to need such a knowledge.

"You appear to be a young and healthy man, but I see

you are dressed as a civilian. Have you fulfilled your military duty, or are you presently on leave?"

"Neither, Your Majesty. I am Mennonite and therefore exempt from service in the armed forces." Anton hoped the pallid glow from the lantern failed to betray his embarrassment.

"Ah, yes, Mennonite. So you served your country as a Red Cross *Sanitäre,* perhaps, or in the *forestri*?"

Heat crept up Anton's neck, into his face, burning the tips of his ears. "I am sorry, Your Majesty, but no." There it was—Anton's greatest shame exposed to Tsar Nikolai himself. How he longed simply to crawl back to the train.

"I was willing to serve, Your Majesty. But as the eldest son, I am exempt from active duty in order to assist in our family's harness factory. I oversee our warehouses and sales office in Petrograd."

He wished that excuse didn't sound so. . .feeble. At this moment, he would surrender the farm, the factory, and all his wealth simply to stand beside his countrymen with honor.

And lose his family and his faith in the balance.

He sighed. It was prudent to curb the passions of his heart, just as his religion admonished and the scriptures cautioned.

"Of course you are willing to defend your country. I sense your devotion, see the fire of patriotism burning in your eyes. The battle between spiritual conviction, family loyalties, and partisan allegiances is one I can appreciate."

The grace in the monarch's gaze burrowed through to Anton's soul.

"Tell me this. . ." His Imperial Majesty let the fore-word hang in the air. "As a Mennonite, you are a man of faith, are you not?"

Anton marveled at just how still a forest in the dead of winter could be. "Yes, sir. I seek to be devout in my Christian faith. I consider myself a pilgrim in search of spiritual truth."

That much was true. He might struggle in espousing all the tenets of his family's Mennonite religion, but Anton saw no need to say as much to the ruler of the whole of Imperial Russia.

"Well, my boy, sometimes God calls upon us to serve in ways we neither choose nor foresee. Perhaps He has set you apart for a special purpose."

Despite the cold, Anton flushed hot under the tsar's scrutiny—scrutiny that seemed to examine him from the inside out.

"As you are undoubtedly aware, I've had my share of differences with the leaders of your sect in the past. All the same, I admire your people for their devotion to seeking after holiness, and I can't help but believe that the Lord, in His mercy, saw fit to answer my prayer for aid by unit-ing our paths in these woods. Some would say it is fate or happenstance, but I personally believe it is Providence that brought you to me."

The tsar took a step back, then another, until he stood just beyond the lamplight's glow. His gaze searched the wall of trees as he motioned for Anton to follow him. "Let me speak to the urgency at hand. I don't expect my war-dens will leave me in peace much longer. I believe they've let me be until now in hopes I might end my life and save them from having to decide what's to become of me."

23

Again he scanned the forest beyond. "I disembarked my train a couple versts up the tracks from here under the ruse of mushroom hunting. I desperately needed some air." The tsar pulled in a deep breath.

Air. Anton could appreciate the need for fresh air.

"All of Russia will soon know, so there's no sense my keeping it a secret now. A few hours prior, I laid down my authority as monarch over our magnificent Fatherland." He sighed, and for the briefest moment, his shoulders slumped.

"I am no longer tsar." His voice lost strength with the pronouncement.

No longer tsar? Anton's mouth grew dry; questions lined his throat. Was German Kaiser Wilhelm overrunning Petrograd? Or had the Russian rebels taken captive the royal family?

Perhaps the Great War, the internal chaos, and the allegations of mismanagement finally had turned the tsar mad.

Anton swallowed around the myriad questions that tickled in his throat. Regardless of the tsar's statements, it wasn't Anton's position to make inquiries of Russia's sovereign or suspect his hold on reality.

"Although I have turned my throne over to my brother, Michael, he has expressed reticence to take control if the people do not accept him. I do not know what might come of the monarchy. I cannot trust those nearest me, and my present circumstance will not allow me to reach those to whom I could turn for help. I am seeking a dependable young man such as yourself to fulfill a mission of grave significance." Authority blazed in those intense eyes of his, belying his words of abdication and daring Anton to refuse his request.

Mission? As in a military mission? Had he not heard the word *Mennonite* in Anton's introduction?

As if reading his mind, the tsar continued. "I do not foresee your convictions of pacifism needing to be compromised should you accept the two charges I hope to entrust to your care. Neither do I believe your services will be required for long. When the disposition of our immediate future is decided, you will be promptly contacted and relieved of your duties and well compensated for your trouble."

Anton strained to keep up. Services? Compensated? Just what did the tsar have in mind?

"Might I count on you? Would you be willing to serve the Fatherland now, as my special emissary, even though I am no longer tsar?" Tsar Nikolai edged closer, his dark eyes holding Anton's gaze.

Anton cleared his throat, buying time. How, exactly, did he expect to refuse the leader—deposed or not—of all of Russia?

Maybe he was the madman for even hesitating.

"Your Majesty, I would consider it an honor and a privilege to be of service to you." He heard the words emerge, saw the tsar's features relax ever so briefly, and wondered in that hiccup of time to just what he had agreed.

Tsar Nikolai nodded, cast another look toward the forest edge, then lowered his voice further. "All right, then. Let's make haste before we are discovered and our plans foiled. First and foremost, I need you to seek out a young monk by the name of Timofea. He lives at a monastery in Pechory—in this region and not far from here, but given my situation, unattainable to me. You won't have any trouble finding him. Tell him Oksana's guardian sends you. He will understand. He must go with you to Tsarskoe Selo and bring out his sister, Yulia, and her coworker Oksana before it is too late. He will understand the urgency and will know what to do. I won't need to give you logistics here." He broke off, shaking his head. "I pray it isn't too late even now. The revolutionaries are making swift work of—" He closed his mouth, eased away.

Of what? A chill brushed up Anton's spine. Of what were the revolutionaries making swift work that the monarch found too horrific to speak aloud? And what miseries had Anton just pledged to assume in his rush to please the tsar?

"I have no assurances that the telegrams I sent my wife have arrived in her hands. She may or may not understand the full gravity of our predicament. Regardless, she and I have discussed the possibility of this very scenario in days past. Explain to her that I've given you charge over Oksana Terekhova's safety. She will see to the departure preparations and will release the young lady into your care. Timofea and Yulia will assist you all they can; however, the burden of the girl's protection rests solely on your shoulders."

The tsar looked at Anton, and his mustache stretched to cover his growing smile. "Don't look so glum, my boy. The task comes with its own rewards. The young lady is fair of face. A true beauty."

Anton forced himself to meet the tsar's gaze and return his smile.

Tsar Nikolai winked, then schooled his features to their earlier severity. "See to it that she is protected. Above all and despite the cost, I want her kept safe. She has served our family faithfully and is an orphan with nowhere else to turn in a dark hour such as this. Not only do we owe her a debt of gratitude, but she has knowledge of such details as would be viewed of having supreme value to my enemies. They will stop at nothing to extract this knowledge from her. Guard her with your very life if need be. Do not abdicate your responsibility to another." He winced in silent censure of his poor choice of words. "Your mission shouldn't last long. I will send for you through Monk Timofea and ask you to escort Oksana back to us as soon as we are safely resettled and out of harm's way."

The tsar fished into his collar and withdrew a gold chain, pulling it over his head.

"Should my wife require some proof that it is I who have sent you, show this to her as a mark of my authority—but use utmost discretion." A jewel-encrusted crest dangled at the end of the necklace. Rubies, sapphires, emeralds, and diamonds sparked a rainbow blaze against the backdrop of lantern light. The tsar caught the dancing colors in his hand and fingered the gemstones as he spoke.

"Until such a time as I send for you, I am hereby appointing you guardian and protector of this, the Crest of Saint Basil the Blessed. I trust the Lord sent His perfect envoy for this task—a man of faith, a Mennonite such as yourself, with no prejudice toward either the Orthodox Church or the State to drive you to forsake this mission in favor of political or monetary gain." The tsar lifted the chain and motioned for Anton to lean down so he could slide the crest over Anton's head. Anton felt the weight of the jewel even before he slipped the pendant beneath his shirt. The precious metal raised gooseflesh as it settled at the end of its tether.

"Take care. For your own safety, as well as the crest's safekeeping, hide it well. The crest would bring no small fortune to the money mongers and fortune seekers who are even now demanding I turn possession of the heirloom over to them. Many a rebel would as soon murder you for it as to ask you for the crest outright. However, far beyond the crest's great monetary value, its symbolic significance is inestimable. For well over a millennium—generation upon generation—the crest has signified the blessed union shared between our church and the crown."

In other words, Anton now wore a golden millstone around his neck.

His expression must have betrayed his dismay, for the tsar cupped Anton's shoulder in his grasp and gave it a squeeze. "Take courage, young man. The Lord will be with you as you carry out your mission."

A crackle of leaves to the north of the clearing silenced Tsar Nikolai and pinned both Anton and the tsar to their shadowed places. The tsar lifted his hand in signal for Anton to stay still and rasped a whispered command. "Hide yourself till you're confident I'm well beyond the woods. Then hasten to Pechory." He took a step toward the clearing but paused and caught Anton's gaze in his. "Godspeed. And may He save us all."

The tsar retrieved his lamp from the clearing and plowed northward through the carpet of frozen leaves, toward the loudening crunches and snaps.

Anton pushed his hand to his chest to rein in his galloping heartbeat, and like a brand, he felt the outline of the crest against his palm. "O Lord, save us all indeed!"

CHAPTER TWO

Anton crouched on a dry patch of ground beneath a tall pine and stared at the fortress parapet surrounding the Pechory monastery. On the other side of the white stucco walls, past the massive arched doors, gold-painted stars glistened against sapphire onion domes. On the hour, chimes rang out from a cupola.

He shook his head for the thousandth time. What had come over him that he would accept this assignment? No—*mission*. He corrected his thought as he recalled the tsar's parting words.

Regardless of whether he'd accepted an assignment or a mission, he knew deep down the real motivation behind his acceptance of the tsar's charge. He saw this as his one great opportunity to be more than the man his father assumed him to be. Weak. Fruitless. Unworthy to bear the Klassen name.

So why was he crouched outside like some sort of vagrant ready to pilfer the monastery's offerings? Just because the rumors of the tsar's abdication—indeed his own words—had been proven true, and just because revolutionaries searched the country for loyalists, didn't mean anyone knew of his quest—or of the jewel hanging against his chest.

Please, let this not be a trap.

He had waited and watched from across the dirt road that ran in front of the monastery as the priests came and went from the compound. This religious garrison looked impenetrable for one such as himself. Even if he managed to get inside, he had no idea how to address an Orthodox priest. Should he bow? Kiss his hand? What words should he say? He hoped he could witness a greeting or exchange of conversation between clergy and laity, but no such opportunity had presented itself in the hour or so he'd stood watch. He didn't see why the tsar believed the removal of a servant girl from the palace was such a matter of urgency anyway. What secrets could she truly know other than what time the tsar rose and retired or how the tsarina liked her eggs? If he could just figure out a way to return the crest—

"May God bless you, son."

Anton recoiled, then looked over his shoulder to see a man in priestly garb, with dark eyes and a long beard that flowed to whispers of gray tangles at his chest. Anton rose to full height and stood eye to eye with the monk, but he couldn't conjure up an appropriate response to save his soul—at the moment, his tortured soul.

"I've noticed you as I've gone and come. You have been waiting here for quite some time. Have you a need with which I might assist you?"

"Uh, yes, sir," Anton stuttered. "*Batiushka*—Father." Anton paused again. "Possibly." He took a deep breath. "I'm looking for a monk by the name of Timofea. I've been told I could find him here."

"Timofea? Yes, I can take you to him." The priest

stroked his beard against his chest. "I'm curious. Why is it you wish to see my son?"

"Your son, sir?"

"Timofea, he's my son."

Confusion knifed a pain through Anton's temple, but he resisted the urge to knead the spot where it hurt. Did this also mean that the Yulia of whom the tsar spoke would be the priest's daughter? Perhaps he referred to Timofea as his son in a spiritual sense. He didn't see how a monastic priest could have children. From all he'd heard, they were celibate. Then again, he could carry all he knew about Orthodox clergy in a slotted spoon.

"I've been sent to deliver a message to him, and begging your pardon, Father, I feel I should speak to him first before discussing the matter with anyone else."

The priest studied Anton. Then he tipped his head. "Follow me."

Anton followed the cleric across the road and through the monastery's garrisonlike doors into an outdoor atrium.

"Feel free to go into the chapel and pray," the priest said, nodding over his shoulder, "or simply wait here." He pointed to a bench along the courtyard wall. "I won't be long." The man turned and strolled down a colonnaded walkway, his skirts swirling like a storm cloud about his feet.

When Anton had the courtyard to himself, he searched in the direction of the priest's nod for anything that resembled a church. He saw instead the entrance to a whitewashed cave. His curiosity nudged him forward, and ever so slowly, he eased toward the grotto and peeked inside. A host of burning candles illuminated the cavern and sent black smoke spirals to the soot-coated ceiling. Mildew and incense weighted the air and gave off a fusty smell. The breath with which he filled his lungs felt more solid than gaseous. Icons of Madonna and Child peered down on him from their gilded frames. He didn't know if he would be welcome to enter the small sanctuary if they realized he wasn't of their faith, but since no other soul appeared to be around, he walked in anyway.

A holy hush fell on him, and whether appropriate or not, Anton felt moved to kneel on the hard-packed earthen floor. He bowed his head, compelled to pray. If he hoped to accomplish the task handed him by the tsar, he needed strength far above any power he possessed within himself. Without help from the Almighty, his chances of success were nil.

He poured out his heart to God, begging for wisdom, pleading for courage, until his appeal boiled down to the same repetition: "Help me, Lord. Please help me, Lord. O Lord, help me, please."

Anton sensed someone had entered the chapel-cave. Heat crept up his neck. He halted his pleadings and stole a glance behind him.

A young man in monk's clothing came toward him, making the sign of the cross. Fire from the candles danced across the backdrop of his dark eyes, and he smiled. "In His holy scriptures, the Lord promises to hear and answer those who truly seek Him."

"Yes, thank you. I am counting on as much." Anton stood, brushing the dirt from his knees. "Without the help of the Almighty, I am lost for certain."

He searched the young man's face to evaluate his sincerity. He always imagined priests as wizened saints with hoary-haired beards, but this one with his scraggy chin whiskers looked to be about the age of Anton's stepbrother Jonas—no more than eighteen or nineteen. Twenty at most. Anton shuddered at the thought of taking spiritual advice from Jonas, who was interested in only two things: fast horses and pretty girls. And with piercing dark brown eyes and high cheekbones, wide shoulders, and a capable build, this man looked more suited for nobility and battle astride a stallion than for service in a monastery. By all appearances, this fellow had forsaken such youthful pursuits, no matter his chronological age. Still, Anton had expected someone older for this mission.

Then again, what mission? The safe transport of a chambermaid from the house of Romanov? It didn't take a cavalry.

"Would you be the monk Timofea?" Anton couldn't bring himself to call someone so young "Father."

"I am Timofea." He crossed his arms and buried his hands within the sleeves of his cassock, wearing a look of calm curiosity.

"Are there any other of the brothers here by that same name?" Anton considered asking for identification. He didn't want to insult the young man, but neither did he want to betray the tsar's confidential mission to the wrong man.

"No, there's not another like me. I'm the only one." Timofea chuckled. When Anton didn't respond in like manner to his laugh, the monk's expression turned serious. "How might I serve you?" He punctuated his question with quirked eyebrows.

Anton thought he detected a tinge of impatience in the young man's voice, but he wasn't ready to accept his word at face value, even for one dressed as a member of the cloth. "Would you mind telling me your sister's name? You have a sister, do you not?"

"Yulia. My sister's name is Yulia." Concern knotted the corners of the monk's eyes. "Why do you ask? Is she in trouble?"

"I'm sorry if I've alarmed you. As far as I know, she is fine." The genuine distress behind the young man's queries dissolved Anton's doubts, but just to be sure, he threw out one more question. "Before I say more, would you please confirm for me where your sister is employed?"

The monk appeared to hesitate, sizing up Anton as friend or foe, those dark eyes sharp in their survey. "She serves the tsar's household as a chambermaid. Forgive my rudeness, but what business is Yulia of yours?"

"I've been sent on a task by Yulia's master to find you and solicit your help."

Monk Timofea's features softened. "What can I do for His Imperial Majesty?"

"He requests you take me to Tsarskoe Selo to bring out the servant girl by the name of Oksana Terekhova. You are to go for your sister, as well." Anton cast a glance left and right, then twisted to look behind him. Though they appeared to be alone, he lowered his voice. "We are to act in all haste. The one who sent me said you would know what to do."

Timofea let a beat of time pass, a moment wherein he considered, or perhaps processed, Anton's request.

The weight of the crest cut into Anton's neck. He fingered it and then, with a rush, pulled it out. "I have this to prove my words."

Timofea stepped back, his mouth open, eyes fixed on the jewel. "Only the tsar—"

"He gave it to me for evidence."

Timofea's eyes narrowed.

"Please," Anton said. "You're going to have to trust me."

The monk sighed. "Put that away at once." He pursed his lips, then gave a stiff nod. "I will inform my superiors, and we will be on our way." He turned and hurried back to the monastery.

Anton pressed the crested jewel against his chest. He wasn't sure how much faith, exactly, he could place in this young man, but for the first time, he felt that maybe he had a chance of completing this mission with which he'd been entrusted.

⁕

Her course had been decided. Her fate sealed.

By way of secret message, an edict came from the tsar, passed down to the tsarina, who, in turn, delivered the news to her. She was to leave the palace with Yulia, Yulia's brother, Timofea, and a stranger. . .a Mennonite from south Russia's steppelands; her safety delegated to the care of a man who refused to bear arms.

Whatever her misgivings, no matter how grave, she must go without so much as a moment's audience with the tsar. When all was said and done, her preferences didn't merit serious consideration. She felt betrayed, abandoned not only by the royal family but by God. Apparently the Almighty hadn't been listening to her pleas from her sickbed.

Outside her window, the early morning sun turned the frost along the edge of her window to diamonds. The room's electric lights glinted off the gold overlay of her chamber icon as though calling her to prayer.

She turned away. Praying wouldn't do her any good now.

Lifting a picture of the Romanov family from the top of her bureau, she traced her finger over each precious member. She planted a kiss on the glass, then wrapped the framed photograph in a satin cloth and tucked it into her suitcase.

Outside, she heard barking, then laughter. It drew her to the window. For a moment, her breath left her, longing so sharp it turned inside like a blade. Gleb, outside with their King Charles spaniel, Jimmy, evidently on a predawn stroll.

The tsar's cousin had, in all likelihood, heard of the dramatic downturn of events in regard to the rebellion and had returned early from his hunting trip with Prince Felix. To get inside the gates, however, he must have had to work his charm on the guards, maybe even offer them a bribe. His commitment to the Romanov family during this dark season touched her heart. As always, he took her breath away with his mysterious dark eyes, his wide shoulders, the way he somehow commanded the sunshine to turn his hair to ebony. He moved with an agility that betrayed his love of wrestling and swimming, while Jimmy yapped about him as he feigned catching the pup. Every young lady in the royal court, including the grand duchesses, had romantic dreams that included Gleb.

He turned, and she ducked behind the drape.

She couldn't think of a time she had ever been away from them all, out on her own. They'd been her life, and the thought of being apart felt as if she might be torn asunder. The very idea pushed tears to her eyes. What if something happened to them—or her? The rebels were advancing on Tsarskoe Selo even now.

If she didn't leave now, she might never.

Even so, how could she leave them? They needed her. She peeked back around the window. Gleb and Jimmy were gone.

Her head swirled with doubts, questions, fears. The tsar's scheme seemed too far-fetched to be believed. Who was this Mennonite assigned to serve as her guardian? Where would they go? When would she return? How could she stay informed of the royal family's welfare? What kind of world would she find beyond the palace walls? This plan, this ruse of monumental proportions, stood as much chance of success as the tsarina's beliefs that the tsarevich would be healed.

She'd been petitioning the Royal Mother against this plan since she first learned of the decision to send her away. Apparently, those petitions had fallen on deaf ears.

"Her Majesty said she needs to finish up her alterations on two more dresses before we can close this bag." Yulia laid a folded blouse on top of an already teetering stack of garments to be crammed inside the suitcase.

"I don't think I have the strength to walk in this heavy skirt. You'd think the Royal Mother had sewn the complete inventory of the crown jewels in these seams. Why she insisted on doing this is beyond me. I don't like assuming such a precious responsibility, even for the little time I expect we'll be gone."

Her words sounded harsh, even to her own ears, but

she didn't believe for an instant that she had fooled Yulia with her bravado. Beneath her gruff tone, her emotions chipped and crumbled—and threatened to give way to a landslide.

Yulia looked up from her work. "Why don't you lie back down? You need to save your strength."

"No, I want to try this wig on first." She choked back the threat of tears. "I look like a clown. A bald, polka-dotted circus clown." The wig's thick locks of straw-colored hair capped her hand and cascaded over her arm. "I can't believe I'm going out in public looking so hideous."

"Here, let me help you with that." Yulia dropped the skirt she was folding onto the bed and reached for the hairpiece. She applied the wig with the same care she took in positioning the grand duchess's crown. "There you go. Measles or no, you'll always look regal—as pretty as a princess to me."

One look in the mirror told the royal Olga Nikolaevna Romanova otherwise. She looked worse, far worse, than the chambermaid Oksana, who had allowed her mistress to borrow her name. At this particular moment, Olga felt anything but regal. Yulia's kind words notwithstanding, all the evidence refuted the servant's claims. Though of royal birth, Olga at present neither looked the part nor could lay rightful claim to her noble title as one of Russia's grand duchesses, thanks to her father's abdication of his throne.

A princess about to turn peasant. Not only stripped of her royal entitlements by the tsar's abdication but about to be exiled from her palace home; separated from her beloved parents and siblings; forced to assume a new name and, along with it, a new identity.

"Regal, you say?" Olga pushed an errant strand of the coarse flaxen hair back into place. "Well, appearances can be deceiving, dear Yulia. At least I hope that's true. Our very lives depend on as much."

CHAPTER THREE

D awn sent slender pink fingers through night's worn shroud and afforded the eldest grand duchess one final glimpse of her palace home before she surrendered to the hurries of her three nervous guardians.

Yulia stood to one side, wrapped in her *dublonka*, stamping her feet against the pressing cold. Beside her stood a monk, a scruff of beard on his chin, his hair long and dark and winding into the folds of his robes. He wore no hat and bowed to her slightly as she approached. Olga readily recognized the resemblance between her dark-haired attendant and this wide-shouldered young monk.

Another man stepped out. With short, cropped blond hair and serious gray eyes, he bore a dimple in his clean-shaven chin. Dressed in a scarf, wool *shuba*, leather gloves, and mink *shopka*, he held out his hand. "*Za tebye*—after you, Miss Terekhova."

She startled at the realization that this Anton Klassen fellow was addressing her. Her new alias would take some getting used to. She shrugged off the stranger's proffered arm and accepted her servant Yulia's assistance instead.

The *troika*'s driver, with his long beard, greatcoat, and square cap of blue velvet, sat on his perch and waited for the signal to depart. Yulia Petrovna's brother, the young monk Timofea, brought up the rear of their entourage and served as scout, keeping a watchful eye on their surroundings as they prepared to board the carriage and leave the palace grounds.

Yesterday's blizzard had thrown down a pall of snow and frost that had yet to be cleared, and Olga had to pick her steps with care. Today marked the first time she'd been outside since she'd fallen ill, and she had no business being up and about even now—save the even bigger threat to her life brought on by the revolutionists. Her legs felt as unsteady as if she were walking on water, but she determined not to let her traveling companions see the extent of her weakness.

Olga motioned to the suitcases littering the ground by the monk's feet. "Keep my luggage in here with us. I don't want it out of my sight."

Mr. Klassen's bewildered expression told her she had spoken with too much authority for one who was supposed to be a servant. Should she hold out any hope of pulling off this deception, she would have to watch her tongue.

Even if her newly appointed protector knew her true identity—which she'd been assured he didn't—she had no call to bark commands. Her mother never could abide rudeness to subordinates.

Then again, the tsarina wasn't here.

The realization hit Olga hard. She gulped down the lump of panic that threatened to cut off her air supply. At the moment, Olga didn't feel up to being polite. She was too sick to care, not only suffering from measles but crippled with worry, incapacitated by fright.

Her head throbbed with the repetitive force of a smithy's hammer, and her ears roared with each painful thud. Her scalp itched beneath her wig so that she could hardly stand the torment. Olga kneaded her temple with her thumb and forefinger. *Please, let them be off soon.*

The men pushed the luggage in ahead of them, then climbed over the bags and situated themselves opposite the ladies in the carriage. Her mother, ever assiduous, had sent her off with baggage sufficient to travel the world, though Olga fully expected to take no more than a few days' leave and travel no farther than a short carriage ride from home.

"We have an hour's drive, at the most," Anton said from his seat across from her. He had gentle eyes, so different from the many soldiers she had nursed.

"Thank you." Olga eased back into the bearskin-covered seat beside Yulia and clamped her eyes shut, willing herself not to cry. She refused to allow fertile soil to the thought she might never pass this way again, but she couldn't help but fill her lungs and her memory with the scent of pine and snow and burning coal that fragranced the air outside the palace grounds.

She kept returning to the hope that she would waken and discover this had all been a fit of delirium, a temporary leave of her senses due to her fever. The reports couldn't be true. With each passing moment, the stability of the Romanov dynasty deteriorated and the threat to her family's safety increased.

Her eyes closed, she turned her thoughts to prayers as she traced the outline of the simple gold cross her mother had pressed in her hand in the final act of their parting.

Olga offered prayers for Father Russia, that the rebellion would soon be squelched and his citizens returned to their senses; prayers for her own health and safety; prayers for her swift reunion with her sisters and brother and for their quick recoveries from their own bouts with the measles; and prayers, especially, for her dear, dear parents.

"Your father and I are more in need of your strength than ever before, Olga." The haunting memory of her mother's words as she'd knelt beside Olga's camp bed pierced her heart and pushed tears to her eyes. One look at Mamma's face had prophesied disastrous news. Olga had feared the very act of relaying the account of her father's abdication might prove fatal to the delicate woman.

Never had she seen her mother so pale and gaunt, her forehead creased, her features drawn, her frame so fragile.

Breakable.

"It's not forever. I promise." She let her mother's assurances find the crevices of pain in her heart, fill them with hope, strengthen her. She realized Maria and Anastasia were probably too young to set out on such a venture away from kith and kin, but she wondered why Tatiana hadn't been asked to embark on a similar journey. Then again, none of the others had been blessed with a double like she had been. Blessed—or cursed maybe.

" 'Now faith is the substance of things hoped for, the evidence of things not seen.' Hold on to your faith, Olga. With it, you have everything. But without it, you'll have nothing." Then the tsarina had held her tight, while long, silent tears streaked her cheeks.

The carriage creaked and jolted forward.

Olga clutched her scarf to her trembling lips. She

suspected her mother watched from the window of her mauve boudoir as they pulled away. She longed to look and maybe even wave, but she remained rooted to her seat. *Why would a servant wave to the Imperial Mother?* she reminded herself.

Other than Yulia's sniffles and her occasional gloved swiping at tears, silence pervaded the carriage cabin. The air dripped with a spirit of sullenness like melting icicles in a Siberian spring. Olga's companions each appeared lost in his or her own thoughts—Yulia twisting her handkerchief in her lap, the monk praying with bowed head and folded hands, the Mennonite looking out the window in a blank stare, and she burrowing down in her coat and blankets. She felt ugly, cold, and bereft. They couldn't arrive in Petrograd soon enough.

The world outside echoed their carriage hush. They'd timed their departure for such a ridiculously early hour that most of Russia still slept. Even the dissidents and rebels must have had sense enough to be in their beds.

As far as Olga could surmise, they'd escaped without more than a cursory survey by the guards at the servants' entrance. A ragtag team of slump-shouldered militiamen had replaced the elite palace sentries whose imposing figures typically stood watch at each doorway. These raucous new sentinels appeared far more concerned with their card game of *durock* than the departure of more fleeing domestics.

Still, their merry little band was sure to garner curious glances and raise suspicions when they disembarked from their carriage in Petrograd. It would have been less risky to travel by train from the family's private station, but the present political chaos had frozen all rail service for the time being. And certainly the rebels would be watching the rail line.

She didn't see how they could possibly succeed at this masquerade—a teenaged monk and his servant sister as her escorts; she, the bundled, bald, and measled princess, disguised as a chambermaid; and guarding them all, a man who seemed more suited to the discussions of politics than defending her against revolutionaries. She probably had the most military training of them all, derived from her father's instructions on weaponry and military maneuvers, her firsthand experience with the trauma of the wounded, and her hours of target practice with the pistol given her by her father.

But she wasn't a princess anymore, trained in affairs of the state, dedicated to the Russian people. *Oksana. I must think of myself as Oksana Nikolaevna Terekhova now. An orphan. A chambermaid.*

The thought rankled. For as long as she could remember, she and her sisters called themselves "OTMA," their code name for the sibling princesses derived from the first letter of each name—Olga, Tatiana, Maria, and Anastasia. Now she wondered if from this day forward, the *O* would secretly stand for Oksana rather than its rightful claimant.

She blinked away the inane jealousy digging at her thoughts.

Among the members of the royal family, only she had a double. For as long as she could remember, the servant girl Oksana Nikolaevna Terekhova had been in training to perform as Olga's surrogate should the need for extreme security precautions ever arise. The few times she'd sent

Oksana Nikolaevna out to those insufferably dull receptions in her stead proved great fun.

Laughter seemed a faraway memory now. Should their ruse be found out. . .

A chill raced the length of Olga's spine as she considered the lethal consequences. Father had the best of intentions by taking these drastic measures, but while she found his concerns for her safety endearing, she questioned his scheme. At the very least, she thought her father had acted prematurely. He hadn't even made it back to Tsarskoe Selo in time to bid her farewell, having been delayed in his return to the palace from his military headquarters in Mogilev, detained by provisional forces. She couldn't imagine what would happen to her if they discovered a grand duchess outside the walls of the palace. Hopefully the rebellion would end soon and her father would once again regain his rightful, God-ordained position.

She knew by her father's way of thinking, if he could save but one, he would take the risk. She, on the other hand, didn't really see the logic in saving only herself if there were no concrete plans to rescue the others, too. Olga's heart raced, and her brow beaded with sweat.

What ever happened to their family's philosophy that they would survive any crisis together? She thought they'd unanimously agreed to subscribe to her father's oft-quoted credo, which had been scratched into the ancient walls of an Italian prison cell: "Better death than life without you."

Surely, however, her parents even now formulated a plot to secure the rest of the family's flight to safety should the political climate continue to spiral out of control. Hadn't her mother's relations, Great Britain's royal family, pledged to come to their aid, despite their recent cool shoulder?

"I didn't even get to give the sisters or baby so much as a proper good-bye." The whispered thought burned Olga's throat like salt in an open wound. Bundled in layer upon layer against the blood-thickening cold, she barely felt Yulia's gentle pat on her arm. If the servant girl offered words of sympathy, Olga couldn't hear past the roar in her ears, brought on by yet another of her symptoms of measles. She didn't have the will to attempt to read the girl's lips and closed her eyes.

The roaring finally subsided, and with it the hot rush of emotions. Olga opened her eyes just in time to catch Mr. Klassen looking away. He'd been staring at her! A flash of heat rose inside her, touched her cheeks. How dare he! Didn't he know how to conduct himself among royalty?

He doesn't know he's in the presence of royalty, Olga. She dropped her gaze to her lap, to her muff. Apparently, remembering her new position might prove to be more difficult than she had imagined. According to her mother, Father had assigned this curious man to watch over her until things were stable enough to send for her. She'd been told only that he came from one of south Russia's Mennonite villages. Supposedly, for her safety, they hadn't told him the truth.

She could understand her parents' sending her out with Yulia and her brother. Yulia had served their family as a chambermaid for several years, and no one would suspect anything amiss when her cleric brother came to take her home, considering the situation. Since Oksana was an orphan, it made sense that she would seek refuge with her friend and coworker. But why employ this other fellow?

Judging by the quality of the black carriage, be it owned or hired, as well as the tailored dress of his driver, Mr. Klassen was a man of some means. Olga searched through her memories, coming up blank. She didn't recall ever seeing him at any of the political or social events. How had her father found him—was he in some secret employ of the tsar's army? She wished she could have had opportunity to learn the details surrounding the circumstance of her father's appointing this stranger to be her protector.

Despite the exodus of troops who had traded their allegiance from the crown to the provisional government, there must be any number of devoted military officers or palace guards who still remained available to the tsar's beck and call. What possessed her father to appoint this unassuming man? He couldn't be much older than she, but he looked, well, stodgy; more like one of the stuffy Duma representatives than her contemporary. Beneath his heavy overcoat and mink hat, he wore a vested business suit and bow tie. His very appearance, added to the fact that his religion didn't allow him to use a weapon in self-defense, robbed her of any confidence in his ability to protect her. Still, the resolute raise of his chin, the eyes that seemed to catch everything—they made her wonder to what manner of man she now entrusted her life.

Olga buried her nose in the rabbit-fur collar of her traveling cloak. She could feel the jewels her mother had sewn into the hem, despite the padding, and they made the cloak feel heavy and cumbersome. For his sake, as well as hers, she prayed she wouldn't have to keep up this charade for long. Well and with her wits about her, she didn't think she could pull off serious deception or secret keeping. And the measles had left her far from well. No matter. She fully expected to return tomorrow or the next day, whenever her father made it home and straightened out all this muddle.

From the carriage window, she watched as the country-side surrounding Tsarskoe Selo melded into the outskirts of the capital city. To her surprise, a queue of restless customers stretched down the sidewalk outside a baker's shop, despite the early hour. Next door, steam rose from the charred skeleton of a ransacked liquor store. Their carriage sank first in one and then in another of the dirty heaps of snow left untended by the road sweepers.

"Where exactly are you taking us in Petrograd?" Olga rasped. She could just imagine herself huddled in some rat-infested ghetto.

Anton Klassen cleared his throat. "My flat is much too small to house us all comfortably, so I've made arrangements for us to stay in the home of my warehouse steward, Sergei Borovsky, not far from Nevsky Prospekt. It's not a palace, but we should find the accommodations more than suitable there. Mr. Borovsky is one of Petrograd's rare citizens who own their own home. He inherited the place from his grandfather."

Mr. Klassen's eyes, as faded gray as the winter sky over Petrograd, had yet to meet and hold her gaze. Instead, he always looked at some spot just over her shoulder when he spoke. A definite Germanic accent laced his Russian, and, her ailing ears further garbling the words, Olga had to focus on his mouth in order to catch his meaning.

"Last week, Mr. Borovsky sent his children and wife to her parents' home in Moscow, and he is sleeping at the warehouse to protect our inventory from the vandals and thieves. So we'll have the place to ourselves, with the exception of his cook. Don't worry. I didn't let on as to your position of royal service. I merely explained you were traveling friends who had been stranded by the rail strike. He's not a man given to excessive curiosity, and my word is sufficient to keep his trust."

Olga attempted a smile. "Please, when you see him, thank him for his hospitality."

Seated at Mr. Klassen's side, the monk Timofea nodded his agreement.

"Yes. Certainly." Mr. Klassen cast a rapid glance her way before he turned and looked out the carriage window.

The deeper into the city they rode, the more the streets teemed with citizens of every class and description, all fighting for life's basic necessities—coal or firewood, bread, cabbage, meat. Gone was Petrograd's quiet, well-bred look. The police appeared to be on holiday, as she hadn't seen a single officer. Mr. Klassen seemed to read her thoughts. He cast a quick glance in her direction, then looked outside again.

"For safety's sake, I asked the driver to keep us off the main thoroughfares as much as possible, but we can't avoid the crowds altogether. I apologize in advance if I frighten you, but quite frankly, the city's gone mad. The quicker we get to Borovsky's home and off the streets, the better off we'll be." He must have seen the frown lining her forehead, because he mustered a small smile. "But don't worry. We'll be fine."

Olga didn't find his assurances very comforting. All traffic had ground to a halt as pedestrians spilled into the roadways and blocked the thoroughfare. Their carriage jostled back and forth with the press of the crowd. Beyond their carriage walls, the angry timbre of the mob filled the tense silence. Olga heard jeers and shouts. Glass breaking.

Squeezing her gloved hands into fists, she fought her rising terror. She wished now she had brought her pistol with her instead of leaving it in Oksana's care.

Even from her quarantined palace bedroom, she had heard reports of chaos overtaking the cities, but her imagination could never have conceived such pandemonium. She threaded one arm through Yulia's and curled into her shoulder. Yulia Petrovna's ample frame provided her a welcome sense of security. Knowing they shared the secret of Olga's true identity, even if they'd sworn not to speak of it, brought its own comfort.

Yulia patted her hand on her arm, again that rare gesture of comfort from chambermaid to charge.

The carriage jerked forward and began to travel again.

"See, we'll be fi—"

The carriage door flew open. Olga jumped, terror squeezing from her throat in a scream. Yulia stiffened beside her.

A snaggletoothed peasant, ripe with the stench of vodka and a month's worth of body odor, pushed his upper torso into the cabin. He wagged a pistol about as he might a dead fish, but fire blazed in his eyes.

Fear's vise cut off Olga's air supply. She gulped for breath.

He pointed the gun at her.

Then at Yulia.

Then back at Olga again. In three quick jabs, he punched his weapon toward her head.

She felt the blood siphon from her face.

"Your valuables or your lives."

CHAPTER FOUR

A nton lingered in the doorway of Oksana's sickroom, overpowered by a combination of antiseptic and incense.

The attack over a week ago still felt so fresh, sometimes the memory made him shudder, a chill brushing down his spine. It had happened so fast. And, paralyzed by some sort of inner restraint, he'd sat there like a. . .a. . .coward.

He felt sick to his stomach.

What manner of man was he that he allowed a monk to do his fighting for him?

Anton's estimation of the monk's presence of mind and his capabilities rose considerably after last Saturday's incident with the gun-wielding drunk.

It was obvious the drunk hadn't noticed the men sitting on the opposite side of the cabin from the women. Timofea sprang into action as Anton sat frozen in his seat, every peaceful tactic in which he'd been schooled flashing through his mind.

Timofea grabbed the peasant's wrist and shook his gun free so that it fell out of reach between two suitcases on the carriage floor. "You chose the wrong target for your thievery today, ol' fellow. There is nothing here for you, unless you're in the market for a contagious disease. Or perhaps you're looking for someone to hear your confession? We have only prayers and measles to offer. So in the words of our precious Lord and Savior, 'Go and sin no more!' "

The drunk's rheumy eyes grew round. He backed away, stumbled to the ground, picked himself up, brushed the dirt from his backside, and then swaggered off into the crowd.

Monk Timofea responded with a laugh.

Anton didn't find anything about the incident funny. To the contrary, whenever he recalled his reaction, or lack thereof, he broke into a sweat. What was he doing trying to protect Oksana? He didn't know the first thing about being a protector—at least the kind this woman needed. He'd been trained in finances, in sales and purchases. He wasn't cut out for the hero business. Less than an hour into his assignment to guard the tsar's servant girl, he'd nearly seen her killed.

At the rattle and chink of dishes, Anton turned and looked down the hallway.

Yulia had reached the top of the staircase and moved toward him. She carried a breakfast tray.

Her flowing black skirts and high-buttoned shirtwaist served to heighten Yulia's familial resemblance to her priestly brother. They shared the Petrovs' wide-set sienna eyes, Roman noses, and tawny hair. However, years spent in the tsar's employ and eating of his food had padded Yulia's frame, while her brother showed the leanness of one who had prayed straight through a good many meals.

"Is everything all right?" Yulia came alongside Anton and peered into the room. "Oh!" She took a step back and lowered her voice to a whisper. "He's still at prayer." A smile played on her lips, and her eyes sparkled. "You realize, don't you, that if you're waiting to speak with him, you might want to make yourself comfortable. You're apt to be here a good long while."

Before Anton could answer her quip, the monk looked up, nodded, and raised his index finger to signal them to wait. Returning to his posture of prayer, he took another moment to finish his supplications.

Guilt twisted Anton's heart as he witnessed the sacred scene. Lately it seemed his own prayer life consisted of selfish one-line cries for help. These past few days had provided him with more time than usual to devote to spiritual matters, but he'd spent his free moments catching up on his journal entries rather than devoting time to the scriptures or bowing in prayer. Until this week, Anton had held to the belief that their Mennonite ways provided a deeper, more personal faith than Orthodoxy. After spending time in Timofea's company, he knew, at least in this instance, such was not the case.

When Yulia's brother moved to meet Anton by the door, Yulia swept past them and deposited her tray on the table beside Oksana's bed.

"She sleeps an awful lot," Anton said to Timofea. He shot a glance toward Oksana. Blankets covered all but her head, and a nightcap hid her baldness. The angry red scars of her illness still blemished her face. Even so, he saw prettiness in the shape of her round face, deep blue eyes, full lips, high cheekbones, and cute, upturned nose. . . . *She should smile,* he thought. *Perhaps they taught their servants to remain solemn. What a pity.*

She'd nearly caught him staring, at least once, but he'd

been ensnared by the mental image of her as she entered his life—walking down the snowy pathway, bundled in furs, her posture and chin erect, as if she expected the waters to part before her. For a chambermaid, she'd spoken to him harshly, and he had to admit to his hackles rising despite his pledge to serve her. Perhaps she'd forgotten that he was a free man in his own employ with sufficient means.

Condescension was the last thing he'd expected from her. He got enough of that at home. Still, the tsar himself had assigned Anton to this task. He'd complete it without a word of complaint, by the power of God.

"Do you think I should go for a doctor again?"

Timofea shook his head. "No, I doubt you'd have much luck, considering the trouble we had trying to find someone last week. Besides, I don't think it's necessary." The monk crossed his arms and tucked his hands into the wide sleeves of his sacerdotal habit.

Despite Timofea's youthfulness, Anton found the monastic garb intimidating. Their Mennonite elders didn't wear such attire, so the uniform of Orthodox clergy, in and of itself, seemed to command authority and gave Timofea an air of maturity, of believability.

"She's showing steady improvement—as far as her physical condition is concerned." Monk Timofea urged Anton out into the hall with a nod. He pulled the chamber door closed behind him. "It's her ailing spirits that keep her bedfast now. She wants desperately to return to Tsarskoe Selo and to the service of the royal family." He shook his head. "According to Yulia, she expected to have received summons by now, and every day that passes with no word leaves her more depressed. I've not yet had the heart to tell her the whole of the Romanov household is under house arrest."

Where Timofea got all his inside information Anton could only guess. He did know the brother had friends in high places—and apparently with sufficient pull to bring him out of the confines of his monastery cell. Every morning while Anton holed up in Mr. Borovsky's study to pore over ledgers and purchase orders and invoices, trying to find some way to keep his business afloat, Timofea would leave the house. When he returned, the news accounts he shared always seemed to be at least a day or two ahead of the city papers. At times, he spoke of things the media could not, or dared not, report.

Someday soon, when the right occasion presented itself, Anton planned to ask the young man about his father; how a monk might come by a son, and a daughter, for that matter. Anton suspected that something about that connection, whatever it truly was, might explain some of the young man's access to insider information and the freedom with which he traveled the countryside.

Timofea bowed his head, sending his unshorn hair into his face. "You know," he said, looking up again, "if we had waited one more day to bring Oksana and Yulia out, we would have been too late. I pray calmer heads will prevail and a peaceful resolution to all this anarchy will soon be reached."

Anton felt the now-familiar press of the crest against his chest. "I have to admit, I never anticipated our wait here to last this long. . . ."

"Even now, many are searching for the palace servants, pressing them for information or even into service against the throne." Timofea gave him a solemn, frightening look.

"I fear we may have to leave Petrograd."

Anton swallowed hard and looked down the length of the hallway to a tall arched window. Through the sheer curtains, he saw the shadows, lines, and forms of Petrograd's street life on parade. "I know my concerns are small compared to those of Father Russia's, but I am, in fact, worried about my business. The phone lines are all still down. I expected a messenger to deliver a box of purchase orders and invoices for me to work on yesterday, but he never arrived. There's been no sign of him yet this morning, either. I realize Oksana is my responsibility, and I hate to impose on you. But would you mind if I were to leave you and Yulia in charge here for a while so I can go to the warehouse and check in with Mr. Borovsky? Cook also needs me to carry some food over to him."

"*Konyeshna*—you must attend to your business." The monk untangled his arms from his sleeves and patted Anton on the shoulder. "I think you should go, if for no other reason than for the chance to get some fresh air. You've been cooped up here for days. It will do you good to get out."

It amazed Anton that Timofea, despite his young age, possessed understanding that Anton's own father still couldn't grasp.

"Thank you, Timofea. I promise not to be long."

Timofea led the way down the staircase. "Your commitment to watch over Oksana is quite admirable, but I'm sure the tsar never expected you to take up residence outside her chamber door. Go. Yulia and I will tend to the patient. She'll be fine. Just take care. You know as well as I do the trouble to be found in the streets. Be ever vigilant."

"I'll follow the advice my father always gives me. He employs a walk-fast-and-look-worried mode when he doesn't want to be stopped or questioned en route." Johann Klassen had employed that mode of communication Anton's entire childhood. Anton should be an expert at mimicking it by now.

The monk chuckled. "I'll have to remember your father's routine when I'm back at the monastery. Being the youngest of the brothers has its disadvantages—one of which is being seen as the resident errand boy."

"Speaking of errands, I'm sure Yulia knows, but I'd better mention it to you as well," Anton said as he followed Timofea down the flight of stairs. "The cook has gone out in search of groceries, and she said not to expect her back anytime soon."

When they reached the foyer, Anton accepted the monk's assistance into his wraps. Then he reached for the muslin-covered basket of food the cook had left by the door for him to deliver to Mr. Borovsky.

While Anton situated his load, Timofea rested his hand on the doorknob. "Mrs. Ivanovna is working hard to accommodate my vegetarian needs, and I know you're paying for our board. I feel guilty imposing on the good graces of you and your Mr. Borovsky and his cook in this way. I'm sure you didn't expect to have to feed and house a crowd when the tsar asked you to see to Oksana's safekeeping."

"Nonsense." The word slipped out before Anton thought to censor his speech when addressing a member of the clergy—even one younger than he. "We are all in this together. I have no doubt that without your sister, Oksana would be absolutely distraught; and without you,

I would be helpless to know what to do to look after her."
Anton offered Timofea a thin smile.

Timofea held the door open for him. "Well, the Lord
sees our goings and comings, and He knows our need before
we know to ask. He will watch over us and guide us as a
shepherd his sheep."

Anton said nothing, nodding instead, biting back his
cynicism. Yes, he believed God watched over them, but he
had to admit feeling that the Almighty seemed more of an
overseer than a provider. Especially since so much of the
fullness of life, the safe pasture, seemed to have been robbed
of him, even before birth.

"Don't worry. I'll hurry back to the fold," he finally
said. He closed the door behind him and joined the throng
on the street.

Anton navigated the short walk from Mr. Borovsky's
home to their warehouse on the quay in the industrial dis-
trict without attracting any undue attention, so far as he
could tell. He skirted down alternate roads whenever he
caught sight of provisional government troops or a cluster of
scowling peasants, but his detours lasted only a street or two
before he was able to return to his original route. The chaos
on the streets reminded him of a New Year's celebration
gone amuck: bottles broken, buildings burned, rabble mill-
ing in unorganized demonstrations. Smoke and the smell of
liquor singed the air.

When he finally reached his company warehouse, he
kicked the snow from his boots against the building's brick
face and paused to draw in several lung-filling breaths.

The iron door, inset into the mammoth shipping and
receiving gate, stood ajar.

"In this cold, one would think people might have the sense to shut the door," Anton growled. The door squealed in response as he pushed it open wide enough to enter, then closed it behind him with a slam. He stood just inside the doorway and waited for his eyes to adjust to the interior's diffused light, straining to hear the customary sounds of labor that accompanied the familiar scents of leather and tempered steel.

"*Prevyeht*—Hello! Anyone here?"

Silence answered.

"Mr. Borovsky?" Anton made his way to the walled-in office area in the southwest corner of the warehouse. He bypassed his own vacant office and headed straight for the shop steward's open office door. "Mr. Borovsky? Are you here?" He stuck his head into the room.

Empty. He stood for a moment, dissecting his tangled thoughts. Had he missed some sort of national holiday? He stepped into the office and around the mohair divan typically reserved for Borovsky's visiting business associates. Anton swiped at the mound of blankets wadded at one end of the divan as he passed by. Any guests today would be hard-pressed to find a comfortable place to sit. Tidiness never had been on the list of the shop steward's numerous outstanding qualities, but after a week of living in his office, the mess had taken the upper hand.

Anton allowed a stab of guilt. Borovsky had been a faithful steward; he could suffer some personal untidiness.

The samovar behind him began to hiss and spit hot water from its release valve. Borovsky could not have gone far. While he waited for Borovsky to show himself, Anton righted a cup, which had tipped and spilled tea across a slew of papers that covered the desktop. Then he returned the swivel chair from over by the row of filing cabinets to its proper place under the desk. Whatever had yanked Borovsky from his office had happened in a great hurry.

Anton set the basket of foodstuffs on top of a filing cabinet, then paced a stripe in the rug, up and back across the empty room. The manufacturing end of their harness business had begun back at their family-owned factory in the Molotschna, nearly twenty years earlier. When Anton had finished school, his father had established the Petrograd warehouse to serve as their distribution center for the metropolitan area. They'd never run a large operation, but it took a dozen employees to run operations during the day. He paused just long enough to look at his watch and then started pacing again.

Where was everyone?

The metallic taste of dread pooled in Anton's throat.

He left the office and returned to the open warehouse expanse. He took slow, noiseless steps at first, listening for the slightest sound.

"Igor?" He called out the name of the floor supervisor and walked another meter, then called out again, fear swelling his chest. "Vladimir? Pavel?" Though he called the names of several employees, he heard only the echo of his own voice off the empty warehouse rafters, the thunder of his heartbeat in his ears.

Passing row upon row of leather straps and metal fittings, his walk turned into a jog. "Hello, anyone?" From one end of the warehouse to the other, his search for workers turned up empty.

He made his way back to the offices and forced himself to calm down. There had to be a reasonable explanation. Maybe their workforce had joined in the rebellious furor of the day and gone on strike. Maybe Mr. Borovsky decided he'd better break such news to him in person and they'd passed each other along the way. It wouldn't be the first time a forgotten samovar boiled dry. But if Borovsky had set out for home, why had he left the warehouse door unlocked—and ajar?

CHAPTER FIVE

Anton waited until his heartbeat stopped thundering against his ears. He couldn't very well go to the police. The provisional government controlled what law enforcement still existed, and Oksana and Yulia's presence at Borovsky's home meant he couldn't raise suspicions. They had to be protected—at all costs, according to the tsar. The ruler's dedication to his servants seemed, at the time, benevolent. Now it seemed overdone. They were simply servants, not royalty. The worst that could happen at the hands of the police was some invasive questioning, right?

Still, he had made a promise. And while he didn't know what that promise entailed exactly or how to fulfill his vow, he planned to be a man of his word.

Monk Timofea might have some ideas as to the whereabouts of his employees—he seemed to know every other secret floating around Petrograd. Anton retrieved a key from his top desk drawer, and securing the building as best he could, he turned to leave. Before he set off toward the house, he surveyed the passersby. Men, capped with ratty rabbit *shopkas,* huddled in wool jackets around canisters of lit coals. Shawl-hooded women in dog-fur *shubas* and wool *valenki* stamped their feet in bread queues. One of them might have seen something, might know some-thing. However, he couldn't manage to make eye contact with a single person. They all employed his walk-fast-look-worried technique and made themselves unavailable for questioning.

A stone's throw out from the warehouse on the frozen river, a humpbacked old man crouched next to a hole in the ice, tending his fishing line. Anton, his feet dancing and sliding under him, walked out to the bundled figure.

"Excuse me for interrupting your fishing, sir, but did you happen to see anything unusual take place at that warehouse earlier this morning?" Anton pointed to the KLASSEN HARNESS sign over the building.

The *dehdooshkah* worked to straighten his arthritic knees and stand. Anton extended his hand, but the offer of aid was waved off.

"Well, son, the unusual's become more typical than routine around here of late, but you could say there was a commotion there an hour or so ago, yes. Same as is hap-pening all over town. They came and carried 'em off."

A slow burn of impatience flamed up Anton's neck. He bit back the desire to shake the man and maybe hurry his explanation along. "Who is 'they,' and what did they do with all my workmen?"

"Provisional forces came through here early yesterday morning. Back again this morning, too. They called it 'enlisting recruits,' but appeared to me they were deliver-ing their draft notices at the end of a gun, marching off any able-bodied men they could find. I watched the whole thing from under the pier, just in case they'd consider me soldier material."

He didn't appear to be joking. Anton wouldn't have laughed anyway.

"Do you know where they've been taken? I've got to speak with—"

The old man poked a gloved finger into Anton's chest. "Listen, son, if I were you, I'd forget about trying to find whoever it is you're after and steer clear of public places. Get yourself out of town if you can. You're just the sort they're looking for."

Anton scanned the quay. The grandfather provided Anton's lone means of defense. They both stood exposed, unprotected, easy targets.

"Yes." Anton moved toward shoreline. "I should go. Perhaps you should consider doing the same?"

"Soon as I snag myself a keeper, I will, but if I don't fish, I don't eat. Simple as that. You take care, though." The man tossed a wave in Anton's direction and turned back to his fishing hole.

Once Anton reached the street, he raced toward Mr. Borovsky's home. He refused to let go of the hope that his employee had managed to escape conscription—if the incident had occurred at all. So many hours out in the cold might have numbed the old man's brain.

If not and the peasant spoke the truth, the city wasn't safe. Clearly the provisional troops were taking control of the city if they had emptied his entire warehouse, and others, by force. Prudence said he and Timofea should bundle up the women tonight and spirit them away. He would talk to Monk Timofea. The cleric might be young, but he possessed wisdom far beyond his years. Together they could decide the best course of action to take in light of this latest horrible turn of events.

Anton let himself in the front door, and without bothering to remove his overcoat, he strode from the parlor to the study and through the dining room in search of Timofea, Yulia, or even Cook Ivanovna.

Borovsky's two-story brick house, set back from the street, muffled the chaos outside and dripped with the quiet slumber of afternoon. The clock ticked, once, twice, again, much slower than his quickening heartbeat. "Hello?"

No one responded to his call. He advanced down the hall, peeking his head into the parlor, then the kitchen. "Brother Timofea?"

He remembered the cook had left to go shopping earlier, and he could safely surmise that the block-long queues might detain her for hours. But Yulia and certainly Timofea should be on hand to look after Oksana. The smell of lemon-oil polish mingled with the scent of coal still burning in the stove from the kitchen. He tasted another swell of panic, so fresh from his visit to the warehouse, and swallowed it back. Certainly the provisional army wouldn't conscript a monk and two chambermaids.

He nearly smiled at his own foolishness. The women were probably resting, Timofea in prayer.

See, another reason why he made a poor protector, if one at all. Paranoia too easily rose to choke off wisdom. If he hoped to act as a guardian, he needed to rein in his suspicions and think with a clear head. Although the world exploded in violence around them, hardly a soul knew Oksana's whereabouts, outside their small band.

One final time, Anton peered into the kitchen. Seeing no one there, he started toward the staircase. But before the swinging door rattled shut, he thought he heard a noise.

He slowed. Listened again. Crying. Or rather. . . moaning?

His pulse ratcheted as he eased the door open once more and stuck his head back into the kitchen. A gust of cold air whistled through the entryway that led into the back garden. Cook must not have shut it tight behind her when she went out. Memories of the warehouse's open door pricked at Anton's thoughts, but he tried to shake them off. Probably the wind.

He took two steps into the kitchen, and the double-leaf swinging doors whomped shut behind him.

"Anyone here?"

A whimper filtered from the pantry.

Whether it was human or creature, Anton couldn't tell, but the sound made something ache inside him. Whatever it was, it had been wounded.

He pulled in a deep breath, bracing himself for attack from whatever injured street creature had found refuge in the pantry. Creeping toward the door, he recognized the cries as female.

Oksana? Could it be Oksana he heard? Surely not. But perhaps she had woken and found herself alone. Or scared. And had gone in search of Yulia. He felt sick. He never should have left his responsibility to anyone else, not even the brave clergyman. Where was Timofea anyway? He tried to quell the sudden flare of anger that burned inside his throat at himself, at Timofea.

Anton steeled his courage for what he would find as he pushed back the pocket door.

Light filtered from the outer room across a female form knotted into a fetal position beside a burlap turnip sack. At her feet, compotes and beans swam around icebergs of shattered glass jars.

A rancid odor, of what origin he couldn't tell, emanated from the pantry. The woman kept her head buried beneath one arm and clutched her blouse closed across her chest with both hands. Her black skirts, twisted and damp, streaked across a puddle of blood.

Oh no. Anton's chest tightened, a sickness in his gut as he fell to his knees. *Not Oksana.* But any relief he felt at the realization it was not her died in his grief.

Yulia.

Clearly, whoever had attacked her had escaped out the back. "Yulia. Shh, you're safe now." He crouched beside her, reached out, and stroked his fingertips across her shoulder. "Yulia?"

"Don't touch me!" Her panicked voice and the way she practically leaped away from him made him jerk back. "Don't. . .touch. . ." Her words dissolved as sobs wracked her body.

Oh, Yulia. Anton swallowed past the fist of horror in his throat. He needed Timofea. No. . .he needed Oksana.

Oksana.

He scrambled to his feet, panic nearly emptying him. "Oksana!"

<hr>

Olga's stomach growled. The hunger pains had interrupted her nap. Her mouth watered at the thought of bread and jam and a cup of hot tea or café au lait.

Hours earlier, Yulia had carried away her breakfast tray untouched.

Now, for the first time in weeks, the thought of food appealed to her rather than left a vile taste at the back of her throat. For the life of her, Olga couldn't figure out why the girl needed so long to fetch a fresh tray.

Well, if the food wasn't coming to her, she would go to the food. She left her bed, and with slow-motion efforts, she slipped into her dressing gown, forgoing the extra effort of donning her wig.

She found the vacant corridor unsettling. The floorboards groaned beneath her as she eased down the hallway with halting steps. She'd never given it much thought before, but in the face of solitude, she realized just how seldom she was ever alone. She reached the top of the stairwell, and clutching the banister with both hands, she started her descent to the ground floor. Olga made it no farther than the third tread.

A rampaging hulk barreled around the corner and took the first four steps two at a time, nearly running her over.

She screamed.

Anton looked up, froze, and the expression on his face scared her. Panic—no, terror.

Alarm bolted through Olga and pinned her in place. Her hand subconsciously went to her naked scalp. Warmth flooded her cheeks. She covered the top of her forehead with her hand. "Mr. Klassen," she said, barely masking her humiliation. "You are supposed to be defending me, not scaring me to death."

He seemed not to notice, for he stepped up to her eye level and, for a moment, struggled to speak, his eyes wild and his breathing hard.

Then he spoke. "Thank God you're okay." For a long moment, he looked like he might actually sweep her up into his arms, so desperate was his gaze upon her. Then he turned, bracing one arm against the wall, and closed his eyes.

"You're scaring me," she said, then realized she'd spoken aloud. She saw him clench his jaw, as if reining in some wash of emotions. He nodded. Straightened. When he turned to her, the expression in his eyes made her hurt.

Something had happened. To him?

He straightened, then blew out a breath. "I am sorry, ma'am."

She had to confess that each time she looked at Anton, she was struck by his demeanor, a quiet strength that he seemed to keep tightly capped. With his solemn countenance, she entertained occasional imaginations of what a smile might do to his gray eyes.

Conversely, even with a smile, she bore a striking resemblance to a skinned potato.

"It's Yulia. She's been. . . She's been hurt." He seemed to stumble on his words. And even now, a shadow of grief clouded his eyes. "I thought. . . I'm sorry I left you. But Yulia needs you. She's. . .she needs you."

Yulia? Olga felt light-headed. *What. . . ?*

He must have seen her start to crumple, because he cupped his hand under her elbow. "Please, come quickly." His eyes said the rest.

Yulia, hurt. And it was bad.

She let him help her down the stairs, fighting a sway of weakness. "What happened?" He hurried her down the hallway. "Did she fall?"

He opened the kitchen door, releasing his hold on her arm, his brow furrowed, shaking his head. "She's there." He pointed to the pantry.

The pantry?

"I'll get a blanket," he said.

"Don't you dare pass out. Not now." Olga spoke the command to herself, but Anton stopped and turned.

"Of course not. I'll be right back, I promise."

His words injected courage into her as she approached the pantry.

Oh no. Bile clotted Olga's throat. She covered her mouth with her hands and sank to her knees, reaching out to the hunched and weeping servant girl. "Oh, Yulia. Oh, Yulia." How could this have happened? She dropped to her knees, aware of wetness saturating her bedclothes, and reached out for Yulia.

The servant's dark hair hung in tangles, a welt across her cheek, her eyes reddened and nearly closed with swelling.

Yulia crumpled into Olga's embrace. However odd it felt to comfort one who had been her attendant, whose station it was to comfort her, a simmering anger built inside Olga. It eclipsed propriety and, shaking through her limbs, made her draw Yulia closer. "Oh, Yulia, I'm so sorry." How could this have happened? Where was Anton? Or Timofea?

Yulia buried her head in Olga's shoulder. She clutched at fistfuls of Olga's dressing gown and sobbed.

Olga choked on her own cries, awash in rage at the monster who had committed this crime.

As far as outward signs of physical injury, she had witnessed far worse in her nursing service: amputations of gangrenous limbs, disfiguring burns, intestines held in place by thread and gauze. But never had she witnessed a woman's spirit and innocence ripped from her by such a base act of debauchery.

Mother, I need you. How can I help Yulia? What do I say?

Oh, she wanted to be home. No circumstance at Tsarskoe Selo could be any more desperate or dangerous than the one that had just occurred under this roof. Her father would be sorry he had ever insisted she leave. She would go back today, and no one—not the whole of the provisional army or the rebel hoards combined—would stand in her way.

Yulia's weeping tapered into jagged breaths. She pulled away from Olga, and with one hand clutching her bodice, she washed her face with her other sleeve.

"He. . .held a. . .knife. . . ."

"Shh." As Olga smoothed out Yulia's torn garments to afford her modesty, she noticed a gash on her leg. "Your leg. . .it's cut. Let me look."

Yulia wrapped her arms around herself, still crying as Olga surveyed the wound—at least this one a surface injury. While the wound ran long, it appeared to be nothing a few stitches wouldn't fix.

Where was Anton with that blanket? And they would need medical supplies to treat her wounds, also.

Yulia swallowed hard. "When I. . .started to. . .scream. . . he. . ." She swallowed again. "He. . .cut me. . .said. . .if I cried out. . .he'd slit my throat." Yulia closed her eyes. The small shroud of privacy she allowed herself seemed to embolden her speech. "Did he. . .did he find you?"

"Find me?" Olga went still. "What do you mean?"

"I told him that you weren't here. That you'd left. I told him—he was. . .so. . .angry."

"Sh–sh–sh." Olga grabbed Yulia's hand and squeezed. "You are safe now. You're going to be all right. I can have you stitched up in no time." *And we'll have Dr. Botkin examine you when we get home. Except, had someone discovered their charade already? Had they come looking for her, the grand duchess?* The thought made her nearly retch. "Are you in a great deal of pain. . .otherwise?" Olga looked away, unable to meet Yulia's gaze.

"No. . .I mean yes, but—"

"It's okay, Yulia."

What was taking Anton so long? Some protection he turned out to be. Olga grabbed up the cook's apron from a hook by the door and gently pillowed Yulia's injured leg.

"Where was Anton when this was happening?" Her own tone surprised her. But he should have heard the struggle.

Yulia used one hand to scoot herself back and lean against the pantry wall. Her body trembled with the force of a seizure.

"D–don't be up–upset with him. H–he's not to blame." She racked in a breath. "If anything"—her chest jerked in faltering heaves—"the fault is my own."

"No, Yulia."

"Anton arranged with Timofea to. . .to. . .watch us. . . while he went to his warehouse. On business, I think. But Timofea received a message, a summons. He seemed. . . upset." Yulia swallowed as if tucking in her spilling emotions. "He wanted to stay until Anton returned, but I insisted he go—that we'd. . .be. . ." A fresh rush of tears broke her voice. "We'd be fine."

Olga stroked the girl's arm. It wasn't her chambermaid's

fault that the two adventurers her father had conscripted to protect them had no more sense than her sister's disobedient spaniel, Jimmy. They'd left them alone.

Alone. To fend off all manner of attackers, it seemed.

Her father would kill them. Probably. Olga's anger seared her chest and made it all but impossible to breathe.

"If Anton hadn't returned when he did, this. . .this might have happened to you, too, and I'd never be able to live with myself then."

She saw, suddenly, that truth—of how narrowly she'd escaped attack—written in Yulia's big brown eyes. Her world tilted. Her own vulnerability rocked her with such force, Olga started to tremble. Her hands shook, and she fisted them and buried them in her lap. Again the thought hit her, and this time it settled deep into the crannies of her heart. What if Yulia hadn't been a random victim? What if someone had found them, had been tracking them, possibly to kidnap her and force her father into horrific decisions?

Had they been stalked? Had the intruder acted alone? Did they know her true identity? She and all within her company may very well be the target of an even grander crime. They had to flee to safety, wherever safety could be found. Now.

"I'm so sorry." Yulia looked past Olga into the vacant kitchen, then reached out and laid her hand on Olga's arm. "The Grand Duchess shouldn't be out of bed," she whispered.

"The Grand Duchess undoubtedly *is* in her bed," Olga rasped. She shot a glance over her shoulder, then gave a quick shake of her head, scolding Yulia with leveled eyes. She hated to reprimand her, especially now, but especially now they needed to be ever more cautious. She couldn't risk their lives on a slip of the tongue. "I'm fine. Don't worry about me. If I arrange it, do you think you can manage the trip back home?"

"Begging your pardon, Oksana," Yulia said, laying a heavy emphasis on the name, her eyes wide at the impudence, "but I don't see the use in returning on my account, nor do I think such a trip is advisable under any circumstance without a direct summons from His Imperial Highness." She winced and lowered her head.

Olga's ears burned. Any other time, she would have condemned such boldness. But just as Yulia had nearly slipped moments before, she, in turn, needed to accept moments of wisdom offered by her attendant. "Yes, you're right, Yulia," she said quietly.

Timofea burst into the room, Anton on his heels. "Where is she?" He crossed the kitchen and excused his way past Olga to kneel at his sister's side. Anton held himself back at the pantry door, his arms laden with blankets and towels.

"The Lord have mercy on us all," Timofea said, making the sign of the cross. He leaned in and kissed his sister's cheek, stroked her hair. "I'm so sorry. Oh, Yulia, I'm so sorry. Are you okay?" While Olga watched, he pulled his sister to his chest, his eyes closed, as if absorbing her pain.

"Is she going to be okay?" Timofea looked to Olga for assurance.

Olga simply nodded. But really, how did she know? Would any of them ever be okay? She tightened her jaw, refusing to give in to tears. Again. She was tired, so tired of tears.

Timofea didn't appear convinced. He clutched his sister's hand in his. "Yulia, I'm so sorry I left you." He looked at Olga. "I'm sorry I left you both unguarded." He kissed his sister's fingertips. "I never dreamed—even in light of the rebellion—I thought sure you'd be safe for just a little... Oh, can you ever forgive me?"

Olga stood and took two steps back. She figured it must be a sin not to forgive a monk when asked, but she found herself angry at him just the same. He'd acted with the impudence of his youth rather than the wisdom of his station. In her opinion, Yulia had a right to bear a grudge.

Even if it was unchristian.

"Why would anyone do this?" Anton stood just feet away, wearing a look of pain. "Who did this?"

Olga glanced at him, the truth of her identity just at the edge of her lips. Perhaps if he knew the danger, the real danger she'd put them in, he'd shuffle her back to Tsarskoe Selo tonight, this very hour.

And then what? Defy her father? She never acted outside the confines of her station. She was a Romanov. A grand duchess. She studied, she attended official functions, she cared for her subjects, she obeyed her authoritarian father.

Besides, what if Anton or Timofea had something to do with Yulia's attack?

The thought nearly took away her breath, crumpled her knees. But they'd both left. Surreptitiously. Without replacement.

She glanced at Anton, at his grim expression, at his hair now mussed, probably from worry, his gray eyes thick with grief. He'd been the consummate gentleman until this moment. If anyone, it was Timofea who seemed rough around the edges, given to secret liaisons. She'd seen him hustle down the street on some errant mission from her bedroom window. Clerics were, after all, well versed in the art of keeping a confidence.

But what kind of confidence? A plot against the head of the church?

She couldn't betray her identity. Not yet. Perhaps not ever.

Even if someone hadn't discovered her identity and she'd succeeded at her ruse as a palace chambermaid, she and Yulia would still possess knowledge of the inner work-ings of the royal household. Knowledge that might prove of grave importance in the wrong hands.

Olga backed away as Timofea helped Yulia from the pantry, took her in his arms, and carried her into the next room.

She followed them, Anton not far behind.

Timofea set Yulia down on the parlor settee, smoothed back her hair. "I'll get some medical supplies," he said softly. Rising, he cast a look at Anton and left.

Yulia laid back, her eyes open, staring at the ceiling, looking bereft.

Olga felt her anger rise, and before she could rein it back, she rounded on Anton. Her voice she kept low, but she hoped he heard her tone loud and clear.

"I hold you fully responsible for this, you know. You should have never left us unguarded. My—the tsar will learn of this, I promise." She felt heat rise to her face as she struggled with her fury.

Anton looked away. On his face, she saw an agony so deep it nearly deflated her anger. "You're right," he said. "I've failed you. I've failed the tsar. I've broken my promise to him to take good care of you."

He turned to look at her, and something in his gaze scared her. "I promise, from here on out, I'll never travel beyond earshot of you."

"That's fine for me, but your promises come too late for Yulia." The words tasted bitter in her mouth. She yanked a blanket from the bottom of the bundle Anton held and draped the cover over Yulia.

She stared at her chambermaid, hot tears burning her eyes. Anger at Anton, anger at this rebellion, this stupid plot of her father, even anger at the measles that made her ugly and weak and—

She felt her head spin, felt darkness closing in on her, saw the floor coming up at her fast. She willed herself not to swoon.

Anton scooped her up a second before the world went dark.

CHAPTER SIX

A nton joined Timofea in wearing a path up and down the vestibule rug. Within moments of her fainting spell, Oksana had sufficiently recovered, and although Timofea had taken over tending Yulia's wound, Oksana insisted on remaining in the parlor to stitch up the gash on Yulia's leg. As they paced, Anton relayed all he knew about the details of Yulia's attack and shared the events of his trip to the warehouse. The best they could figure, the attacker broke in through the kitchen door and found Yulia.

"I must have frightened him off," Anton said, forcing from his memory the image of Yulia broken in body and spirit, lying on the pantry floor. "Why? I don't understand. Why would someone do this?"

Timofea looked positively undone. His hood had fallen back; his youthful eyes burned with anger. He'd said little and balled his hands into fists when he walked. Anton could imagine that, if it had been his sister, he might fight the urge to tear her attacker limb from limb.

He stopped pacing and glanced at Oksana now bent over Yulia, then out at the street where the sun threw shadows across the cobblestones. "We need to leave. It's not safe. With the provisional army breaking into homes, businesses. . . I want the women out of Petrograd."

"I agree," Timofea said, his voice more of a growl. "Immediately." He stopped, and Anton watched him draw a finger and thumb across his eyes. For a moment, he did not speak, just stared at Yulia through the open parlor doors, his shoulders rising and falling. "I had just received those orders today, seemingly as my sister was being attacked." He shook his head. "We should have left days ago."

Anton stared at him. "Orders? From whom are you taking orders?"

"Word came down from His Imperial Majesty himself." Timofea reached into his cassock and withdrew a packet of letters. "You should find your own set of instructions here." He offered Anton the top envelope on the stack and fanned the others. "These are addressed to the women. I assume they contain letters from various parties under house arrest at Tsarskoe Selo." He slipped them back into their hiding place.

Anton ran his thumb over the envelope's elaborate seal. "How. . . I mean, where did you get these?"

"I'm not at liberty to say. I don't actually know. For the protection of all those involved, the channels of delivery are kept secret from me."

Anton nodded, but he wasn't entirely sure he could accept that answer. Ultimately, the Imperial Highness had asked *him* to protect Oksana. Timofea was supposed to be his sidekick. "I should have been told about your liaison, Brother."

Timofea turned, considering him with a frown. Then quietly, he nodded. "I understand. When I arrived here, I approached a brother—an acquaintance of my father's. He sent word through the channels of the church that we were well. The tsar used this route to secure communications."

Anton went still, staring at him. "Did it occur to you that you could have alerted someone from either the rebel faction or provisional forces that we were here?"

Timofea's mouth opened, his face blanching. He shook his head, showing his youth for the first time since Anton had known him. He felt a spear of pity for the monk.

"I know you're just trying to do your duty. But from now on, please, trust me. And don't tell anyone else where we are. I don't know why it is so important that I protect Oksana, but I made a promise, and I intend to keep it."

Timofea looked at the papers in his hands. "Certainly. Forgive my boldness."

Anton placed his hand on the monk's shoulder, feeling a brotherly kinship to the boy no older than his kid stepbrother. Timofea carried so much responsibility, Anton easily forgot his age. "Of course. But we must be away, and soon."

Anton started to break the seal but paused, his hand poised in midair. "May I?" He waited for Timofea's nod before proceeding. His heart sank a bit when he saw the text consisted of only a few short lines. For a moment he'd hoped for an epistle filled with the monarch's advice.

> *To My Forest Friend,*
> *Fire threatens. Leave your present woods. The Lord will guide your steps as you seek refuge. Take the sisters and follow your brother home.*
> *My sincere prayers for your safety.*
>
> *Yours truly,*
> *A Fellow Woodsman*

Anton reread the note several times, then, scratching his head, he passed the cryptic letter to the monk. "I think I'm being told that we're supposed to follow you. Home? Where are you from?"

Timofea studied the message, then returned the note to Anton. "I have to concur with your translation," he said. "And I believe it agrees with the instructions I've been given. For now, we'll go back to Pechory. Rail service seems to be up and running again, at least somewhat. If the women can manage the trip tonight, I will arrange a private car through the help of the local diocese. Yulia and I have an aunt and uncle who live in the village there, just down the street from the monastery. They are trustworthy souls, and Uncle Maxim is a physician. They will do whatever it takes to keep the women safely hidden and nurse them both back to health."

"Am I to have no say in this matter whatsoever?" Oksana stumbled into the foyer from the drawing room and sank onto the receiving bench. "Have you no intention of consulting me before deciding my fate?" Though her eyes flashed, exhaustion shadowed her face and frame.

Anton had a sudden flash of memory—Oksana collapsing into his arms, her lithe body as he swept her up, the moment of her complete dependence on his strength as her head bobbed against his chest. She'd fit well there, and he couldn't deny that watching her surrender to his embrace had surfaced unfamiliar feelings. Tenderness perhaps.

Not that he knew, exactly, what tenderness toward a woman felt like. He hadn't known his mother, and, well, he'd never let a woman close, fearing perhaps the hard-edged criticism he would receive from his father and stepmother.

But when he'd held Oksana in his arms, her head against his chest, watching her dark eyelashes drift down, feelings churned in his chest unlike any he'd ever before experienced.

Until Timofea reentered the room. The young monk had stood in quiet shock, a frown on his face.

Timofea had said nothing as Anton set Oksana down on another sofa, then wet a cloth for her forehead. She came to moments later without comment.

Probably she didn't even remember being in his arms.

Especially judging by the way she now glared at him. "I am not going with you to. . .Pechory or wherever." A tear traced the outline of her nose, and she brushed it away with the back of her hand. "You can take Yulia to run and hide if you want, but I am going back to Tsarskoe Selo."

"The Lord bless you, Oksana," Timofea said, his voice soft and low, "but there are things you need to know about the situation at Tsarskoe Selo. Maybe you should hear the news and read what those who are still there have to say before making up your mind."

Oksana snatched the tendered envelope from the monk's hand and ripped open its seal.

Anton watched her eyes dart back and forth as she read the handwritten lines.

She refolded the pages, slipped them back into the envelope, and used it like a scepter to stab at the air, first at Timofea, then at Anton. "I don't care what it says." She raked her teeth over her quivering lower lip. "I'm going home." Her shoulders shuddered when she pulled in a deep breath. "There has to be a way back into the palace. They need me."

Three times Anton opened his mouth to speak, but no words came out.

Such brash defiance from a servant girl.

He understood how she could speak with peremptory bluntness in the heat of a crisis as she had in the pantry. And he wanted to give her the benefit of the doubt now. But would she speak and act with such boldness if standing face-to-face with the tsar and tsarina? Somehow, he didn't think so. If Oksana always exhibited this proclivity toward disrespect when addressing her superiors, how she had managed to keep her position with the royal family, much less warrant the tsar's concern and attention at the hour of his abdication, was beyond Anton's comprehension. Surely, the code of conduct for the Romanov domestics wasn't all that different from the behavior of servants in the general populace. Not once had he observed Yulia exhibiting impudence of any kind, either through her actions or through her demeanor.

He would have sent the chambermaid Oksana packing long ago, orphan or not, had she shown such insolence while under his authority.

"Begging your pardon." Anton crossed his arms. "I understand you are distraught, but perhaps you need to be reminded that the decision to return is not up to you."

Oksana stared at him, eyes wide, tears running down her face. With her shorn head and high cheekbones, her dark blue eyes looked huge in her head. Perhaps beautiful, when not angry.

She put her hand to her mouth, fighting the flow of tears. Anton's heart as well as his tone softened just a bit. "Look, I know this is hard. You are concerned for the Imperial Highnesses as well as missing your home, but I have my orders.

I am to keep you safe and out of harm's way until such time as the tsar sends me specific instructions as to how I am to deliver you back into his hands. I wish I could comply with your wishes and escort you back to the palace immediately, but I made a vow to the tsar."

She pulled a handkerchief from her pocket and dabbed her nose. "Don't lecture me on the importance of obedience. You aren't the only one committed to carrying out the tsar's requests. My devotion has never been questioned, and I am insulted by such insinuations now." Fury glinted off her tears. "The tsar obviously does not realize the extent to which my safety has been compromised while under your care."

"Now, Oksana, please." Timofea extended his arm and motioned for her to stop. "We are all upset over what's happened, but—"

"But what?" she fired back. "But you can ensure I'll be safer in Pechory than I would be under house arrest with the royal family?" She huffed and shook her head.

Her accusatory tone riled Anton, and the heat of his anger melted away any sympathies elicited by her tears. He could abide no more of her condescending airs.

"Listen, Your *Highness*—"

His sarcasm hit target. Oksana closed her mouth. Her eyes grew wide.

"After consulting with Timofea, I believe our best option is to go to Pechory, and that is where we are going. Like it or not, you'll just have to trust us."

❦

In truth, he felt sickened by what he'd done. Just a bit.

The little tramp. Gleb whipped his hands down his face, remembering again her screams, feeling her struggle beneath him.

Last week when she looked out her chamber door and saw him in the corridor, she had waved and ducked back into her chamber. His curiosity aroused, he waited in the shadows. But not for long. Within moments, the tart of a maid crept into the hallway and down the stairs—accompanied by another most interesting palace resident. They and their peculiar entourage hadn't been all that difficult to trail to their Petrograd hideaway.

Ah, the royal family's little plot.

We should all be so lucky as Olga to have such a contingency plan. He leaned against a building, thankful the shadows in the alleyway concealed him. Across the street, a mob gathered in front of his home, some throwing bottles at the windows. His mother had barricaded the windows, the doors, and probably was packing right now.

Or hiding her jewels—from him, as well as from the rebel forces and provisional government. Nowadays, loyalty ran thin among the Romanovs. Aunts and uncles, cousins and stepsiblings from around Europe were testing the strength of their royal ties, seeing how far they could pull before the Romanovs might snap off and free-fall without the safety net of family connections to protect them.

Lesser royals like himself, far down on the feeding chain, were left to survival of the fittest.

Gleb lit a cigarette, pulling in sharply when he saw how his hands shook. He had not meant to hurt the maid when he investigated their hideaway. Not really. His anger and frustration at being a royal left behind had simply consumed him, poured out into violence he hadn't expected. He had thought he could use Yulia's obvious affection for him. He had flirted with her for years, never realizing she might become important.

Then again, who had ever dreamed that Russia might rise up, behead their very benefactors? The masses, just like the servant girl. Ungrateful.

Infuriating.

Because of her, he had barely escaped. He still bore a welt on his chin where the chambermaid had scratched him. But at least he had confirmed the truth.

Olga, the grand duchess, had evaded house arrest. And if his hunches, bolstered by the clues he'd coerced from the maid, proved accurate, the tsar's daughter secreted thousands of rubles worth of jewels in her garments. Jewels that would give him a new life in a new land. A royal life, like the one he should have had. If only Mother had married better. She'd compromised her position for love. And discovered that love didn't buy bread, or homes, or even protection.

Compromises. One choice at a time had landed him in this alley, watching the mindless peasantry erupt in chaos. Forcing him to become a man he never thought he'd be.

He threw down the cigarette and crushed it under his boot. He would wait with their secrets. Olga couldn't hide from him forever.

According to her coveted letter from Mother, Olga's family now served as prisoners in their own home, their future as unpredictable as the spring weather. She felt like a traitor of sorts, traipsing to the bathhouse behind Dr. Petrov's home, not so far removed from the spot where her father had abdicated his throne.

In this world where cataclysmic events stood as commonplace, the mundane tasks of everyday life now seemed surreal. Still, she saw no virtue in smelling foul when she had the means to get clean.

Olga walked arm in arm with Yulia.

Owing in good part to all the two chambermaids had endured together in the past week, their relationship had changed from that of servant/superior to one of friends. The two of them, bundled against the cold, picked their way down the muddy path that led from the cottage, past the pigpen, and to the Petrovs' rustic *banya*.

Beyond the yard, a flock of sheep grazed on tan grassy patches that pushed up through the snow-coated field like toes in a holey sock. The early evening sky held just enough hint of spring to lighten the spirit and delude Olga into dreams of grass between her toes and trips to Livadiya. Instead, most likely the next weeks would see a spring blizzard and probably more gray days of grim news, or none, from home.

No hope of future days on the Black Sea, swimming with Anastasia or Maria or even Cousin Gleb, who made a practice of tossing each of them from the dock until exhausted. She remembered him in the yard, playing with Jimmy right before she left, and her heart twanged.

Any other time, Olga might find the Petrovs' home quaint, secluded as it was and welcoming in the pastoral countryside. The mindless days of sewing, reading, and recuperating from her illness seemed nearly maddening with their numbness. Especially when she freed her thoughts to imagine the chaos and terror her family might be enduring.

Please, O God, don't abandon us.

She slipped her hand into her coat pocket and fingered the edges of the envelope she had tucked inside. Mamma's words, written with such care so as not to give away Olga's identity should it fall into the wrong hands. Only the Lord knew when she might receive another.

Olga caressed her mother's calligraphy as though in touching the strokes she might be transported home. In the days since she'd received the letter, she must have read the scripted lines and the hidden meanings between them ten thousand times.

She still couldn't believe their message: no one allowed in or out of the palace, her family under house arrest and threatened with imprisonment in the dungeons of the prison of the Palais de Justice or worse. For all her determination to race home after Yulia's attack, she found herself a several hours' train ride farther removed from home, farther from her hopes of reunion.

She blamed Anton. Despite his charge to keep her safe, it felt easier somehow to resent him, to pile on his shoulders all the frustration and grief this masquerade caused.

Two weeks ago, her father had ruled an empire. Why could he not at least affect a political asylum to Romonov-on-the-Murman or maybe Japan? He must have some ally left among the rulers of the world.

If her father wielded no power sufficient to gain their freedom from house arrest and reunite his family, she felt utterly powerless.

Hopeless.

Olga listened to the two men behind her, thankful Anton and Timofea followed close on her heels. Although the distance between the residence and the outbuilding covered no more than a ten-meter span, she feared that a spy lurked behind every tree, that every shadow hid the enemy.

Despite her resentment of him, her distinctive cold shoulder, Anton had been accommodating, gentlemanly, and, to a fault, protective. Since Yulia's rape, Anton held true to his word not to stray far from Olga's sight.

She felt rather as if she had inherited one of her father's guard dogs.

Still, the longer Olga stayed in Anton's presence, the more she could see past his reserve to the positive qualities of his personality. His serious, quiet nature hid from casual observers this man of deep thought who took his responsibilities to heart.

She had seen how he agonized over his regrets in leaving the house unguarded during Yulia's attack, had watched him in his sensitivity in dealing with her after the fact, had witnessed his compassion and noted his quick thinking, his level head. He seemed just the sort of fellow her father would appreciate—one given to logic with a curious mind. Maybe the tsar had chosen wisely, after all.

Monk Timofea kept the women company, and Anton ran ahead of them to check the security of the bathhouse, stoke the fire, and raise the steam. "Ladies, the place is yours," he said, motioning for Olga and Yulia to enter. "Enjoy." Then he parked himself alongside the monk against the trunk of a linden tree, where the pair promptly resumed their running theological discussion.

Olga could see a wispy spiral rising from the smoke-stack from whence the wood fire burned, and the smell beckoned to her. With its rough-hewn exterior, the two-roomed bathhouse resembled nothing like any of the banyas she'd visited up until now. When she opened the door, however, she was pleased to see a planked wooden floor, hooks for her clothing, a small table and a samovar for tea between the various baths, and freshly drawn tubs of cold water. Inside the second room, which led to the steam sauna, small washing tubs of heated water sat upon a large rinsing trough. Olga could nearly feel the hot water running over her, washing away the sweat and grime of the past week.

The women engaged in small talk about the day's weather and Aunt Vera's too-salty *bitochki* as they removed their outerwear in the thin-walled anteroom. Yulia disrobed with calculating slowness, still favoring her bruised and wounded limbs.

Olga stripped out of her black apron and scratchy woolen skirt, both items on loan from Yulia's aunt. She hadn't needed to make up some excuse for not wanting to wear her own jewel-lined wardrobe. Aunt Vera deemed that both Yulia's and Olga's clothes were made of a fabric too high quality for average village wear. She had insisted the girls wear some of her "more suitable" garments and, turning a deaf ear to their protests, had set about making alterations.

Olga checked her coat pocket one last time to make sure her mother's letter remained buried deep in its recesses, safe from the effects of the bathhouse steam.

"I can't wait," Yulia said, stepping into the inner *parilki*.
Olga nodded in agreement. "The last banya I took was

after the New Year celebration. Right before we all fell ill."

In the few days' time they'd been in Pechory, both Olga and Yulia had made significant progress toward healing from their ills and injuries, but Yulia had yet to recover her quick wit and ready smile. Her hands still shook. She went about her day silent and somber, assisting her aunt with the cooking and household chores.

They made quite a team, she and Yulia, as in good measure Olga's disposition echoed that of the chambermaid's. Consumed with worry for her family and the need to get home, her fears now reached beyond desperate to the point of hysterical. All Olga's energies poured into trying to maintain her calm facade; she had little strength left to manage a smile.

Olga gathered up her towels and trailed after Yulia to the sauna room. The hot air stole her breath, immediately biting her skin, but the warmth poured over her, soothing. Once positioned on the upper-tiered bench, she laid back and inhaled the medicinal vapor of the birch-branch-and-eucalyptus-scented steam. It relieved the itch of Olga's crust-pocked skin.

Yulia stretched out on the bench opposite her. Her hair fanned around her head like a diadem.

The splendor of that glorious tawny crown sent a blast of envy through Olga. She scratched at her bristly fuzz of dark blond hair, so like her baby pictures.

Yulia cast a glance her way, then turned back and stared at the cedar ceiling. "I wonder how our Olishka is doing now."

Olga jumped at the use of her own nickname, even though Yulia meant it in reference to the "other Olga" and not her.

"I'm sure she's fine, Yulia. She was already well on the mend when we left home. Her complications weren't nearly so severe as mine."

"Um. Yes, I know. I can't help but worry about her, though."

Olga knew Yulia's concern went beyond anxiety over Oksana's physical infirmity, but she couldn't bring herself to speak aloud of the other, more threatening dangers. She saw no use in fueling Yulia's fears for her best friend.

Until Yulia had allowed her to read the letter she'd received from Olga's surrogate, she had never really stopped to consider the bond the two servant girls shared.

Despite the need for discretion when she penned her every word, the "real" Oksana's dismay over her imprisonment—and the missing of her closest friend—came through loud and clear. She wrote to Yulia with the same affection Olga might use toward Tatiana—not just her sister nearest in age but her soul mate and confidante.

In reading Oksana's letter to Yulia, Olga comprehended perhaps for the very first time the scope of their deception. And the horrible truth. In order to carry out her father's wishes and flee the palace, she wasn't the only one forced to endure the pain of separation from the ones she loved. The orphaned Oksana gave up the one relationship she had ever known that most closely resembled family. At a time when Yulia desperately needed her best friend, the servant girl Oksana was sacrificing herself for Olga's security.

Oksana, the real Oksana, might never see freedom again if rumors came to fruition.

Olga had an obligation by virtue of her royal birth to face the fate of the Romanovs, whether death or exile. Such were the risks of her life station. But this servant girl gave up a proffered chance for freedom and willingly chose to bear as her own whatever sentence was handed down to the royal family. Not by force but by choice, she had taken Olga's place.

Had Oksana willingly sacrificed her dreams of love, of marriage, to serve the crown? What were the girl's hopes for her future? Olga had never bothered to ask. Her self-centeredness condemned her now.

"I wish I had known her better," Olga said. "She attended our lessons, and sometimes we played at pretend, but I never thought I would seriously require her services."

"She was ready and willing, Your Highness."

Olga glanced at Yulia, thankful for those words. No matter how upset she might be at her parents for insisting she escape and leave her family behind, Olga had to admire and respect Oksana. Such sacrifice resembled that of the Lord Jesus Christ, who took upon Himself the undeserved penalty of death so that His loved ones might be saved and set free.

Olga thought of the verse in the Epistle to the Romans that spoke of the rarity of such a selfless offering: *"For scarcely for a righteous man will one die: yet peradventure for a good man some would even dare to die."*

Might Oksana be forced to pay the ultimate sacrifice on her behalf? Olga felt neither righteous nor good. She didn't deserve such mercy. . .not from Oksana. Not from Christ. Especially after her deception in assuming the identity of a servant. Not only did she deny her station in life, but the deceit before Monk Timofea made her evermore guilty. The thought now felt heavy upon her sweaty body.

Yulia eased down off her bench. "I'm ready for the tub.

You?" Yulia's face had flushed redder than beet borscht.

Olga nodded and exited behind Yulia, the heavy wooden door banging behind them. The individual cold-water bath sat in the anteroom, freshly drawn from the local Velikaya River. Her breath caught when she dipped her toe to test the temperature, but she braved the shock, climbed in, sucked her breath, and plunged in all the way. The water closed over her, and she launched up even as needles of cold found her pores. Still, the awakening of so many nerve endings, the feeling of invigoration, made her laugh. "Oh, I feel clean!"

Yulia climbed out of her bath, shivering. She looked up at Olga and gave the smallest of smiles. "It is good to hear your laughter again."

Olga met her eyes, saw in them the longing, too, for easier times. Of innocence and hope. Her smile dimmed. "You will laugh again, too, someday, Yulia."

Yulia said nothing as they returned to the sauna. Olga lay down on the bench while Yulia picked up the *vyeniki* —a spray of oak branches tied together with a strand of twine—and began to beat on her back, releasing more heat, improving the flow of blood. She felt even more invigorated.

"I managed to catch Timofea alone in the yard as he was coming over from the monastery." Yulia said. She dipped the branches in a bowl of hot water, then repeated her ministrations. "He says no fresh word from Tsarskoe Selo yet again today."

Olga sighed. "I see."

Her hopes of hurrying home dissolved a little more each day that passed without good news. Any news. The not hearing proved harder to bear than when she first learned of her family's arrest.

Olga sighed again. "So we wait another day."

Yulia ceased her swatting. Olga turned and met Yulia's eyes.

"I never would presume to tell you what to do, but I can't keep from thinking. . ." She hesitated and raked her lower lip between her teeth. "If you aren't summoned back soon, maybe we need to separate. I've given serious thought to entering a convent."

"What?" Olga sat up from her prone position on the bench. "You can't be serious. Why?"

Yulia looked away, her face glistening in the meager light. "I was thinking that maybe. . . Well, since my attack, my prayers seem to be frail. Perhaps it was some sort of punishment—"

"Don't say that." Olga sat up, took Yulia's hands in her own. "Don't ever say that. You are a devout believer. I don't think God punishes His children like that."

Yulia looked away. Her chin quivered. "I feel hollow inside. Empty and broken. I can't think of another way to feel whole again."

"But a convent?"

"My father and brother chose a pious life. I can also."

"There are other ways to serve God, Olga. Your service to my family is a holy calling in a way."

Yulia looked at her, a glint of surprise in her eyes.

"Of course, Yulia. My father is the head of the church, chosen by God to lead Russia. You are serving the family of God's chosen people."

Except, well, even Olga had to admit her words felt

raw and painful against current events. Apparently, God had forsaken His chosen people and left them in the hands of the rebels.

Maybe they were all better off at a convent. Maybe Yulia was right—maybe God was punishing them. Or worse yet, had forgotten them all.

CHAPTER SEVEN

Anton stamped his feet and scrubbed at his arms with gloved hands. His breath froze in a vapor cloud as it left his mouth. The women seemed to be taking their sweet time in the banya, although he didn't mind nearly as much as it might appear to Timofea. The tense silences enveloping Yulia and Oksana felt suffocating. More than once, he felt as if his very presence kept Yulia from healing from her trauma. He ached for her in a way he never thought possible—not just for her wounds and shame, but for his failure. And he blamed himself for the fear in poor Oksana's eyes.

He'd seen that kind of fear before through his own eyes. That kind of fear had held him captive. Not fear for safety so much as a haunted, chafing aloneness that hollowed him out—the fear of being forgotten.

He'd been wrestling with such fear since birth, it seemed. How could he not? His father could barely stand to be in the same room with him. Father had shipped him off to live with his uncle Franz; his mother's sister, Aunt Agata; and his four cousins for the first five years of his life, only to have them send Anton back when Aunt Agata died. Sometimes in those early years, he'd wished he'd been sent away again, even to an orphanage. There, at least, he wouldn't have had to face a daily dose of disdain and rejection. There he wouldn't have had to be reminded of the pain he'd caused.

Oksana had grown up an orphan but had been adopted, in a way, by a family of royals. Yes, a servant, but she'd obviously earned a place of honor for the tsar to request her safe passage. She even carried herself like a woman of value, of respect. So why the haunted look in her eyes?

Next to him, Timofea sat on a stump, leaning on his knees. He'd pushed back his hood, his long hair hanging below his ears, his beard scruffy and patchy, youthful. Now he looked every inch like Anton's eighteen-year-old stepbrother, Jonas, perhaps devising his latest scheme. But his gaze never missed a thing.

"You're restless, Anton," he said, his voice puffing into the cold.

Anton stamped his feet, and they crunched in the sticky spring snow. The smell of smoke laced the air. He, too, should take a banya, maybe tonight after the ladies were tucked in.

"No. Just tired of conversations revolving around food and clothing and local gossip. And if I hear one more story from Uncle Maxim about Babushka Millie's gallbladder, I might forever lose my appetite."

Timofea gave a small smile. "They are only trying to avoid asking questions, trying to keep our privacy. I counseled them on the need for secrecy. I believe their inane chatter is cover for the inquiries that tempt them."

"Of course. I'm grateful for their hospitality, Timofea. It's just that I'm worried."

"About your business."

"About Oksana and Yulia." He pushed away from the

tree, paced out a few steps from Timofea. "I keep thinking that their attack seemed. . .planned. Not random. Or at least not the random event that we all want to believe." He turned, staring at Timofea. "I think someone followed us to Borovsky's home, maybe tipped off through your contacts, and meant to attack both the ladies. The question is why."

Timofea looked up, shook his head.

"And if they were after something, why rape Yulia?" Anton ran the palm of his hand over his forehead. "What if I hadn't shown up?"

"By the grace of God, you did, Anton. I just wish it had been moments sooner." Timofea's grim expression betrayed his feelings about his sister's attack.

Anton sighed, looked toward the banya. "I hope I did the right thing in bringing them here. I keep thinking maybe we should go south to my hometown. No one would suspect us there, and Oksana would be safe. Yulia could heal."

"Perhaps I should bring Yulia into the monastery with me. My father is still here visiting on a short sabbatical from the seminary where he teaches, and neither of us have seen her in many years. The reunion would be healing for us all."

"So he's really your father? Not just in a spiritual sense?"

"Yes, that's correct." Timofea smiled at the look of confusion Anton wore. "My father is also my brother. Makes quite a profound riddle, doesn't it?"

Anton shook his head and groaned. "So is your mother a sister, too?"

"No, sadly." Timofea's smile dimmed. "My mother

passed away three years ago."

"Oh." Anton cringed. "I apologize for being crass. I should have asked before now."

Timofea waved off the apology.

Anton smashed his boot into a melting patch of snow, then sculpted the slush around the crater into a bowl. "Tell me to hush if I'm prying too far into personal matters, but seriously, do you mind explaining? How does such a thing happen, a monk with offspring?" He caved in his icy art-work and looked at Timofea. "I realize I'm unfamiliar with your ways, but I thought priests who lived in monasteries were celibate."

"Yes, those who accept the vows of the ascetic life and enter a monastery, such as my father and myself, agree to practice that which we call the evangelical counsels: obedi-ence. . .poverty. . .chastity. . . ." Timofea's eyes took on a distant glaze.

Anton absorbed the depth of commitment revealed by Timofea's words. "Sounds like a tough row to hoe to me." He figured he wouldn't have the fortitude to live his entire life as a monk. He looked forward to the day when he would settle down, get married, have children. Continue the Klassen legacy.

His father would laugh to hear him—seeing how he was nearly twenty-six and still unmarried—but he'd had plenty of prospects in the Molotschna Colony, plenty of women willing to marry him if no other reason than for the fortune attached to his name. Look at his father's wife. Papa Klassen didn't suppose that Hilda Penner truly loved him, did he? Even Anton could see ulterior motives on both sides when the Widow Penner brought herself and her three able sons to the Klassen farmstead.

Anton didn't want a business transaction for a marriage. He wanted someone who could see the man he wanted to be. The man he would be for her. He wanted a woman who believed in him. And loved him. Till death did they part.

No wonder he was still single. He nearly laughed at his own foolish idealism. "So, then, your father received his calling to become a monk later in life?" he asked Timofea.

"My father didn't enter his present calling until three years ago, after my mother died. Prior to becoming a monk, my father served as a parish priest. But according to church law, without a wife, he had to resign from parish ministry. He chose to accept the monastic life rather than turn to secular pursuits." His gaze traveled to the grazing sheep and on past to the darkening horizon, then back to Anton. "I joined the brothers when Yulia went to serve in the tsar's household and my father assumed his teaching position. I could have moved in here with my aunt and uncle after Mother died, but I've always felt that God's plan, His purpose for my being, lay in devoting my days in prayer through total surrender and consecration of my life." Twilight darkened his features, made his eyes less readable.

"You know, Monk Timofea. . . ," Anton said as he fished a matchbox from his pocket. He lit the two oil lamps they had carried with them from the house. "I'm impressed with the maturity and wisdom you demonstrate for one so young. And I admire your faith and commitment. I like to think of myself as a devoted follower of Christ, but I couldn't live like you do."

Timofea waved off Anton's compliment. "I am nothing to be admired; only God is worthy to be praised." He bowed, then lifted his head to look at Anton again. "Each of us must find his own way to faith and service. Every true follower of Christ will do nothing less than obey." He rocked his head up and down. "If we long to discover the will of God in our lives, we must search for that high calling He has deemed right for us as individuals. As it says in Philippians chapter two, verses twelve and thirteen, 'Work out your own salvation with fear and trembling. For it is God which worketh in you both to will and to do of his good pleasure.' So anything I am, I owe to God's work within me."

Timofea gave him the slightest smile, void of condemnation. The lamplight sharpened his features, added warmth to his eyes. "I see in you this same desire, to seek God's will and please Him by allowing Him to work His good pleasure in you. Why else would you accept responsibility for Oksana if not to serve the greater good of another above your own ease and comfort? I know you well enough after these many days to understand that you didn't do it for the possibility of monetary reward."

No, not for monetary reward. But he had let the whys of his actions toss him in his bed at night, pushing back the hours of darkness into sleepless eternities. Why? For love of country? Certainly. Especially since he had been forbidden by his religion to serve in the fight against Germany's Kaiser Wilhelm in the Great War. This seemed an apt substitute. Because His Imperial Highness had asked? Of course. Anton couldn't deny the swell of importance he had felt that moment in the woods when Tsar Nikolai suggested God had answered his prayers.

But as Anton had dug into his heart, he also discovered

a reason that he could never speak aloud—to prove to Johann Klassen that he, his only son, Anton Johannovich Klassen, was not a son of shame, leaving a legacy of failure. Perhaps he might establish a new legacy, one of courage and strength. One that, should he ever marry, the Klassen generations might bear with pride.

All the same, even if his motivation to look after Oksana's safety had been noble, this short-term assignment was quite different from a lifetime of self-denial such as Timofea had committed to.

"I don't care what you say; I could never give up my dreams of a future family in exchange for the lifestyle of seclusion you've chosen."

Timofea shook his head, looking away. "Don't be so quick to glorify my actions. Sometimes it is easiest to fall into a life that is expected of us, even when we know it is right. In fact—" he steepled his fingers over his lips for a moment before extending his open palms "—now that I'm accustomed to the cloistered life, I find I much prefer it over those times when, in order to fulfill missions of special service, I must be out in society, as I have been this past couple of weeks."

In a motion Anton had come to recognize as a trademark of Timofea's, the monk leaned back, crossed his arms, and plunged his hands into the depths of his cassock sleeves.

"Even so, I seek only to make myself available as clay in the hands of the Master Potter. No doubt, the Lord knew I needed this discipline lest I stray from the narrow way." In the dusk and flickering lamplight, his smile danced beneath his beard. "I am doubly blessed, not only to be able to draw daily from the knowledge of the abbot and the older monks, but now for a short time to also reap the benefits of my wise father's spiritual insight and understanding. He will only be with us for another three months. I hate to be away, even for a day, while he's here."

Anton pondered Timofea's words as, beyond the orbit of his lamp's light, the colors of day bled to evening gray. He nodded. "I envy your relationship with your father. I wish I could have the same." He pinched his lips together and shook his head. "I know my father loves me, but it seems he and I are always at odds with one another. If I have an opinion, he's sure to take the opposite side. I should have telegraphed him by now about Borovsky and the troubles at the warehouse—and I will tomorrow if I can get through—but I know when I do get around to breaking the news, he'll find some way to lay the blame on me rather than on the rebels."

Timofea stared at him in the flickering lamplight. Anton cringed, realizing how pitiful that sounded. Thankfully, the monk could be counted on to keep that confidence. He hoped so, anyway.

"What happened?" Timofea said softly.

Anton frowned at him. Shook his head.

"Why would your father blame you for things outside your control?"

Why, indeed, would a man blame his infant son for the death of his mother? Anton turned away; his voice fell. "My mother died giving birth to me. She was the love of his life. He never forgave me."

Behind him, Timofea stood silent. The wind gathered the chill of the evening and brushed it over Anton, raising gooseflesh.

"Your father is a weak man, Anton. I promise you, you're nothing like him."

Anton let that thought sift through him, saying nothing as the night closed in.

❦

Olga and Yulia sat in silence as Olga conjured up life in a convent. Surely God had other plans for her. A family. Perhaps marriage to her cousin Gleb. Yes, she wanted to marry a prince—someone handsome and strong. But she also wanted a man who didn't *have* to marry a princess. Who could see beyond the crown to the woman who simply wanted to love and be loved.

Maybe she could find a man who would share her love of poetry and literature, someone who would see past the pomp of grand duchess and be charmed by the real Olga, the quiet, sometimes stubborn, serious one who would rather spend her days imagining shapes from the clouds than attending a ballet or ceremony. Of the two of them, Tatiana had always been the social one.

Still, Olga had always felt that she'd been given a position of grace, a place to shower upon the Russian people the mercy of their heavenly Father. Such as the time she had used the meager allowance allotted to her by the tsar to send a cripple to sanatorium. Or her fund-raising project in Crimea, selling white flowers to benefit tuberculosis patients. Her father had always taught them to live a frugal lifestyle, despite the family's wealth. Now, she considered that, perhaps, God had, from the beginning, planned a life for her in a spiritual conclave, renouncing worldly benefits, as He had for her aunt Elizabeth Feodrovna, who had founded a convent after her husband's assassination.

Olga couldn't deny, however, the way her throat closed at the thought of a cloistered life. "Yulia, it's too soon to make these decisions. Wait until you're healed, until my family is freed and this rebellion choked out. Wait until we return home."

"What if we never return home?" Yulia spoke softly, the hot air eating her words. "What if whoever. . .attacked. . . me. . .is still following us?" Yulia dropped her head, soggy strands of her long hair falling forward to hide her face. Her hands trembled. "I could never forgive myself if such a horror were to befall you. And I can't help believing we're in greater danger together than apart." She shook off a shudder.

Olga watched Yulia compose herself, becoming once again her chambermaid with a precarious secret.

"With His Imperial Highness now officially in custody and charged with crimes against the Fatherland, I'm sure either the provisional government or the rebels or both will soon begin to search for those with any ties to the tsar. Even if my attacker doesn't return for us, servants like us will no doubt be of special interest. The least they'll do is bring us in for questioning. More likely, they'll throw us in jail."

She picked up the oak branch. "When that day comes and we're together, if they find one of us, they find us both. We need to separate, and you need a better escape plan. . . a hiding place no one would suspect."

The hot, heavy air left Olga woozy. To keep from falling, she grabbed hold of the bench on each side of her knees. "Where would I go if I were to leave you? If what you say is true, every single person I know who might be willing to take me in would also be a suspect—with the possible exception of our mysterious Mr. Klassen."

"What if. . .what if Mr. Klassen is your answer?"

"What? I don't understand."

Yulia stepped off her bench and reached for a towel. "The tsar knew what he was doing when he appointed Anton your guardian. He has no connections to the royal family, no obvious reasons to be called into question." She dabbed at her face before wrapping herself in the cloth. "Go home with Anton to the land of the Mennonites. No one would ever think to look for you there." She paused and met Olga's gaze. "Consider it, Your Highness. I believe it's the only way to truly keep you and your secret safe."

When Yulia opened the door to leave the inner sanctum of the banya, she let in a surge of cold.

Go home with Anton? To live among the Mennonites? She had learned of the German sect from her father. Back in the late 1700s, her ancestor and reigning monarch, Catherine the Great, offered the industrious Prussian farmers free land, partial autonomy, and exemption from military service if they would settle colonies in the frontier of south Russia and establish model farming communities. The Mennonite colonies were in the middle of nowhere.

Distanced from her family, hiding among Anton's people; this might be her safest option. Should an enemy—Yulia's attacker, or an envoy from the current provisional government—decide to seek them out, she might very well be better off to separate from Yulia and Monk Timofea. Considering the Petrov family's longtime service in various capacities to the Romanovs, they might not prove too difficult to track for someone with due diligence.

And if by some horrific turn of events, the increasingly

powerful rebel Bolsheviks realized the captive Oksana's royal facade, they'd begin a hunt for the real Olga. And her missing chambermaid.

All the same, she couldn't very well follow Anton home. If he were to show up in his village toting a female stranger on his arm. . . Well, talk about raising suspicions.

Unless. . .

Olga climbed down from the bench, reached for her towel and cloak, and followed Yulia from the room. The cold air of the anteroom caused her flesh to prickle. Yulia was just rising from her cold plunge, and Olga quickly followed her, glad for one last cleansing despite the chill that ran over her body. She hurried to pull on her clean attire, rubbing the towel over her head, trying hard not to envy Yulia for her long wet locks. With each moment bathed in quiet contemplation, a gathering notion emerged and took on defining shape in her mind.

"You've been awfully quiet since my little tirade," Yulia said. She stood dressed and by the door, coat in hand, waiting for Olga to lace up her shoes. "Please accept my apology if I've troubled you. I'm sure we'll all be safe here. I realize I'm jumpy and tense."

"No, I appreciate your advice, and I can see where we should be concerned, even out here in the Pechory backwoods." Olga paused and offered Yulia a smile. "I've even thought for a moment about joining you in a convent, but that's not a calling I aspire to, nor do I think my new guardian, the indefatigable Mr. Klassen, would take too well to the cloistered life."

Yulia laughed. "Yes, he seems bound and determined not to let you out of his sight, and I don't think the sisters would approve of a male houseguest hovering over you."

"I might have a plan. I need to think through the logistics a bit more." Olga straightened and brushed at her skirt, then retrieved her coat from its hook.

Yulia frowned at her as if to tug the plan from Olga's thoughts. Olga smiled.

Such times demanded courage and invention, from her family in particular. However, considering the far-reaching ramifications of her plan, she needed to know she could trust Anton's integrity before she voiced her idea to him. Was he truly the gentleman he seemed to be?

Yulia accepted Olga's offer of assistance into her coat. "I'm praying the summons comes for you and me to return to the royal family before we need to decide any further course of action."

Olga turned to her, grateful for this maid God had given her. "Amen. I, too, pray it shall be so."

"Speaking of praying. . ." Yulia paused with her hand on the doorknob. "Timofea says he'll walk with me over to the church near the monastery for evening prayers. Would you like to join us?"

Prayers? So far her prayers had gone unanswered, despite her begging, pleading, beseeching the Lord to right the wrongs foisted upon her family, to free them, and to restore order to Russia. Especially to destroy the Bolshevik faction and their treasonous activities.

The tsarina's prayers, too, appeared to go unheeded, though her mamma had to be the most devout person Olga knew, bar none. God appeared to be punishing her family, perhaps as retribution for the Rasputin scandal or as penalty for her cousin Dmitri's role in the starets' death.

What if God had turned away because of her deception, this grand lie that might cost the life of another? For whatever reason, God's favor no longer appeared to rest on the Romanovs. She didn't know if she presently had the energy for another futile round of appeals.

Clearly, she had to take the matter of her protection into her own hands.

CHAPTER EIGHT

Anton rounded like a shot when the banya door squealed open and Oksana, then Yulia, emerged. A shabby woolen shawl framed Oksana's face, and when she stepped into the lamplight, the navy plaid of her head covering accented the blue of her eyes. Her cheeks bore a healthy glow, all but hiding her measles pocks, which faded and healed a little more each day. She may have been just a servant to the royal family, but her carriage and demeanor spoke of stateliness and breeding. After spending a lifetime among the ruling class, she had obviously assimilated their ways and graces as her own.

Oksana came toward Anton until she stood toe to toe with him. She looked up and met his gaze. "Thank you for waiting for us and standing guard out here in the cold. I feel quite refreshed."

For the first time since Anton laid eyes on the servant girl, she offered a genuine smile. He swallowed hard and smiled back at her, suddenly struck by those eyes that seemed to look right through him. His heart pounded as if he were dancing the *trepak*.

"Yes, you look. . ." He swallowed again. "Refreshed." He cleared his throat. "A steam always does a body good."

She smiled, a gentle uplift of her face, a small light in her eyes.

Oy. He hadn't felt this way since the time he'd invited Katrina Loewen to the *Jugendverein* social at his home church.

He took a step back from Oksana and tipped his chin toward Timofea. "We were happy to wait for you." He waved his lamp toward the back door of the doctor's home. "But we'd better get you out of this weather and into the house."

He watched as she turned to Yulia and said, "Do you and Timofea mind going on ahead? I need to speak with Anton for just a minute. We'll be right behind you."

"Certainly," the pair replied in unison.

Oksana reminded Anton of someone he ought to know. . .a face he couldn't quite place. "After all you've been through, we can't have you catching your death of a cold."

"Yes, we'll go." She stood on tiptoe and lowered her voice just one notch shy of a murmur. "But I need to ask you something first, away from well-intentioned friends and their relatives' inquisitive ears." Oksana lowered her heels to the ground and glanced over her shoulder to confirm they had the yard to themselves and the pigs. She tugged on the ends of her head scarf and pulled it tighter around her face. Her speech came in raspy whispers. "Yulia and I were discussing the idea that maybe we. . .that is, she and I, for safety's sake ought to separate."

Her words caught him off guard, and his thoughts raced to take in what she meant to imply. Was she still insisting on trying to return to the palace? Did she want him to take her there?

"All right. I am listening." He lifted his lamp to provide

a better view of her face and urged her on with a nod. "What are you suggesting?"

She sighed, looked away. "Just how serious is this commitment you made to. . .the tsar? Will you do anything to serve him, regardless of the cost?"

She looked so frail standing there, the wind pushing at her scarf. What would he do for her?

He would surrender his business. He had probably already done that. Which meant he would also surrender his father's respect. Then again, he had never had that to begin with.

"Would you be willing to surrender your freedom for a season to obey his request?"

In the silence, Anton felt the weight of her words, the chill of it in his bones. Yes, provisional government troops might hunt them down and arrest him for stealing away a chambermaid in the royal service. He'd already failed to protect her once. Yes, he would surrender his freedom for her.

She stared up into the night sky punctuated with crystals of light, looking so vulnerable yet strong, unlike any maid he had ever met. She intrigued him and revealed in him feelings of fear like none he'd ever known. Yes, he would protect her. Sacrifice anything. Everything.

"Of course, Oksana. I would protect you. . .with my life. Even if it meant going to prison."

She closed her eyes. He saw turmoil ease from her face and the slightest smile lift the corners of her mouth. Sighing, she turned to him, seeming to consider him in the lamplight. He wondered what she saw. A man of no profound build, cold to the bone, dressed in a wool coat, with his *shopka* pulled down around his ears like a village idiot, his gloved hands clasped together. Some hero. Some protector. He tried a wan smile.

"Yes, Anton, you are a gentleman."

He raised his eyebrows at this, not quite sure what she meant. Had he behaved otherwise?

She smiled. Cleared her throat. "Anton Johannovich Klassen." Oksana paused and hauled in a deep breath. "Will you marry me?"

<hr>

The sun filtered in through the faded brocade and lace draperies, already on its ascent for the day as Olga passed through the living room on her way to the kitchen. Dr. Petrov, finished with breakfast, perched now at his desk with his nose in a book. She'd delayed her entrance this morning, taking extra time to affix her wig and attend to her morning toiletries before joining Yulia and Anton and the Petrov family.

As if composing her outside appearance might mask the turmoil inside.

What had she been thinking? Asking a man—and not any man, but a common merchant of immigrant descent—to marry her? She had obviously stayed in the banya much, much too long.

Vera Petrovna hovered over the ancient wood-burning stove, stirring a pot. Her plump frame served as a testament to both her good health and her culinary skills, although the bare lightbulb that swung from the ceiling cast a jaundiced pallor on everyone in the room. She looked up from the stove and nodded at Olga as she entered.

The village doctor's home did not betray a physician's

bourgeoisie status but more closely resembled a peasant farmhouse. Throughout the residence, moldy wallpaper featuring faded chrysanthemums pulled away from the walls. Teetering pillars of books rose from the floors of both bedrooms, leaving just enough space to walk around the beds. Medical supply cabinets ringed the combination living room/office/study, while the kitchen, according to Yulia, often served as a makeshift operating theater.

The quarters were likely built when Olga's great-grandfather, Aleksander II, still ruled as tsar. Never in her life had Olga set foot in such a humble abode, but she imagined her brother, Alexei, would have loved the chance for an adventure such as this.

Oh, but she hoped nothing had happened in her absence to compromise the tsarevich's delicate health. Alexei had succumbed to the measles after her. However, she didn't fear his recovery from the childhood disease. The measles he could handle. A fall from the bed might kill him. As a hemophiliac, the slightest bump or bruise sent him into fits of bleeding and pain-filled shrieks that made her want to weep. No one slept, no one truly lived when Alexei suffered.

Always before, her mother believed Alexei owed his survival of his bouts with the inherited disease to the prayers and ministrations of the starets Grigory Rasputin. Olga, on the other hand, was never fully convinced that the cleric's healing capabilities stemmed from supernatural power. Regardless of whether the mystic's sway over her brother's physical condition amounted to spiritual healing or mental persuasion, Olga worried how her mother would cope should Alexei fall ill now that Rasputin had been murdered.

For the time being, Olga pushed her frets and fears aside. She would drive herself crazy if she dwelt on such things. She had to keep her promise and stay the course regardless of the outcome.

Even if it made her look like a fool.

She sent a sideways glance in Anton's direction as she joined him and Yulia at the kitchen table. Ashen pillows drooped beneath Anton's bloodshot eyes. Spikes of his blond hair shot from the back of his head. His good dress shirt, so starched and crisp at their first meeting, now stood in grave need of a washing and ironing. She raised one eyebrow in surprise at his uncharacteristic appearance.

Anton had asked for a night to sleep on her proposal before giving her an answer, but he didn't appear to have so much as dozed in his makeshift bed on the living-room divan.

She'd spent the night wide awake herself, tossing in guilt and feeling the idiot for her marriage proposal.

Squeezed onto a thin strip of mattress, she had tried to lay prone, not disturb Yulia, but looking into the blackness and listening to the groans and creaks of the old house only made it worse. Her mounting pile of deceptions weighed on her chest like an anvil.

Loyalty to her family didn't absolve her of guilt over her deceit, guilt first for this charade and then for her willingness to sell another person into marital slavery. Although she'd made her intentions perfectly clear to Anton that the marriage would be in name only, such a union still felt overwhelmingly intimate and placed another burden upon her already weary shoulders.

He understood her plan to annul the marriage as soon

as she was sent for by the Romanov family. Even so, by using Oksana's legal name and assuming her identity, she had, in essence, offered to stand as surrogate for Oksana in a wedding ceremony that would legally bind the servant girl in marriage to a total stranger. As if that weren't enough, she would be carrying out this lie at the altar of the church and before a man of God.

Her guilt turned even more bitter when she awoke this morning to her bristly stubbled head pocked with measles scabs. Oh, she looked the princess, she did. Anton probably couldn't wait to accept her offer.

Somehow she had to find a way to renege on her latest scheme. She knew, glancing again at Anton, that he would feel relief. She'd have to steal him aside and hope he accepted her apologizes without rebuke. Or laughter. Because really, he'd been propositioned by a servant girl.

Anton's distress, written on his current disheveled appearance and so uncharacteristic of him, could probably be accredited to his desire not to hurt her. He probably spent the night working out how he could remind Oksana of her station in life without being rude. . .and point out the absurdity of a merchant marrying one born to serve.

She had to admit that thought had humbled her in new and unfamiliar ways. For the first time, she realized how deeply her identity as a princess had branded her soul.

All this gave further proof to her realization that she, Princess Olga Nikolaevna Romanova, could not marry a commoner like Anton Klassen. Ever.

Yulia's aunt Vera dished up bowls of kasha at the stove and handed them to her niece to pass along to the others.

Olga breathed deeply of the smells of brewed tea and

simmering breakfast fare. The comforting scents carried her back home. Could her family take meals together while in their captivity? Worry about her family seemed to hound her every waking moment. The tension sometimes caught her around the chest and squeezed out her breath.

"Oksana, would you feel up to walking with me over to St. Nikolas Church this morning?" Anton looked at her as he blew on a spoonful of the hot buckwheat mush, then took a bite.

"Yes," she nodded. "I believe I would." She met his gaze but couldn't discern his thoughts before he looked back down at his porridge.

Of course, praying wouldn't do her a bit of good now. But maybe she could summon the courage to apologize.

Yulia glanced up from her work of digging troughs in her kasha with her spoon. "Oh? If we're going to church, I'd better hurry and put on a fresh apron."

Olga made sure Aunt Vera's back was turned before she shook her head at Yulia. "I don't want to keep you from worship, but I thought you planned to finish that letter you were writing so you could post it in this morning's mail."

Yulia's eyes grew wide as she looked back and forth from Anton to Olga. "You know," she said, drawing out her words, "you are right. If you don't mind going without me, I believe I'll stay here with Uncle Maxim and Aunt Vera and work on my correspondence." She shot a glance at her aunt, who stood at the stove humming.

Anton seemed not to notice Yulia's change of mind. He finished his kasha in silence.

Olga pulled on her coat, wishing she had a carriage to bear her over the mud and snow. The cross she wore at her neck seemed cold and heavy this morning as she pulled on her boots. Anton bent to help her, and she let him, remembering how he looked as he stood in the yard yesterday as she had considered him for matrimony.

Dressed like a gentleman, as usual, in his wool coat, his mink shopka covering his blond hair, he'd given her a gentle, even kind, smile. "Of course I would protect you." Gloved hands clasped before him as if trying to hold in heat. He'd stood out in this cold for nearly an hour yesterday, waiting for her. Chapped and hungry and patient.

That thought, and the memory of all he'd surrendered for her—his time, his business, and the fact that at any moment the provisionary forces might find her and arrest them both without his having the slightest inkling he had been protecting a princess. It felt unfair. Even so, at that moment, the thought of marrying him disguised as someone of no importance, the idea that she could just be Oksana, charmed her. Like those times when she and Oksana had switched places and she'd watched her maid stand in ceremony or travel out for public events while Olga stayed at home to read. Freedom like none she would ever know reeled out before her. And something akin to calm or peace entered her heart.

Probably it was that other Olga, the one who longed to be out of the royal light and find a man who would love her for herself, who had prompted her to propose.

The real Olga had spent the time since wanting to strangle her.

Olga followed Anton from the house, and they traveled across the snow-crusted yard and through the gate. He opened it for her, and she stepped out into the dirt road, smelling the farm animals and the gathering of spring in the still, cold air.

"I spent all night considering your suggestion." Anton's Germanic accent seemed heavier than usual this morning.

His coat pushed up one corner of his shirt collar, and Olga had the strangest urge to smooth it back into place. "And?" she asked, disgusted by this romantic vein. *Remember your station, Olga!*

"I don't want to appear uncooperative"—his words came in labored puffs—"but I have some concerns."

Relief whooshed through Olga. He was going to say no and rescue her from her own incrimination. If Anton turned her down, she would view his refusal as a divine pardon of her foolish proposition. There had to be some other way she could ensure her safety without compromising her integrity any more than she already had.

"It's all right, Anton. I understand." She tried not to let her emotions into her voice. Olga continued walking, unwilling to look at him lest those feelings show on her face.

They passed the Petrovs' neighbors' house, the white stucco walls of the monastery coming into view. A few short meters beyond the monastery, the spires of St. Nikolas Church rose above the horizon like citadels.

Anton glanced at her from beneath the thick fur of his mink hat. Falling snow dandruffed his shopka, coat shoulders, and eyelashes.

The intensity in Anton's gray eyes took her aback, the concern in them, the haunted look that betrayed how she sometimes felt of late.

She would say it for him, wishing she had never landed

them in this mess. "Marriage is a lot to ask of anyone, even in this circumstance. I'm sure we can think of some other plan."

"Oh, I'm not saying no."

He wasn't saying no?

Olga's face must have registered her surprise. Anton smiled.

"I believe there is merit to your idea. If we were to marry, we could travel together without the need of a chaperone, and no suspicions would be raised." Anton drew a breath. "Besides," he said with a soft smile, "if I were to show up at home with such a beautiful bride on my arm, I have no doubt my friends and family would have to rethink their meager estimation of me." Color rose in his cheeks.

Meager estimation? Of this man? The thought rattled her and filled her with sadness. She suddenly longed to soothe the pain that lingered in his eyes.

Besides, she wasn't beautiful, and his words only made tears fill her eyes. She shook her head and looked away. "You're kind, Anton. But my eyesight wasn't damaged by the measles. I know how I look. You don't need to flatter me with empty praise."

"It's not flattery." He hooked his finger under her chin, raised her gaze to his. "Perhaps you simply don't see what I do."

Oh. She felt heat press her cheeks, painfully aware of his hand at her chin, the soft smile he gave her, the smell of him—he must have taken a banya last night—clean and scented. He had shaved this morning, and the fact he didn't wear a beard and moustache like her father and so many Russian men intrigued her. Made him seem younger, even exotic. And the cleft on his chin only made him striking.

She swallowed and stepped away from his touch. Anton was a gentleman; she knew that. But she was a princess, and she couldn't marry a man who wasn't royalty.

She resolved to remember that.

He smiled, his hand returning to his pocket. Then, his expression turning serious, he said, "Yes, Oksana, I will marry you."

CHAPTER NINE

Anton had expected to find Timofea at church and easily spied him among other faithfuls standing in corporate worship among a congregation of two dozen or so.

In stark contrast to the chapel cave where Anton first met Timofea, the St. Nikolas sanctuary reflected the extravagant gilt and the classic art and architecture typical of many Orthodox churches. Unlike the utilitarian meeting room of Anton's church back home, this sanctuary had no pews. The expansive domed room inspired reverence and worship with its echoing voices, candles' glow, and pungent incense.

Anton stayed near the entrance while Oksana traveled deeper into the sanctuary and lit a candle, then made the sign of the cross, folded her hands, and bowed her head.

As he basked in the holy sights and sounds, a recent revelation overtook him afresh. Perhaps the Mennonite way wasn't the only way of the faithful in Christ. Anton joined his heart with the other worshipers and began to pray.

When the murmurs quieted, Anton raised his head. His gaze fell first on Oksana and then on Timofea as the service ended and they, too, ceased their praying.

Anton watched as Timofea spied Oksana. The monk's expression conveyed surprise, then worry, and he scanned the room until he caught sight of Anton. They acknowledged each other with a nod.

Timofea's frown deepened.

Anton offered a quick smile in hopes of setting Timofea's mind at ease. Not only did he worry about his sister more than he supposed anyone knew, but last night, after Oksana's proposal, Anton had confided in Timofea. And asked him to pray for wisdom.

The monk excused his way through the small crowd and fell into step alongside Oksana. Together they moved toward the door to meet up with Anton. The trio walked outside into the falling snow and turned in the direction of the monastery a few short meters away.

"Where's Yulia?" Concern edged Timofea's words. "Is there a problem? Is something wrong?"

"Yulia's fine. Your uncle is home to watch out for her. Oksana and I needed to talk to you in private, so Yulia stayed behind. May we speak to you for a moment?"

"Certainly. Follow me." Timofea guided them through the front gates of the monastery, across the courtyard, and into a chilly, antiseptic-looking chamber devoid of any furnishings other than a simple wooden table, four rickety chairs, and the standard icon corner that adorned most Orthodox rooms. A *rushnyk*, or ritual towel, draped both the artwork of Christ the Savior and that of the Virgin and Child, and flame danced from the icon lamp on its stand.

"Have a seat. Please." Timofea and Anton both reached for the same chair to offer Oksana, but Timofea beat him to the task. He pulled the seat away from the table and motioned for Oksana to sit.

Anton could see his breath, and though he removed his hat, he wasn't yet ready to give up his overcoat as well.

"Accept my apologies for the cold room. We don't have drop-in guests here very often, so the fires are kept low." Timofea rubbed his hands together and blew on his palms. "I'm glad to see you out, Oksana. Your strength seems to be returning a little more each day." The legs of his chair screeched across the stone floor as he took a seat.

"Yes. My main ailment now is my lack of energy, but I am sure this, too, shall pass." She unbuttoned her coat but kept it on with her scarf still tied under her chin. Her blue eyes seemed huge in her beautiful face.

"I caution you not to overdo." Timofea's expression changed from serious to bright. "Then again, I don't suppose you came here seeking medical advice from me." He chuckled. "You can get that from my uncle Maxim, and I'm sure he's said those very same words to you more than once." He rested his elbows on the table and steepled his fingers, shifting his attention from Oksana to Anton. "So what is it I can do for you two?"

Anton cleared his throat and leaned forward in his chair. He wasn't sure how Oksana might feel about his discussing her proposal with Timofea, so he started at the beginning. "Yes, well, Oksana and Yulia were discussing their predicament yesterday, and naturally, Yulia has grave concerns for both her safety and that of Oksana, as do we all. I don't know if she's discussed her feelings with you about this matter, but she fears sooner or later all those who served in the tsar's household will be sought out and likely arrested and their possessions confiscated. In light of this possibility, she believes the two women might want to consider separating."

"I agree." Timofea nodded. "My sister has gone so far as to ask our father to inquire at a nearby convent about her becoming a novice there."

Anton stood, compelled to pace away his tension. "To tell you the truth, in light of all she's been through, I can see why Yulia would want to go into seclusion. Her fears are well founded." He paused and leveled his gaze on the monk. "So there will be no doubt, let me say that I remain committed to keeping the vow I made to the tsar to look after Oksana until such time as she is sent for, but unfortunately, that day seems further removed now than it did even a week ago. I think we all know I can't stay here indefinitely, cadging on the good graces of your uncle and aunt. And with the situation deteriorating as it is in Petrograd, neither can I return to my flat or to Borovsky's."

While Anton spoke, he shed his coat and draped it on the back of his chair. "Excuse me if I sound self-serving at such a time, but if there's any possibility, I still need to find some way to save my business." Clamminess swept over Anton. "As much as I hate to face my father and report bad news, I have to discuss the situation of our warehouse with him and get his advice on what can be done." He scrubbed at the back of his neck. "However, in my conservative hometown, eyebrows are sure to rise if I travel all that way with an unmarried young lady." Anton swallowed hard and took a deep breath. "So Oksana and I, we've come to you with an idea. . . ."

He looked to Oksana. She sat picking at the tassled edges of her shawl, separating the colors of the plaid. She glanced at him and offered a thin-lipped smile.

Anton feared his pacing exacerbated her nervousness. He stood by his chair.

Timofea's expression remained stoic. He made a fine confessor.

"Oksana thought of it first, but I believe she may have stumbled onto a good plan." He poised over the chair, bracing his hands on its back. "What would you think if we were to marry, Oksana and I?" He searched Timofea's face. He'd given the monk plenty of time to consider it and now hoped for an answer. Even waited for it, seeing Oksana bow her head in prayer from out of the corner of his eye.

"In name only, of course," he added, glancing at Oksana. "And then I could take her home to Alexanderwohl. No one would expect to find a servant of the tsar's household married and living so far off in our sleepy little village in the Molotschna Colony. If there's any safe place in Russia where she could hide, it would be there." He fell silent and waited for Timofea's response.

The monk tipped his head back and looked heavenward for what seemed to Anton an interminable length of time. When Timofea lowered his head, his gaze seared into both Anton and Oksana, as though attempting to divine their innermost thoughts.

"Anton, have you thought through all the implications of what you're proposing here?" Timofea had asked him the same last night. Anton hadn't an answer. "I know you're committed to fulfilling the tsar's request and keeping Oksana safe, but I could arrange for her to be well cared for until such time as permanent arrangements are made, either for her return to service with the tsar's household, her exile, or her assimilation into a new life."

Like last night as he stared at the darkness of his room, the weight of the Crest of St. Basil drilled into Anton's chest, his ever-present reminder of his pledge to the tsar. In the end, that pledge gave him the only clear answer. "With all due respect and appreciation for your offer, I made a promise, and unless providentially hindered, I plan to fulfill my vow, no matter what that entails."

"I understand," Monk Timofea said with a nod. "Your devotion is admirable."

Anton squirmed under Timofea's scrutiny. He knew he didn't deserve admiration for his determination to look after Oksana. Once he traversed past his obligations, he could admit he rather liked the idea of returning to Molotschna with a woman on his arm.

No, that wasn't entirely accurate. The moment Oksana broached the subject and offered her idea, his mind had leaped upon the thought of spending time with her, enjoying her smile, coaxing the light into her eyes. While such a marriage might serve to protect Oksana, perhaps it would do more to encourage his lonely heart. He wouldn't presume that she would, or could, come to love him, yet a friendship with such a lady as Oksana felt in many ways to be a treasure in itself. But could he keep her safe, even as his wife? That thought had caused him to toss the rest of the night away in sleepless agonies.

It was possible that right now he was so tired that he might not be thinking with all his faculties.

Timofea studied Anton another long moment, then turned his attention to Oksana.

"Oksana, I want to hear from your own lips." Timofea

leaned forward. "Would you be entering into this union willingly and without coercion?"

She stopped her fidgeting and let go of her shawl. After sending a quick glance to Anton, she cleared her throat. "Yes, *Batiushka* Timofea. I am willing."

"And what happens when, or if, you are called back to serve the Romanovs? What then? You know as well as I that personal attendants to the royal family are required to be unmarried."

Oksana shot a glance at Anton, her eyes so very blue while the blood seemed to drain from her face. She moistened her lips before looking back to Timofea. "Anton and I spoke of this, and I believe we are in agreement. Since ours would be a marriage in name only, we likely would have the union annulled."

Timofea folded his hands, bowing his head as if praying. Anton waited, his heart thumping. What if he said no? Although Anton wasn't bound by the Orthodox Church, Oksana was, and she wouldn't do anything without the Church's consent. But God would give them another plan, wouldn't He? Perhaps he should be asking.

Timofea looked up. "I would need to consult with my elders before I could give an official answer, but you asked what I think, so I will be frank. I have my reservations. I understand your rationale, and believe me, I sympathize with your thinking. Marriage would be an easy answer to the thorny situation you both find yourselves in. I am not opposed to marriages of convenience by matter of principle. Oftentimes such unions breed lifelong loving and committed relationships. But while the Church makes provision for annulment of a marriage in certain situations, for you to enter into marriage already thinking of a dissolution—well, it gives me pause. Marriage is a sacred institution and not to be entered into without a commitment to permanency. Besides that. . ."

Sending another glance heavenward, Timofea then shifted his attention back to Anton. "There is one big obstacle to be overcome before the Church could give her blessing to this idea." He hesitated. Took a deep breath. Cleared his throat. "Anton, I know you to be a righteous man with a heart bent toward God and spiritual things, but you are not Orthodox, and therefore, there is no record of your birth in our archives. In the eyes of the church, it's as if you were never born. Hence, we cannot perform a marriage ceremony for you." He looked down. "I'm sorry."

Anton caught himself strumming his fingers on the table. Painfully aware of the sting of Timofea's words. As if he'd really hoped. . .

How had he gotten into this predicament? He fisted then released his hands and rubbed his palms together, wondering for the hundredth time what had possessed him to go into the woods to investigate a bobbing lantern. He looked at Oksana, her head downcast and her lips pursed. She hadn't asked to be thrust into this unconscionable situation any more than he had. Poor woman.

He remembered her words from just last night: *Just how serious is this commitment you made to. . .the tsar? Will you do anything to serve him, regardless of the cost?*

How far would he go to bring honor to his family name, to redeem his history of shame, to prove to himself and his family he had the wherewithal to be a real patriot despite his Mennonite commitment to peace?

"Would you be willing to surrender your freedom for a season to obey his request?"

How far would he go to see Oksana smile, an expression of peace on her face?

He turned his undivided attention back to the monk. "What if I were to convert to Orthodoxy?"

Her new husband sat across from her in their railcar compartment, writing in his journal. Every so often, he looked up and sent a glance and a weak smile her way. Other times, he paused to stare blankly at his reflection in the window, which had been mirrored by nightfall. She'd noticed his leather-bound journal more than once on this. . .journey. Wondered what a man like Anton might write. Of course, she, too, kept a journal, but she felt a jealousy for this book that contained his deepest secrets.

She wondered if she might ever possess the courage to inquire about his secrets. The ones that hung in his gaze when he wasn't aware she was looking.

In all likelihood, however, she would never ask, and he would never reveal his entries. They were both better off if they kept their emotional distance. Why further complicate their already muddled situation by becoming friends? Bad enough she had married him.

She twisted the plain gold band round and round on her ring finger. The deed was done. Married. In another woman's name. Her cache of lies expanded yet again.

No matter the rationalizations she used to bolster her courage, she had half-expected a lightning bolt to strike her for her deception as they proceeded with the ceremony in the presence of the Petrov family, Yulia, and Timofea, and under the authority of the parish priest. Among the things in her trunk, she'd found a white satin and lace tea-length gown that she'd worn for afternoon concerts last spring. It served as her wedding gown. As they moved through each portion of the marriage ritual—the prayers, the recitations, the ceremonial traditions, the "I wills" and "I dos," and especially the sacrament of Holy Communion—she lost a little more control of her tremulous emotions. When they reached the moment of the marriage kiss amid their small wedding party's shouts of "Many years," Olga could no longer restrain her tears.

Aunt Vera assumed they were tears of joy.

Olga had let the postulation stand.

It didn't help her guilt when Yulia repacked Olga's bags and noticed her camera stowed in the bottom. She edged it out and suggested a picture.

Olga nearly yanked the camera from Yulia's hands. She'd been given the folding Autographic Kodak as a gift from her father. However, this was one memory she didn't want to capture. With luck, she would someday be able to erase it completely from her memory. She had shoved it back into the bag and hid it under her green ball gown.

She leaned back against the scratchy upholstery of the train berth and unbuttoned the jacket of her navy tweed and velvet traveling suit.

"Why do you keep a journal? I know the tsar does, but few other men I know do."

He looked up at her, a curious look on his face. "You know other men's habits?"

She felt a blush and looked away.

He sighed. "I'm sorry; that was rude. I am just surprised at your familiarity with the inner lives of the royals."

The statement resonated with her, reminding her to watch her words. "I have been accused of being observant on more than one occasion."

Anton acknowledged her smile. "I keep a journal for my heirs so that I might detail the lessons I learn in life and in my walk with God. And maybe they can learn from me—even avoid some of my mistakes."

For some reason, that touched her, a man so concerned for his future family that he might consider them in his daily life now. Clearly, having a family meant a lot to him.

She hated the fact that she had stolen that opportunity from him, at least for a time. She stared out the window as he went back to his writing. A mere three hours into a two-day ride to Anton's home, the silence between them stretched out before her, long and uncomfortable.

If only they weren't alone.

Through wrangling on the part of her new husband and probably at a cost she didn't want to know, Anton had secured them a coupe-class four-berth semiprivate compartment, the best available in these frenzied times. A family of four had been assigned to share the compartment with them. However, despite Olga's insistence that she was no longer contagious, when the mother caught sight of Olga's scabs, she insisted for the health of her children that the conductor reassign them to another compartment. No doubt, the mother also thought she was doing the newlyweds a favor.

Olga's gaze rested on the food basket that occupied the seat next to her. Yulia's aunt had prepared an army's worth of rations for her and Anton's two-day journey to the Molotschna Colony. On top of the bundle lay a cloth-wrapped parcel of bread and salt, good-luck presents from their wedding guests.

It was beyond Olga to know how Yulia had been able to present her gift with a straight face, since she knew the full extent of this sham, including Olga's true identity. Timofea, at least, seemed to be working under the assumption that she, as Oksana the servant girl, had taken his cautions to heart and had entered into this union with a mind toward permanence.

Olga closed her eyes. Oh, but she was worn out—body, mind, and soul.

Even the hardiest and healthiest would be exhausted after all the hubbub that had transpired in the days leading up to today's events: Anton's decision to convert, his rushed catechism under the tutelage of Timofea, followed by his baptism into the Orthodox faith on Sunday. . .and her own four-day mental tug-of-war over whether or not to go through with these rash wedding plans.

In the end, she couldn't bring herself to back out after seeing the lengths to which Anton was willing to go in order to accomplish her safety. He thought he was marrying a servant girl, and still he had offered her his name. The generosity of that nearly took her breath away. And made her realize that indeed her father had chosen wisely this man Anton to carry out his request.

She wondered what her parents would think of this latest turn of events. Would Papa commend her for taking such a bold step as marriage in Oksana's name to secure her own safety? Or would he chastise her for the extremes to which she carried out the masquerade? If she had to guess, she imagined Papa would back the idea, while Mamma, in typical motherly fashion, would protest her daughter marrying even as a surrogate bride.

After Mamma's extensive but as-of-yet unsuccessful scheming to forge a union between Olga and the likes of Prince Carol of Romania or Prince Edward of Wales, the only time she would want her daughter walking down the aisle would be to exchange vows with a man of the nobility, not as a stand-in for a servant paired with a common merchant.

Still, perhaps mother would approve of Anton's character despite his meager pedigree. While Anton might not have the gentry's social graces and sophistication, he was faithful. And kind. And honest. So unlike the shallow and superficial phoniness she saw in many of society's privileged upper crust.

A lurch of the train sent Anton's knee bumping into hers.

"Excuse me," he said, closing his journal. "Are you okay?"

She nodded, feeling a blush. He'd been careful since their marriage to be only the perfect gentleman. She knew even he was aware of their close proximity. Alone. Married.

An attack of shyness forced her to look away.

From among her gentlemen acquaintances within the nobility, she could never imagine any of them willingly placing her interests above their own, even in light of her position as a grand duchess. Yet that's just what Anton had done for her as an orphaned chambermaid.

One thing was for certain: Papa would like Anton, would admire the man's commitment, which rivaled even her father's protective care and precautions for his eldest child.

If her mother could see past any objections to their wedding scheme, she might very well like Anton, too, and not only for the devotion with which he carried out his commission. Anton shared a couple of distinct parallels with Tsarina Alexandra. For one, both her mother and Anton had agreed to convert to Orthodoxy for the sake of marriage, although her mother's decision sprang from love, while duty and honor drove Anton.

And both the tsarina and Anton were of German descent.

Unfortunately, since the start of the Great War, most Russians questioned the patriotism of their fellow citizens who claimed German heritage. So strong was this xenophobia, not even her mother was immune to accusations of treason on the basis of her ancestry. They rarely used the German language at home anymore due to the suspicions sure to arise if overheard.

Sympathy for Anton seized her heart as Olga studied him out of the corner of her eye. No doubt he had also suffered prejudice on account of his German Mennonite roots.

"*Kannten Sie mich sprechen Deutsches?* Did you know I speak German?" Olga floated the question at Anton, then tipped her head to one side. "If what I learned about the Mennonites is accurate, German is your native tongue, am I correct?"

A smile curved his face, looking oh, so much better than the grim look he normally wore. He was handsome today in a black suit and silk ascot at his neck. His blond hair, however, refused his ministrations and remained mussed from their departure.

"*Ach du lieber!* Oh my goodness!" he exclaimed in his native tongue. "No, I had no idea you spoke German. Your pronunciation is perfect. Actually, our people use Dutch, or what we call Low German, at home and High German, the language you're likely familiar with, at church, but I'm sure if you speak German, you'll be able to understand us for the most part." She heard pride in Anton's voice and felt a warmth inside her chest. Yes, she liked it when he smiled. At her.

"Where did you learn?"

She hadn't anticipated the question, and her mind raced ahead to formulate a safe response. "The royal family is fluent in several languages besides Russian. I grew up hearing French, Italian, German, and English, as well as Russian, spoken in the palace. While His Royal Highness conversed with his children in Russian, I'd say, as a whole, the family actually used English most often. They had English-speaking nannies and were expected to function with dignitaries in their languages. Her Imperial Majesty did not learn Russian until her marriage betrothal, so she has never felt very confident in her Russian language skills, and although she has a good accent, she speaks it very slowly."

Even as she described her mother, Olga could hear the halting Russian speech.

"Of course, she spoke German, having been born Her Grand Ducal Highness, Princess Alix of Hesse, but since her mother died when Her Majesty was a young child, she spent a good deal of time with her grandmother, who was

Great Britain's Queen Victoria. As a result, the tsarina prefers English as her language of choice."

Anton raised his eyebrows in a teasing expression, and she realized that she might have spilled out too much information. "I learned it as a part of their household," she finished.

"It's okay, Oksana. I know you miss them."

His kind words sent a rush of emotion through her. She put a gloved hand over her mouth and stared out the window. She did miss them. So much that it made her ache inside. Every time she thought of her family under house arrest, she wanted to retch. Only knowing that her father via her mother had asked her to be brave, to save their family by saving herself, did she summon the courage to continue this farce.

Anton reached out, touched her knee. His hand there made her nearly jump. "You will return in due time. I'm sure of it."

He leaned back, capping his pen while she composed herself. "I have to say, you've certainly lived a fascinating life. To be able to speak so many different languages. . ." He tucked his book into his jacket pocket. "I find you intriguing, Oksana."

She wondered how much more intriguing she might be if he knew the truth.

"I've often thought I would like to learn English. Over the past thirty years or so, many citizens of our village have emigrated to America. If the government follows through on their threats to confiscate our lands, or if the political situation continues to spiral out of control, I could see myself maybe following them someday." He met her gaze, his lips pursed. "But not until we have our. . .arrangement. . .concluded."

Yes. Of course. But she couldn't deny that the idea of traveling across the ocean with him felt adventurous, even tempting.

Impossible. She had a life here, responsibilities here. She needed to remember that, not let her heart reel out too far. Or she might never get it back.

Even so, she wanted to remain friends, neutral friends. The kind of friendship that wouldn't be too invasive, the kind they could both walk away from without wounds.

Anton held her gaze, his expression serious. "When we get home, I suggest you keep your varied linguistic abilities a secret between the two of us. If you keep your German hidden and use Russian exclusively when interacting with anyone but me, you'll save yourself from undue prying by my family, particularly on the part of my father's wife, Hilda." He couldn't hide his sigh. "She doesn't speak much Russian, and believe me, you don't want to deal with her any more than necessary." He made a face, and she did her best not to smile.

Did this Hilda have something to do with the pain that sometimes flashed across his face? Anton referred to her as his father's wife rather than as his stepmother. That clue alone signaled a warning to steer clear of the senior Mrs. Klassen as best she could. Olga wasn't known for her vivaciousness and runaway jabbering as Tatiana was. She could hold her tongue—if she wanted to. She resolved to smile, to make Hilda like her. And to speak only Russian.

A knock sounded at their compartment door, and Anton, shifting back into the use of Russian, excused himself from their conversation. Ever acting the part of her protector, he rose. "Yes?"

Upon the response, he opened the sliding door first a crack, then all the way, to allow entrance to a female conductor, her bosom straining the buttons of her gray uniform. In her wake, a noxious blast of creosote fumes mixed with cigarette smoke billowed in from the narrow passageway. The conductor handed Anton their *belyo,* the packet of linens and blankets with which to make up their beds for the night, and wished them a *spahkoynigh nochee.*

Good night? Olga's mouth opened even as her throat clogged. Good night. . .together. Here, in this compartment.

She closed her eyes, willing back shame. He might again see her uncovered head, her stubbled crop of hair, her ugliness. . . . But she'd put them in this situation; she'd have to bear it.

Before he closed the door, Anton stuck his head into the aisle, then turned back to Olga. "I see the *prodyetstvya* coming. Would you care for tea?"

She could hear the tea lady's pushcart rattling closer, bringing with it the spicy aroma of hot *chai.* Her mouth began to water.

"Yes, that would be nice," Olga answered. "But I'll get it." She was, after all, supposedly the servant among them. And maybe some time in the hallway would clear her head.

She moved to stand, but Anton waved her back down. "I can manage. You're tired. Keep your seat."

His consideration took her by surprise. He appeared to be taking his role as a newlywed husband to heart. Hopefully not too much to heart.

Anton deposited two steaming glasses of tea on the small fold-up table beneath the window and between the two berths, while Olga fished in their food basket for dried apple slices and sweet bread. He helped himself to the cake and settled back into his seat. He washed his food down with a sip of tea, watching Olga over the rim of his glass. "By the way, I'm not asking you to lie to my family, just not to bother mentioning that you speak other languages."

Hard as she tried to appear aloof and calm, the suggestion troubled her. Olga took a sip of her tea, but the hot liquid failed to dissolve the knot in her throat. Would there be no end to her deceit?

Anton kept his head down, and she couldn't help but notice his bare right hand, where a ring should be. A pledge of his bride's love and commitment. But she didn't love him, and although she'd nearly succumbed to a splurge of romanticism, wanting to take from the hem of her traveling cloak a man's gold ring, inset with rubies, she wasn't committed to him, either. A ring would have been yet another farce. She had the traveling cloak bunched beside her in close guard. She wasn't sure how many of the crown jewels her mother had sewn into the hem and trim, but she knew that any vagrant wouldn't hesitate to kill her for such a fortune. Piquing Anton's curiosity might also put them both in danger.

"I just think the fewer suspicions we raise, the better," Anton continued. "The family is sure to have all sorts of questions as to how we met and who you are and where you came from, especially considering they've been badgering me to marry one of our local girls for years now. I was, after all, home less than a month ago, yet I never spoke of a serious woman friend then." A sigh lifted his chest. "This morning, I sent my father a short telegram in which I mentioned that the trouble in Petrograd necessitated my return home. I also said I would be bringing my new wife with me. Who knows what type of reception we shall find waiting for us at the train station tomorrow?"

She imagined past receptions. Parades. Carriages. Throngs of people out to cheer or jeer depending on the political mood. Perhaps it might be nice to disembark in anonymity.

"I am particularly worried about how I am going to explain my conversion to Orthodoxy. When Father learns I have rejected my family's faith to marry a servant girl. . . Who can say how he will respond?" He gave a slight, chagrined smile. "He'll probably see it as one more shameful act by his only son."

Olga's heart went out to him, and she fought an attack of guilt over her consuming self-absorption. She hadn't given a thought to the sticky situation in which Anton might find himself as a result of their union.

Her true identity burned in the back of her throat, and she ached to tell him. To share with him the full extent of his mission and the importance of his task. Perhaps such knowledge would make the humiliation and ridicule he was about to face worth enduring. And frankly, she longed to have a confidant, especially with Yulia no longer at her side.

"So what shall you tell them? About us, I mean." She blew on her tea and took another sip.

"I haven't yet decided the best tack to take. I'm hoping between the two of us we'll be able to come up with an idea before we reach Molotschna tomorrow evening." He let his gaze meet hers, and his gray eyes softened. "I'll protect you from their questions as much as possible, but we might do well to think through an explanation ahead of time as to how we met and who you are. I'm inclined to advise you against telling anyone that you served the Romanovs, especially in light of the revolution and the rising popularity of anti-tsarist sentiments. To avoid my family's condescending airs, you might not want to divulge that you are a servant at all."

She clenched her jaw and swallowed a rise of mortification. Probably that should make her extra grateful that her husband—husband!—was a man of kindness. When she finally did make it back home, she planned to treat her subordinates with much more admiration and respect.

Anton looked at her, then down at his hands again. "I think the less said about your background, the better, especially if our association ends up being a short-term project, so to speak."

More and more, Olga realized the embarrassing predicament in which she would leave him when she rejoined her family and had the marriage between Oksana and Anton dissolved. Even so, the extended Klassen clan must never know the truth behind Anton's decision to wed Oksana—or the reason to have their union annulled.

Anton himself would likely never hear the whole story.

She had a hard time keeping it all straight herself.

As she thought about Anton and the humiliation he would suffer at her hands, another crazy possibility kept floating around in her mind.

All in all, Olga believed she had married well for Oksana. What if Oksana were offered the choice of honoring the marriage contract Olga had entered into on her behalf?

By Olga's own way of thinking, it was far better to be a servant in the tsar's household than married to an untitled merchant from the far-off reaches of nowhere. But the real

Oksana might have another point of view, especially if the Romanovs must exile to another land and forsake their royal entitlements. When this convoluted mission came to an end, perhaps there could be some way Oksana might be offered the choice of trading places with her yet again. She might welcome the chance to accept the marriage vow Olga had made in her stead and settle down to lead a quiet, comfortable life with Anton.

For some inane reason, Olga felt a flare of hot jealousy. She looked up at Anton, sipping his tea cupped in one hand, staring out the window. Solid. Kind. Dependable. And accepting. Yes, Oksana could do much, much worse.

Only, would Anton accept the idea of a true and permanent union with the real Oksana? How could she go about presenting such an offer to him?

Perhaps she and Oksana could make the switch without Anton's knowledge. On the other hand, didn't he have a right to know when it concerned the woman with whom he would spend the rest of his life? They would surely have a moral obligation to explain.

Maybe she could make him fall in love with her—as Oksana—first and let him be the one to propose the idea of making their union permanent. Oh, there was a frightful thought—and too far-fetched for her to hang on to. Her romantic and overactive imagination at full gallop. What was she thinking? She and Oksana weren't so identical that someone who spent much time around her would not be able to tell the difference between the two.

She rubbed her forehead with the heel of her hand. Her head hurt trying to figure out the various options. Perhaps the Lord would hear her prayer, and a telegram calling for her to join the family would be waiting for her when she and Anton arrived at their destination. They could catch the next train back to Petrograd and avoid any introductions and detailed explanations to Anton's family.

She hoped so, because she feared that playing the part of Anton's doting wife just might be the one deceit for which she couldn't forgive herself.

CHAPTER TEN

With his rucksack slung over his shoulder and lugging Oksana's suitcases behind him, Anton followed his bride down the train's steps and onto the station's open-air platform. The rural outpost smelled of coal dust and manure, but after nearly two full days in the confines of a stuffy berth, he found pleasure in even the earthy fragrances of home. He dropped his hold on the bags and scanned the crowd for a familiar face. Seeing no one from his family, he watched Oksana out of the corner of his eye.

She fidgeted with her fur hat, tugged at her wig, and cinched her coat tighter around her waist. Her breath appeared in cloudbursts against the morning chill. She cast a glance and a wan smile his way.

He gave her elbow a gentle, protective squeeze.

She looked ready to bolt and hop the next northbound train back to familiar territory. With her lashes fluttering over those wide-with-fright blue eyes, Oksana reminded him of a helpless moth caught in a spider's web.

Anton bore the blame for her fear. He hated to guess what manner of cretins she expected to greet her when he first introduced her to his family—thanks to the earful he'd given her. Probably he should have been more. . .private.

But he found Oksana easy to confide in, told her things about his upbringing that he'd thought he'd never reveal. Like how, when he was twelve, his father had brought a new wife and three brothers into their house. And how Johann Klassen took those brothers, his stepsons, hunting, fishing, and even on a trip to Kiev, leaving Anton at home. How he had never felt as if his father had forgiven him for living. How he had tried to be the son Johann wanted, embracing the family business, setting up a successful distribution in Petrograd, and even toeing the Mennonite edict for nonenlistment when all his chums from the School of Commerce he had attended in Gross Tokmak were abroad, fighting for Russia.

He even told her his dreams about someday bringing honor to the Klassen name.

And she had listened, that beautiful mouth tweaked in a gentle smile, those eyes upon him trusting him, drinking in his words. Everything a man could want in a wife.

Well, everything he could hope for, at least. Because he was ever aware of their boundaries, especially last night as he'd stepped out into the hall to allow her to dress for bed. He had returned, Oksana already wrapped in her bedclothes, and for a moment watched her sleep—although he felt certain she hadn't been sleeping. She had pulled up her covers over her head, hiding her baldness, and he ached for her and her wounds.

She deserved a man who would love her. Cherish her. And as he stood above her, he wondered if it could not be him.

He had gone to bed not daring to pray that thought, that minuscule dream inside his chest. But all the same, the thought of Oksana in his arms made him smile.

Maybe God would fulfill the promise He had given Anton the morning of his marriage. The one that fairly leaped from Psalm 100 as he'd been reading and asking for God's peace over his conversion to Orthodoxy: "For the LORD is good; his mercy is everlasting; and his truth endureth to all generations."

Klassen generations? He didn't want to ask if perhaps those future generations might start with this woman, but the thought burned into his chest even as he pledged to protect her and become her husband.

Anton understood enough about the walk of faith so as not to take this as a promise of comfort and ease. Yet he had to believe that even in their darkest hours, God would prove faithful and true.

Like the day when Oksana would leave him to return to the tsar's service and have their marriage annulled. A day of public humiliation and shame. It seemed he attracted those twin distresses in new and horrific ways.

Still, he'd made a promise—many promises—to Oksana. And the first was to return her safely to her tsar. He would keep that promise, regardless of the cost.

Another scan of the crowd failed to harvest a glimpse of his relatives. "Don't worry," he said, looking down at Oksana. Her pasty color and slumped shoulders bore testament to her weariness and her need of a hot meal, a warm bath, and a clean bed—regardless of the early hour of the day.

Where was his father? Could he have not received the telegram?

"I'm sure someone will be along to meet us soon. Why

don't we move away from this crowd and wait by the road on the other side of the station house?" He hiked his rucksack higher on his shoulder and reached for Oksana's bags, nodding the way she should go.

If need be, he would hire a troika to carry them home so he could tend to Oksana's needs without delay. The rail station closest to his home was located here in Halbstadt, and they still had a forty-minute ride before they reached the Klassen's rural estate near Alexanderwohl. Anton hated to keep his wife out in the elements any longer than necessary.

His wife.

The term had a nice ring to it.

His wife.

For the time being anyway.

They might not be in love, but now that the deed was done, he could see himself spending a lifetime with her. The tsar's words had been true. Oksana was fair of face and a beauty to behold, in spite of her measles. She looked like an angel dressed in white on their wedding day, taking his breath away. Once she fully recovered and her hair returned, she would own rightful title as the most gorgeous woman in the colony. And though she possessed a feisty spirit and strong will, characteristics he found most peculiar in a servant girl, she also demonstrated unswerving devotion and loyalty, the two most valued qualities he sought in a wife.

He certainly could do much worse in the choosing of a bride. At least she had not married him for his money. That thought made him smile.

He could not, would not, go back on his promise to

the tsar. He promised to protect and defend Oksana until such time as she was sent for by the royal family. And he would.

Anton closed his eyes. *Lord, please show me how to be the man You want me to be. The man Oksana needs.*

"Hello, Anton! Over here." He recognized his stepbrother Jonas's voice before he opened his eyes. The gangly youth had extricated himself from the driver's seat of the buggy and made his way to them, unabashedly gawking at Oksana.

"It's true, then. You weren't just trying to get Father's goat with your telegram. You've gone and married a Russian girl." He let out a low whistle.

Anton glanced at Oksana, saw her blush, and moved to put his arm around her. "Jonas, have you no couth whatsoever? That is no way to meet my wife for the first time." He gave him a mock glare but couldn't help smiling. Jonas was a less-tamed version of Timofea, young, brash, bold, and capable of wooing every heart in Molotschna with his smile. He wore his hair cut shorter than Timofea, and the wind mussed his capless head. He made a perfunctory bow to Oksana. "I apologize, Mrs. Klassen. My manners are abysmal, but my intentions are honorable."

"Pick up her bag, Jonas, and let's be off." But Anton winked at his stepbrother. Despite the rift that Hilda wanted to create between the two, Anton had felt so relieved to have another soul to share his chores and wrestle with in the barn, the two had forged an easy friendship. Sometimes he felt as if Jonas was true kin.

In fact, he would trade his father for Jonas any day.

Jonas loaded their luggage in the carriage, and Anton

helped Oksana aboard, tucking a blanket around her legs. Although here in Ukraine, March delivered real springtime fragrances, and along the river the ash and oak were budding, the unhindered wind sweeping in off the flat steppes could still make Oksana ill. "It's not a long trip," he said and settled in beside her, daring to put his arm around her so she could lean against him.

Jonas climbed up onto the driver's seat of the *verdeck-federwagen*, gave Anton a wink, then took the reins.

For all his travels north, the desire to live in his beloved Molotschna Colony never left Anton's soul. The villages' perfect tree-lined roads, the painted wooden houses, and the smell of coal smoke trickling from stone fireplaces as they traveled away from Halbstadt brought back the memories of Uncle Franz's home. He had lived with his relatives in this village until Aunt Agata had died in the fire that destroyed their family-owned bakery. Left with no livelihood and no wife to tend his children, Uncle Franz had been forced to send Anton back to his father.

Life on the Klassen farm and factory estate was difficult and lonely, their situation unlike the typical *wirtschaften* farms located within the Alexanderwohl village limits. The village farms shared communal farmland on the outskirts of town, and the landowning farmers worked the fields together. In order to accommodate their harness factory enterprise, the Klassen family owned an estate and working farm to the north and west of the village proper. Anton's father hired serfs to work the land, and later, when Tsar Nikolai rewrote the laws, they stayed on with their plots given in exchange for labor.

His father often used to leave him on the farm alone

or sometimes with their nearest neighbors, *Herrschaft* Wedel and his family of seven. But Anton had his first taste of ridicule and torment at the hands of the Wedel children, and he found it easier to crawl home, licking his wounds. "Turn the other cheek," his father had said when he returned from his day at the factory to find Anton, cold and hungry, waiting for him on the porch. The few times he had gone against his father's admonishment, when he had struck back out of fear and desperation, he had received chastisement on both sides.

When Anton finally reached sufficient age and education, he convinced his father it would be in the best interest of them both if he were to be allowed to enroll in the School of Commerce in Gross Tokmak. There, he dove into his studies. If he could not farm—or at least not bear to be on the farm—then he would excel in business management.

Maybe, someday, he would earn his father's respect.

He should have given up trying by now.

"Why didn't Father come?" Anton asked, aware that sometimes he was his own worst enemy.

"He received your telegram about Petrograd." Jonas looked over his shoulder. "Says that he'll speak to you when you get home." Jonas made a face intended to lighten those words, but Anton sighed and looked away. Oksana had her eyes closed, nestled next to him, and he longed to stay right where he was with the fragrances of the fresh-turned fields and wild prairie grasses, the buds on the trees, the birds singing, the sunshine warm on their faces lulling him into believing everything would work out.

How would he explain a wife and a failed business without betraying Oksana's confidence?

They rode in silence broken only by the *thud* of the horses' hooves upon the road. The village houses became scarce and overrun by rambling fields of wheat, barley, oats, and rye. "I see the Halbstadt farmers have opened another field," he said as they passed a freshly plowed *kagel*.

"They are expanding their spring wheat crops in that field. We are plowing new ground to plant more wheat, as well. Father says with the war on, we must do all we can to help in the patriotic effort. We need to do our part to supply food to the front."

His father said that? Well, it stood to reason that he'd try to do his part for the war effort so long as it didn't include sending his sons to fight.

"What do you think, Jonas? Will you join the *forestri* or the Red Cross *Sanitäre* when you are called to serve?"

"Me?" Jonas turned, a grin on his face. "I'm hoping with the overthrow of the tsar and a new government in charge, they'll end this war and I can avoid service altogether, like you did. I don't want to leave my soon-to-be bride."

"You're getting married? This is news to me. To whom?"

"End of the harvest season. I'm marrying Gertruda Regier."

Gertruda. Of course, the girl Jonas couldn't stop torturing in their village school, the eldest daughter of a nearby neighbor. "When did this happen?"

He thought he saw Jonas's neck redden. But in typical Jonas style, he shrugged. "Why not? I'm likable."

"To Wilhelmina, the sow."

Jonas glared at him. Anton grinned, but he couldn't help feeling a shard of jealousy. Yes, he was married. . .but, well, not really married. Somehow that made a difference.

They turned down the tree-lined road to the Klassen estate. The big house, once a meager, single-story Mennonite dwelling with rooms built around the kitchen in an L-shape that connected the barn to the house, had been expanded after the arrival of his stepmother. Now it stood two stories tall on one end, with a large bedroom for his parents above a cellar of fieldstone. The thatched roof had been replaced with wood shingles, and two years ago they had painted the house a bright blue that looked like the sky. The breeze brushed the tops of the trees, and in the fields surrounding their house, he saw the buds of early potatoes just rising over the mounded rows.

Closer to the house, he made out Daniel and Peter spading the kitchen garden. They turned at the sound of the horses' hooves and raised their hands. Although Anton had never created a kinship with them like he had with Jonas, they were affable and treated him like an older brother. With wary respect.

Only their mother, Hilda, seemed to detest him.

Thankfully, at present, she was nowhere to be seen.

They pulled up to the house, and Jonas climbed down, moving to untie their bags. Anton expected Oksana to rise and follow, and when she didn't, he noticed she'd fallen asleep. His heart twisted in unexpected tenderness. Bringing his finger to his mouth to shush Jonas, he took Oksana in his arms, stood, and carefully climbed from the carriage.

"I will put her in my room for now," he whispered to Jonas. Jonas opened the door, and Anton carried her in, smelling the musty cellar, the lingering scent of freshly baked bread, the lining of wood smoke on the plaster walls. The kitchen was empty as he crossed it, and he felt a swell of relief.

He would just lay Oksana on his bed, then seek out his father. That would be a delightful conversation he wasn't especially anxious for his new bride to hear.

Bending to open his door, he heard movement behind him. Then, "Well, the prodigal returns."

He straightened, turning slightly. "Hello, Hilda."

The woman's lumpy figure cast a huge shadow as she strode into the kitchen. She wore her hair pulled back in a bun so tight it made her harsh features look even more pinched and severe. She glowered at him. Then her gaze dropped to the package in his arms.

Her lips twisted in a warped smile, and she shook her head. "What kind of waif have you brought into my house?"

"I never should have sent you to run the warehouse! What were you thinking? Again you have disgraced me. Soiled our family name. You make me ill."

Olga sat at the edge of Anton's single bed, feeling cold to her very bones, shaking with horror. The raised voice on the other side of the closed door felt as though it invaded her very soul, and she could only imagine what the words might be doing to Anton.

She wanted to storm through the door and scream in his defense. Her mother always called her hotheaded. Now, perhaps, that vice would be appropriate.

But the woman's words the moment she had seen Olga churned inside her, paralyzing her. Waif? She looked like a waif? She had to admit she'd never been called that, at least to her face, and when the woman went on to look her up and down like a stray dog, well, she'd desperately wanted to return to that soft place she'd been moments earlier, nestled in Anton's arms.

In Anton's arms. She still smelled him, the aftershave he used. Or maybe it was his room, simple and tidy like Anton. A single bed pushed up to the white plaster wall was draped with a handmade quilt. A wooden *sckoff* held his personal belongings, one door hanging slightly ajar. And on a table next to his bed, a book of poetry. She wasn't sure why, but that found a soft place in her heart and set down roots. She wound her arms around her waist, remembering how his grip around her had tightened as if wanting to shield her from Hilda's attack. Instead, her eyes flew open at Hilda's words, and she had stared at her wide-eyed and horrified.

What kind of life had she married into?

She cupped her hands over her ears, unwilling to hear more, unable to shut the words out. According to Anton's father—whom, although she had not seen him, she guessed by his voice might be a portly man, with dark eyes and a scowl—his son had single-handedly destroyed the family business, and they'd be paupers in a week.

Why didn't Anton defend himself? Raise a voice against the accusations, maybe tell them about his promise to defend her?

Because then he would betray her secret. And make her life that much more difficult. Hot tears burned her eyes and spilled down her cheeks. "Oh, Anton, what have I done to you?"

She closed her eyes and let the tears drip off her chin.

She heard neither the door open nor Anton move into the room. He startled her as he touched her cheek and wiped away her tears with his thumb. She opened her eyes to see him kneeling at her feet.

She looked down at him, her husband. He wore a sad smile, his face flushed from the verbal assault. Such kindness in his eyes made her cry even harder.

"You're not a waif, Oksana. I promise you, your hair will grow back. And you are already lovely to me. Don't listen to her."

She sat up, suddenly angry. "She's wrong, you know. They're both wrong."

"Of course they are. You're beautiful. Don't listen—"

"Do they not know what is happening in Petrograd? You are hardly to blame for your business misfortunes. Didn't you tell them the provisional army conscripted your entire workforce?" She wiped her eyes with force and stood, pacing. "I am so sorry, Anton."

He stared up at her, blinking, as if just realizing she wasn't crying over her appearance. Then he stood, brushed another tear from her cheek. "I am going to sleep in the barn. You can have this room. If my parents ask, we will tell them that you are still weak from your illness."

She stared at him, mouth sliding open, then closed it quickly, ashamed at her anger. Where had God found such a noble man without a title?

"Thank you, Anton. But this is your room also. I feel I shouldn't—"

"No. My place is in the barn."

She nodded and then watched as he gathered his belongings.

"Try and rest. I'll fetch you for dinner." He turned and exited the room, closing the door behind him with a soft *click*.

She didn't deserve him. How strange did that feel. . . she, royalty, not deserving a commoner. But after all he'd surrendered for her, he deserved a real wife. A woman who could love him. A woman who believed in him.

She believed in him. And she might not be the perfect wife, but she could make his life easier by trying to be. At least during the daytime.

CHAPTER ELEVEN

He had kept his promise to Oksana. With her hair regrowing in maize-colored curls about her head and the cheerful June sun on her face drying up her scabs and turning her skin to a healthy golden glow, she had become beautiful. And he had to admit that her inner beauty made him pause, as well, when he saw her plant beans or onions, when he watched her gather eggs, and especially when she pulled up a one-legged stool to milk the cows. She had a quietness about her, a determination and a smile for every mean word Mother Hilda said to her, whether it was about accidentally spilling the barley and oats she milled to bake bread, or startling in fear as the chickens scolded her for stealing their eggs, or having a clumsy hand at milking.

Admittedly, for a chambermaid, she seemed awkward and unaccustomed to the simplest domestic tasks of farm life. Anton had tried to protect her, intervening as best he could when Mother Hilda reproached her time and again, her sharp tongue leaving scars. It only made him appreciate Oksana more when she refrained from snapping back.

So different from the girl he first met in Petrograd, the one who had torn him open with her claws after Yulia's attack. She seemed to accept their situation and even embrace it, willing to sacrifice alongside him for the mission.

Like now, as she emerged from the barn, carrying two pails of milk from the midday milking. She wore a scarf around her head, curls peeking out from the top, and held the milk out from herself, trying to keep it from sloshing on her skirt. Her face was set in a grim look that made him stop planting his seedling tomatoes and smile.

"Let me help you," he said, dropping the spade and jogging over to her.

"I'm okay," she said, but he took the buckets anyway, and she released them into his hands, flexing hers to work out the strain. "Thank you."

They turned, walking toward the house. "I was thinking that I'd like to take you for a picnic along the Begim Tchokrak River tomorrow. It's not far from here, and we both need a day of rest."

She stopped short and glanced at him with a frown. "No one else is resting," she said, gesturing with her chin at Jonas, his silhouette atop the waving wheat.

"Yes, but Jonas does not have to travel fifteen miles for church every Sunday." Since his father had decreed that Anton, having converted to Orthodoxy, and Oksana were not allowed to attend the local Mennonite gathering, they had begun traveling the fifteen-plus miles to Gross Tokmak and the nearest Orthodox Church for the two-hour standing mass every Sunday. The round trip, the service, and the hour Oksana spent in prayer, lighting candles for each member of the Romanov family, sapped any time for napping or light recreation meant for a Sabbath rest.

Usually Anton returned hungry and tired, ate the cold meal Mother Hilda had left for them, and retired to his new quarters in the barn's tack room to read or perhaps write in his journal. Occasionally they would go for a walk, but most Sundays, Oksana preferred to retire, as well, quietly shutting his bedroom door to be alone with her thoughts.

Thankfully, neither Jonas nor any of his stepbrothers made mention of the fact that Oksana and Anton slept apart, although he once saw Jonas standing just outside the tack room, watching him dress, and felt questions in his stare.

Anton wondered how long they could continue the charade of their marriage. He'd used the excuse of her illness and weakened condition as the reason why he slept in the barn. But with Oksana taking on a healthy glow and managing the chores, well, Mother Hilda would soon begin questioning their separation. He hated to give the woman another reason to ridicule Oksana, even if he felt certain Oksana preferred him to sleep in other quarters. However, he hadn't discovered a way to broach the subject without offending or having her assume other intentions.

Mostly, however, he missed their conversations. Even the long trips to Gross Tokmak didn't afford time for casual conversation, as Oksana strove to teach him English during their round-trip journey to church.

"How about tomorrow? I'll make a picnic, and we'll take the day off."

"What about Hilda?" Oksana crossed her arms over her stomach, rubbing them in a gesture he'd come to recognize as worry.

"Hilda has her once-a-month sewing circle. She will be in the village the entire day." He smiled at her, hating the fact that he didn't have the courage to simply stand up to Hilda and demand time for Oksana and himself. But sometimes a soft answer—and in this case a soft departure—seemed the best way to avoid her wrath and any perilous questions.

Oksana met his gaze, and the worried expression faded. Then to his delight, she nodded. "I would enjoy a chance to escape for a day. Shall I bring something?"

He so longed to reach out, touch her cap of soft hair, see if it felt like silk against his fingertips. "Just your smile."

She rewarded him with the slightest hint of a smile.

The morning dawned with a streak of lavender across the sky, pushing into the lingering bath of night and hinting at a glorious, sunny day. Anton greeted it as he sat outside on the swing that hung from the towering oak. He had his Bible open, reading again the verses from Psalm 100 that God had given him the day he and Oksana wed. "Make a joyful noise unto the LORD, all ye lands. Serve the LORD with gladness." It seemed all of the heavens agreed with him, alighting his spirit with the flush of the day, the scent of peonies and jasmine on the morning breeze.

He had been dreaming a dangerous thought over the past month. What if he could convince the tsar to allow Oksana to stay with him and remain his wife rather than return to a life of servitude? Surely the tsar wouldn't deny her the opportunity to live in peace and comfort if she so chose? Should he prove trustworthy in his mission of safeguarding both the Crest of St. Basil and Oksana, perhaps when he met with the tsar to return the crest, he could beg the favor of Oksana's hand in exchange for his promised monetary reward.

Whatever secrets she harbored, he would respect and vow to guard her so long as he had breath. The thought of her having to sacrifice any hope for a normal life—for marriage and children and a home of her own—to protect the deposed tsar seemed too harsh a requirement even for a lowly servant girl. While it was true his family didn't live in a palace or bear claim to titles of nobility, they did make a comfortable living and enjoyed the benefits of living in peace and comfort on their estate.

These musings, these internal dialogues, nudged him further into forbidden hope with each passing day.

Oksana appeared at the door even before he knocked. Hilda and Johann had already left for the village, and Anton felt a surge of delight that Oksana had not worn her head scarf but had left her curly short hair uncovered to frame her face. Her huge blue eyes twinkled as she greeted him. "Ready?"

He held out his arm, thankful he'd already loaded lunch into the carriage. "It's a beautiful day," he said, not knowing how to address her attire—a white dress with a blue velvet jacket, trimmed at the neck with faux diamonds. He had to admit that for a chambermaid, she had exquisite clothing.

He settled her into the open carriage, then climbed up beside her and set off. "Begim Tchokrak River runs through Alexanderwohl, but I know a secluded place away from the village where we can picnic without being disturbed. When I was young, I'd sometimes escape for days to camp there, fishing for trout while my father took his trips into town."

She looked at him, melancholy in her eyes. "It pains me to know that you grew up without a mother."

He shrugged but felt touched by her words. As an orphan, she probably knew how that felt. "How old were you when you joined the Romanovs for service?"

She looked away from him, clasping her hands together. "Uh, I'm not. . . I think I must have been about six years of age. I don't really recall. My earliest memories are in the Romanov court, being groomed for service."

"Six is so very young to begin a life of servitude." He felt a pang of sadness for her. Did she have a childhood, a time of freedom and unfettered play?

"Oh, it didn't feel like servitude most of the time. I had many happy moments. The Romanovs are a grand family. They love to play and have many pets. I remember Tatiana's little French bulldog, Ortino. He loved to play and would sleep on our feet as we took lessons." She let out a giggle. "He loved poetry. Pushkin, of course, as any good Russian would, and Robert Browning." She leaned back on her hands and began reciting Browning's poem "Rabbi Ben Ezra":

> *Grow old along with me!*
> *The best is yet to be,*
> *The last of life, for which the first was made:*
> *Our times are in His hand*
> *Who saith "A whole I planned,*
> *Youth show but half; trust God: see all, nor be*
>   *afraid!"*

The words spilled out, and with them the sweetest smile. She closed her eyes.

He was silent beside her.

She opened her eyes and caught him looking at her, a frown on his face. "That's amazing, Oksana. I, too, have

read Browning but have never committed him to memory."
He studied her. "I find it intriguing that you were allowed
to take lessons with the grand duchesses."

Her eyes widened, and for a moment, she looked
afraid. He touched her hand. "Oksana, you don't have to
worry about me repeating anything you tell me. I am your
husband, although in name only, and your secrets are mine.
From what I deduce from your stories, you had a rather
unusual relationship with the Romanovs as a servant, and
it is only to your benefit that they took you under their
wing so completely. Frankly, it makes me reevaluate my
estimation of the royal family."

"Is that so?" What had been a relieved smile turned to
a frown. "How did you see the family? As the tyrannical
despots the provisional government claims?"

"Of course not!" He wasn't so stupid that he didn't
know she might feel deeply about slander against the
Romanovs. He schooled his words, still aiming for honesty. "I actually didn't give them much thought. They
felt far removed from my life other than the tsar's edict a
couple of years ago concerning property liquidation. The
law demanded German colonists sell their property within
eight months, but fortunately for us, those laws have yet to
be enforced. You can understand why the tsar lost favor in
the eyes of many Mennonites at that time."

He cast a glance her way and saw dismay in her expression. He rushed to disarm the sting of his words. "Myself,
I know there is always more to politics than meets the eye.
No doubt the tsar was under pressure from the Duma to
make a public denial of the pro-German sentiments of
which he'd been accused. The law was likely never more

than a toothless gesture." Anton offered Oksana a smile, and she nodded in silent agreement with his words.

"Whenever I think of the tsar's family," Anton continued, "my mind carries me back to a day when I was about twelve. The royal train passed through Molotschna on its way to the Black Sea. Their train stopped in Halbstadt, and I remember sneaking off to the station with some of the other boys in hopes of catching a glimpse of the grand duchesses." He remembered, also, the feelings of jealousy at the protective hover of their mother as they stood at the back of their car, waving to the crowds. And from the way the tsar had taken care to rescue one of his servants, Anton felt no doubt that the man had made similar arrangements for his family. Their house arrest seemed only an inconvenience, and Anton felt sure that Tsar Nikolai had a plot to rescue them all, even if it meant sending them into exile.

Which meant they would send for Oksana, also. He couldn't deny the stab of pain at that thought.

"I remember the girls," Anton added, "not so much younger than myself and dressed in white dresses with identical bows in their long hair. I remember how they looked so regal standing there, perfect replicas of each other, waving to a crowd of drooling boys."

"I remember that," Oksana said softly. "It was hot. And Mother wanted to stop for fresh fruit. Peaches, as I recall."

Anton looked at her. "You call the tsarina 'Mother'?"

Oksana took in a quick breath. "Yes, of course. She's the Imperial Mother to us all, isn't she?"

Anton nodded despite his frown. Yes, the Romanovs through Oksana's eyes seemed a close-knit, loving family. So different from the wealthy aristocrats bent on subjugating

172

the masses as the rebel leaders and provisional government claimed.

"I am amazed at the life you led with them, Oksana. You must have been only eight or so at that time. What an incredible gift to be adopted into a family of royalty as you were, even as a servant."

She wore a far-off look. "They are a. . .remarkable family. I traveled with them extensively as a personal attendant. They never knew when I might be needed."

Anton looked at her. "What exactly could a young child of eight or ten do in way of service for the tsar?"

Oksana's expression turned sad. "Mostly I played with the grand duchesses. And I protected them."

"Protected them?"

She seemed to understand his question, for she put a hand on his arm. "Sometimes protection isn't in might but in choices. What we're willing to do for each other. Like what you've done for me, Anton. I can't thank you enough for taking me here despite what it has cost you. You've given me the gift of safety. And helped me believe that despite the chaos of our current world, there are still gentlemen willing to help a lady."

You're my wife, Oksana. Of course I'll protect you. The thought was on his lips, and for the first time he realized that yes, although he had a mission, he no longer was in service to the tsar. These days, he was obeying his heart.

***

Olga helped spread out the picnic of cheese, meat, brown bread, butter, fresh milk, and a jar of raspberry jam. They sat on a blanket he'd pilfered from Hilda's chest of linens.

The lake beckoned as the sun glared overhead; the water barely rippled with the slight breeze. The smell of field grass and wildflowers tinged the air, and she could nearly taste memory in the laughter of children swimming at the beach not far away. She had passed through this country before on more than one occasion. The route to their vacation paradise in Livadiya passed through the Molotschna Colony, and she wondered if she'd seen a towheaded teen in the crowd that day they had stopped. If she remembered correctly, Oksana had accompanied them—in fact, she'd joined them on nearly every trip they took for the vague purposes Olga had elucidated to Anton. So she hadn't really lied, not really.

Still, she felt ugly inside. He deserved to know the truth, and that had rankled her since coming to Ukraine. The fact that he had not derided the Romanovs when the rest of the world seemed to rejoice at their captivity—that gave her hope. All the same, probably the less he knew about her family, the better.

Anton made her an open sandwich of sausage and cheese on bread. "I know it's not fancy. I just wanted to get away, perhaps recline in the sunshine."

Olga ate in silence, nearly ravenous. She tried hard under Hilda's hawklike eyes to be as unseen as possible. Life at the Klassen farm hadn't been easy. Most nights, she retired to her room exhausted, curling into a ball and crying silently in the darkness. She ached with worry for her family, for Yulia, and for their future. Her prayers seemed to gather on the plaster ceiling, even when she attended church and lit candles in hopes the smoke might carry her petitions to heaven. She had never felt so rejected by God, so empty. So hopeless.

Only Anton gave her reason to smile. She felt his watchful eye on her as she passed through her days, confirmed by the moments when he appeared to offer her a hat or carry the milk or simply push her on the swing she'd collapsed onto a few times. She knew he worked tirelessly to keep her out of the reach of Hilda's stinging words, although the time the woman had upbraided her for getting shells in the *pljuschky* batter. . . Well, there were times Olga wished she didn't understand German.

The sun and farmwork had given Anton a farmer's look with tan forearms and sun-bleached hair. He leaned back on the blanket, raising his arms up to pillow his head, stretching out to cross his ankles. He'd divested himself of the fine attire he wore in Petrograd and on their trip south. Now he wore cotton work pants, boots, and a white blouse rolled at the arms. The look suited him. Strong, confident, and for a moment, she felt a stirring of warmth inside her. Her husband. Despite the farce in that term, she could not help but enjoy it. He would make the real Oksana a wonderful husband.

She sighed, pushing the thought away before it could grab hold and turn her inside out. She had no claim on this man. He belonged to her chambermaid, even as Oksana's current position as royalty under house arrest belonged to Olga.

"I suppose, then, you've been to the Black Sea?" Anton spoke, his eyes closed. "Ever been stung by a jellyfish?"

Olga took a spoonful of raspberry jam, licked it off, and let the flavors explode in her mouth. "No. Maria was once, however. One summer right after we arrived, she ran out into the sea before the Imperial Mother could stop her and immediately emerged with a jellyfish on her back. Screaming, she fell on the beach while my fa—the tsar and her cousin Gleb tore it off her and piled sand on her back. She was sick for a week, and the tsarina prayed her back to health. I don't think Maria went back into the water the rest of the trip."

Anton turned toward her, shading his eyes. "Is the tsarina as religious as everyone says? They say she prayed away the tsarevich's hemophilia."

Olga thought of her brother, of the days when after a fall he would be confined to his bed or wheelchair or carried by his constant bodyguards and attendants, the sailors Derevenko and Nagorny. Tears pricked her eyes as she remembered his screams of pain. "I don't know. She believed the starets Rasputin had the power to heal Alexei. I have to wonder if the starets' murder didn't turn God's wrath on the family."

She looked away toward the happy scene of swimmers, unsure why she'd finally spoken that fear aloud. But it plagued her—especially since it had been alleged that her uncle Dima had been involved in Rasputin's murder. She had even heard her father speculate on Cousin Gleb and his involvement. The thought that her second cousin, the favorite playmate of the grand duchesses, could poison, then shoot, then drown a man—especially a holy man—made her nearly ill.

"I am sure that God has not turned his back on the Romanov family, Oksana." Anton had turned, propping his head up with one arm. "I was just reading this morning from Psalm 100: 'For the Lord is good; his mercy is everlasting; and his truth endureth to all generations.' God set up the

Romanov family, and even if they fall from power, it doesn't mean that He doesn't love them. We so often assume that because something bad happens, God doesn't love us anymore. We have to hang on to faithfulness, believing He has a plan. Verse 3 of that psalm says, 'Know ye that the Lord he is God: it is he that hath made us, and. . .we are. . .the sheep of his pasture.' That's a proclamation that we are in the hands of God, and He knows how feeble we are. He's not going to forsake us. We need to look to the future—sometimes to the next generation—but we can believe in Him."

The question leaped to her lips before she could stop it. "Do you ever think of the future, Anton?"

He considered her, those gray eyes holding hers with such intensity that she felt heat run up her spine. Her mouth dried. Then he sighed and looked away. "If you mean, do I hope to have a family someday, the answer is yes. I long to have an heir, someone to carry on the family name." His voice had become distant, even cold. She couldn't dodge the idea that she had thwarted those dreams for him. Trapped him into a marriage that ate away his time to find a bride.

Unless, of course, her plan worked and Oksana took him as her rightful husband. She would have to put her trust in that possibility. "You'll have a family someday, Anton. And I know you'll be a wonderful father."

He looked at her, and the smile on his face sent a blush to her cheeks. "And I suspect you'll be a wonderful mother."

Oh. Olga licked her dry lips, hating how much those words touched her. "Hopefully I'll be kinder than Hilda." Olga frowned, thinking of Anton's stepmother. "What keeps you silent before her and your father?"

He gave a sad smile. "I am silent before my father because he is my elder and I am his son."

"But he treats you with such disrespect. The Holy Word also says for fathers not to exasperate their children. Even I am driven to exasperation by his words spoken so harshly to you."

Anton sat up and drew up his knees to lean on them. "Thank you for your patience with my family. I know it isn't easy. The truth is. . ." He sighed. "I've always struggled with that response. Yes, inside me I long to raise my voice, defend myself. Perhaps I've been quietly trying to prove him wrong all my life. But as a Mennonite, I always believed that God would fight my battles."

"Is that why you didn't join the imperial forces and fight in Germany?"

He nodded, and she sensed more inside his expression. He stayed silent for a long while, and she felt tempted to fill the gap with an apology.

"The truth is, Oksana, I wondered if I had the courage to fight in the war."

What? She stared at him, trying to wipe the horror from her face. "Anton, I think you're the bravest man I know."

He shook his head, looking down. "I didn't react when the drunk attacked our carriage in Petrograd. And when Yulia was attacked—what if I had arrived minutes sooner? Would I have known what to do?" He clenched his jaw. "When I was young, my religion taught me to turn the other cheek. I spent my childhood pretty bloodied and earned a reputation for cowardice."

Olga could not resist the urge to touch his arm. He

had strong, farm-etched muscles. "Just because you don't fight back doesn't make you weak."

"It doesn't make me strong or brave, either." He shook his head. "The truth is, I don't know what I would do if someone I loved was challenged. If I was forced to choose between fighting and staying silent. Not because I don't have the strength. At times it takes all my strength to stay the course of peace. But because I can't reconcile the tenants of my upbringing with the realities around me. What makes a man brave, Oksana? His ability to wield a gun or sword, or his faith in God?"

She went silent, his words leaving her blank. Indeed, she had seen her father, the head of the Orthodox Church, lead his country in battle and had not thought a moment about it.

He sighed. "I don't mean to burden you with my struggles." He cast a look at her, wearing a grim smile. "There are times, however, I wish the tsar hadn't asked me to take on this task."

She felt as if he had slapped her, taking her breath. He regretted the task? Protecting her? Marrying her?

Olga withdrew her hand, feeling sick. But of course he would feel this way. She was a burden to him, one too great for him to bear. For anyone to bear. Hot tears stung her eyes as she closed them and looked away.

"I'm sorry," she said softly.

He said nothing in reply.

CHAPTER TWELVE

I s there something amiss between you and your bride?" Jonas sat beside Anton on the wagon as they drove to the Klassen estate from Alexanderwohl. The sun hovered at their backs, burning their necks, plastering their cotton shirts to their sweat-drenched bodies. Anton longed to turn the horses south for a trip to the river and cool himself before he arrived home. Then again, Oksana's reception might be cool enough.

"Is it that obvious?" Anton held the reins, staring at the horses' sweat-slicked bodies, laboring to carry the wagon of supplies. In the fields around them, flaxen heads of grain barely shoulder high waved in the hot August breeze.

"Well, other than the fact that you're still sleeping in the barn, I don't think anyone but me would notice. She barely looks at you at dinner, and I've seen her twice hiding in the barn with pails of milk, waiting until your back was turned before she ventured out." Jonas pulled off his wide-brimmed hat, running a hand over his brow with his handkerchief. "Did you offend her?"

Anton shrugged, giving a long shake of his head. "I don't know, Jonas. Perhaps."

"Please, tell me what you did so I can avoid making the same mistake with Gertruda." Jonas smirked at him.

"I don't plan on spending one night in the barn after we're married."

Anton tried to smile, but jealousy filled his throat, nearly choking him. How he longed for a family, a real marriage. Oksana, despite her demeanor, continued to intrigue him, to wind through his thoughts when he didn't hold them captive. Sometimes in his dreams, he returned to their picnic, replayed the words right up until she went quiet.

"I think I might have told her, somehow, that I was sorry we were married." He hadn't exactly said those words. He had meant that he feared he would fail her, fail the tsar, disgrace the family name. He had meant that she had crawled so far inside his heart that letting her go might leave him crushed.

She had asked him if he thought of a future. He had skirted the truth, speaking with hope about a family, per-haps extending invitation into his words. In truth, he saw in his future only heartbreak.

And for that, there were times he regretted the tsar's call on his life.

"You told her that you were sorry you married her?" Jonas shook his head. "Even I know better than that."

"I simply meant that this wasn't the life I'd planned for us." In a manner of speaking.

Jonas leaned forward, his forearms on his knees. "I know things look bleak with the war and the rebellion and all, but farm life isn't bad, Anton. You will build a house of your own, raise a family."

"A farmer's life is a fine one, Jonas. I'm not saying that. It's. . .complicated."

Jonas cast him a look, remaining silent for a long moment. "Do you love her?"

The question arrowed to the soft places Anton had so long guarded, especially since knowing Oksana. Did he love her? He thought her beautiful with her golden-brown hair now curling around her ears, her beautiful blue eyes, her soft smile. He loved her determination, her elegant, nearly regal bearing. He loved the fact that she seemed loyal to her family, and even to him, staying silent in her service to his family. Her belief in him had touched him. And when she'd told him that he might be the bravest man she knew. . .he took those words and buried them in his heart.

But love her? He dreamed more often than not about a future with her. He imagined how their children might look—towheaded with her big blue eyes, her smile. He thought of those few times he'd carried her in his arms, how she felt warm and perfect next to him.

Most of all, until recently she'd been his confidante. Even now, he couldn't imagine sharing with anyone so freely the things of his heart as he had with Oksana.

This ache he felt inside when he thought of losing her. . .the way his pulse leapt every time he saw her, even if she looked grimy and disheveled from weeding the garden—yes, perhaps he did love her.

Perhaps.

He didn't look at Jonas as he gave a slight nod.

"Then, brother, it is not complicated. Move into the house with your wife. Make a family. A life. Make her smile again."

Anton swallowed the ball of pain in his throat.

Even if he declared his love for her, took her in his arms, erased those words he had said in a moment of foolishness, he felt sure she would never smile again. Not after the news he'd received in town today.

The Klassen farm had flourished, the summer sun and rains fertilizing the fields. Barley and oats rimmed the fields, and the flower garden, filled with gladiolas and roses and hollyhocks, sent its heady scent into the air. Even from this far away, Anton could make out Oksana bent over the vegetable garden, weeding the tomato plants.

He dreaded their conversation, words already clogging in his chest. They pulled up to the house, and he and Jonas unloaded the sack of sugar, the fabric Hilda had ordered, and canning supplies. Then they drove to the barn and stacked the extra provisions of wheat seed for the fall planting in the barn. He hoped Jonas's idea would work. With the closing of the Petrograd warehouse, they needed any extra income they could muster until they could reopen it when the chaos died.

Anton had to admit he felt grateful he wasn't in the capital city these days, although Lenin, their new leader, had moved the capital to Moscow just weeks earlier. He wondered at this new leader, at the reforms he promised. They seemed far away from life in Molotschna, and Anton hoped they'd stay far away. However, he'd heard rumors of the civil war, of rebel forces surging south. The population feared both the Red Army, which represented the Bolsheviks, and the White Army, comprised of the imperial forces. Both armies would sweep into villages and conscript every able-bodied man to fight one against the other as well as against their German enemies in the continuing

Great War. Certainly, however, they wouldn't touch the Mennonite communities, knowing how their citizens felt about violence and war.

Anton finished stacking the seed, then unhitched the horses and rubbed them down. The sun was inching into the western horizon when he finished and wiped his hands and face with his handkerchief.

Oksana sat on the swing, moving it slightly back and forth with her feet on the ground and her back to him. She stared at the sunset.

He stood for a moment, sighing, gathering his courage.

He approached her slowly, not meaning to scare her, grief weighting each of his steps. She held on to the ropes of the swing, and he noticed how her elegant hands looked scraped and roughened. His heart twisted. Still, she bore herself with grace befitting a servant of royalty. He wondered if he would ever believe she belonged on the farm like Jonas suggested. With everything inside him, Anton longed to take her to the city and outfit her in clothing and supply her with her own set of servants.

He touched the rope right above her hand. "Oksana?"

She turned to look at him, and he saw that a long tear had made a trail down her cheek. Alarm rang through him. "Are you okay?"

She nodded, wiping her hand down her cheek and leaving behind fingerprints of dirt. "Just tired, I suppose." She offered him a weak smile, warmer than any she'd given him in more than a month, and it made him want to cry, too. He turned and crouched before her, holding on to the swing's ropes with each hand.

Her face tightened in a frown.

"I have some news for you," he said before his mouth dried completely. "About the royal family."

She said nothing, but worry filled her eyes. She swallowed.

He closed his eyes, willing any moment but this for her. Then he opened them and moved his hands to touch hers. "The reigning government has sent the Romanov family and all their remaining servants to Siberia as exiled prisoners."

⬦

Olga stared at him, unsure of what he might be saying, trying to unscramble his words. Exile? To Siberia? No, that couldn't be correct. They had family all over Europe, especially in England. Her father would have sent them out into the hands of relatives. Not to Siberia.

"What? I don't understand."

Anton crouched in front of her, the expression in his eyes gentle but worried. She felt his touch on her hands, warm and strong, and she realized again how much she missed his companionship. He'd come to mean more to her than even Yulia and perhaps in many ways her sisters. Although they were comrades in her royal life, she never had feelings for anyone that compared to the way this man stirred her. The knowledge that he regretted taking on the mission only made her respect the way he continued to protect her, even if her growing feelings for him frightened her. She shouldn't become so emotionally attached to someone who viewed her as no more than unwanted baggage.

The compassion in his expression made her eyes fill

with tears. "The provisional government sent the entire family to Siberia. Some say this will eventually lead to exile to Japan. Others say not."

Siberia? She knew so little about that vast area within Russia. Cold. She knew it had to be cold and barren. And cruel. What about Alexei's condition? Had Dr. Botkin traveled with them? If not, would there be capable doctors? And her sisters alone without her? She felt sick and curled her arms around her stomach. "No. I don't understand. Why do they hate us so? What did we ever do to them?"

"No one hates you, Oksana. This has nothing to do with you." He tugged at her arms from around her waist and took her hands in his. His hands were rough and work worn, so different from the smooth hands that had held her the day she'd collapsed after Yulia's attack. She felt vastly removed from that girl and from the years of royal privilege before. How foolish she'd been to leave the palace, to obey her father without a thought. Had he known even then that they might never be reunited?

Tears blinded her, and her face crumpled as she fought to keep down a wail. Pain doubling her over, she tore her hands from Anton's grip and rocked. "No, this can't be happening. No."

She felt Anton's arms go around her, felt him lift her, settle her on the ground next to him. Still she kept her eyes closed, grief shuddering out of her in sobs. She covered her eyes with her hands, giving over to the sorrow that dogged her through each day.

"I never agreed to this. I never said I could live without them." She felt Anton pull her close, tighten his grip around her, and she let herself give in to his comfort. He felt so strong, so protective as she laid her head against his chest. "He was wrong. He was so wrong." She dug her hand into Anton's work shirt, pulling herself into his embrace. "They never should have sent me away."

"Shh, Oksana. Don't cry." Anton's arms tightened around her, and she felt his chin on the top of her head, then the soft press of his lips against her hair.

"You don't understand, Anton." She let those words linger, aching to tell him, needing to tell him. "I have to be with them."

"No, Oksana." He put her away from himself, meeting her eyes. "*Doragaya*, your life with them is over. They have a different path now, one that releases you from their service. Probably they'll leave the country from the east and travel abroad. You need to accept this and think about your future."

Her mouth opened, and a gust of pain leaked out. Fury gathered, raced up her arms to push against him. She jerked out of his arms, scooted back in the grass. "No!"

"Oksana—"

"No, Anton. I belong with them! They need me. They are my future."

Anton sighed, his lips pursed. He looked away from her, his expression grim. Then he shook his head.

"Yes, Anton. Take me to them."

"To Siberia?" The look on his face, incredulous, horrified, only solidified the words that had stumbled out.

"Yes, to Siberia. I need to return to my family."

"They're not your family, not anymore. I know you loved them probably like your own flesh and blood. And

I know you believe you have no one else, but you're not alone, Oksana."

She stared at him, at his desperate expression, hearing his ragged voice. She swallowed, frowning, not sure—

"You have me." He put his hand to his chest. "Me. I'm your husband. And I know it was just a ruse, but I—I care for you. And you're not alone. I will take care of you."

She felt herself hiccup, his words finding all the wounds she had nursed over the past month. He cared for her? Another rush of tears made her blind, and she covered her face with her hands, confused.

What if her family was sent to Japan or returned from Siberia when the imperial troops vanquished the provisional army? She couldn't be Anton's wife. Her parents would never approve of their marriage. An annulment they would understand, perhaps, but Anton, a commoner, as a son-in-law?

Her sobs came harder, and she felt Anton come close to her, take her again in his arms.

"I promise I'll build you a fine life, take care of you, and give you a future, Oksana. Be my wife. My real wife."

She heard his words and ached inside. But she shook her head quietly, painfully. "I can't, Anton. I can't."

She felt him stiffen, then sigh, as if something had left him. She tightened her jaw, willing herself to composure. She let herself remain just a moment longer in his arms, smelling hay and sweat on him, feeling his muscular embrace, honed by hard work, comforting her.

Then she pulled away, raising her chin and meeting his eyes. She was a princess, and even if he did not know it, he was still her subject. And under her father's command.

"I want you to take me to Siberia. It's time for me to join my family, Anton."

The frown on his face, the dark look in his eyes, scared her. "Is there something you haven't told me about your relationship with the royal family, Oksana?"

She swallowed and looked away, hating herself. "Not a thing, Anton." Using the swing, she pulled herself to her feet. "I'll expect to leave in the morning."

He sat there in the grass at her feet, the sunshine turning his blond hair to bronze, his sculpted face in a hardened expression of anger, his gray eyes as stone cold as she'd ever seen them. Despite the heat, a shiver rippled up her spine.

He shook his head and said quietly, "Then you'll be sorely disappointed, Oksana. Because as long as you're under my care, you're not going anywhere."

She stared at him, her world tipping. Drawing in a shaky breath, she nodded. "So be it." She turned and started toward the house, drawing up her escape in her thoughts. She had money in her valise and jewels sewn into her traveling cloak, even one of her corsets. She easily had enough to purchase her transport to Siberia.

She felt Anton's gaze on her and, for the first time since leaving Tsarskoe Selo, knew she was utterly alone.

⚜

Anton felt bereft as he watched Oksana over dinner. Something had changed between them, something irrevocable and heart wrenching. Yes, he knew he'd hurt her before when he said he regretted accepting the tsar's mission. But he thought he'd made his intentions toward her clear as he took her in his arms. "Be my wife, my real wife," he had said, his heart in his words.

And still, she remained fixed in her service to the crown. As if she hadn't a choice.

Or rather refused a choice. Refused him. The *tweeback* tasted like ash in his mouth, and he ate nothing, excusing himself early. He felt Jonas's gaze on him as he bid his family good night and exited to the barn.

Climbing into the loft where he could watch the night bathe the estate, he looked into the heavens, seeking God's plan. He ached for Oksana, wanting to do her bidding, to see happiness on her face even if it felt like tearing his heart from his chest. But he couldn't take her to Siberia. Not without risking her life. And even if he couldn't marry her, he still felt the burden of the tsar's request. *"Protect her."*

As a reminder, he pulled out the crest he had secreted inside a book of poetry in the barn and slipped it again over his head. Perhaps he had lost focus, and the cold weight against his skin would help him keep his head. He watched Oksana's light extinguish and imagined her getting into bed. For the briefest moments, he'd thought she might agree, might lift her face to his, joy on her countenance, and accept his proposal.

"I can't, Anton."

The words still stung.

The breeze carried with it the scent of barley and the coolness of late summer. Soon they would harvest, and then Jonas would marry and bring Gertruda into their home. Perhaps another woman might lessen the sting of Hilda's tongue. Still, he knew that Oksana missed her "family." He had to admit, however, how odd her attachment to them was. Clearly he had underestimated the bonds between the family and their servants. Most of all, he hated the fact that he had refused her request. Hated to see the pain—even shock—in her eyes. Hated that he longed for her to trust him, and he'd just snuffed out any possibility of that.

So much for wanting her to love him. She'd looked at him like she just might hate him.

He was watching her room when he saw the door open. A figure edged out into the night, cast a look at the barn, then headed for the road. He recognized a cloak, a traveling case. . .Oksana.

Oh no. What was she up to now? He knew she had a feisty spirit about her, that she'd bottled it up for the good of their plan. But apparently it had bubbled out into a rash decision to escape.

Escape him.

With a sigh, he climbed down from the hayloft and exited the barn, quietly on her tail. She hustled down the drive toward the road. What? Did she hope to walk all the way to the train station in Halbstadt?

He stole quickly behind her, running lightly, his breath tight in his chest.

She turned out of the drive and started down the road, the moonlight lining her cloak, a phantom in the night.

"Oksana!" he hissed.

She froze, turned, her eyes wide. Then she sighed, her spirit sinking visibly in her expression. "Let me go, Anton."

He closed the distance between them, and when she took a step, he planted himself in front of her. She looked so defiant, so angry, it shook him to his core. Her eyes snapped in anger. "Get out of my way."

"*Nyet.* I made a promise to the tsar to protect you. And I will."

"Then take me to Siberia."

"No. You are in danger there. Anyone associated with the royal family is in danger."

Her eyes glistened, but she refused to look away. Her jaw tightened. "They need me."

I need you. The words nearly left his mouth, but he caught them. He sighed, blowing out a frustrated breath. "Stay. For now. When I feel it is safe. . .I'll take you to Siberia." He ran a hand through his hair, disbelieving he'd actually said that.

A tear ran down her cheek. She brushed at it, anger in her posture. "Really, promise?"

He closed his eyes, feeling a fool. A heartsick fool. And nodded.

"Thank you. Oh, thank you, Anton." The tremor in her voice made him open his eyes a second before she dropped her valise and lunged at him, her arms around his waist. She pressed her face into his chest, and he wondered if she could hear his heart thumping against his rib cage in wild amazement.

His arms went around her, holding her, relishing this moment. Oksana in his arms. He tightened his hold on her, burying his face in her hair. She smelled sweet, freshly washed, and feminine. He closed his eyes. Oksana.

He'd been a fool, spoken out of desperation. Because he knew the promise he'd just made might kill them both.

CHAPTER THIRTEEN

A nton looked like a prince sitting with the other Klassen men in the first aisle as his stepbrother Jonas repeated his vows to Gertruda. She wore a crown of yellow chrysanthemums in her long blond hair and a simple dress made of white cotton. Still, the girl—probably a year or two younger than Olga—looked radiant.

And why not? She was marrying the man of her dreams. Olga would feel the same if she could only tell Anton that, yes, she wanted to be his wife. And if he accepted her back.

She sat in the second row next to Hilda in the small Mennonite church. Already they'd endured two sermons, prayers, and two choral numbers. At the front of the church, Gertruda held a simple bouquet of late-blooming dahlias and chrysanthemums—a mix of purples and oranges and whites that only accented the rather simple attire of the bride and groom. Simple only by royal standards. Olga would gladly sacrifice the gems of her supposed bridal gown to marry a man she loved.

She let a melancholy smile touch her lips. She *had* married the man she loved.

Anton.

She had finally admitted as much to herself one day as she watched him work with the other hands harvesting the barley. How freeing the realization. As if, for the first time, she might be true to herself. She loved Anton. Since the moment he'd held her, agreed to take her back to her family regardless of the cost, he had become again her friend. They had taken walks to the duck pond on the far end of the property with the twilight closing in, bringing with it the smells of autumn. She had helped him harvest pumpkins and mow down the kitchen garden for the winter, turning the leftover stalks to fertilizer in the ground. His strong arms lifted her into the hay during the harvest hayride, and his laughter filled her soul, buoying her spirits even as her hope felt feeble. She hadn't heard a word about the royal family in weeks, although Anton did his best to gather what news he could when he went to the village.

Her father had been scheduled to be tried by the state. *Tried*, like a criminal. The thought turned her stomach. Currently, the Bolsheviks and the provisional forces waged battles in every hamlet in Russia. Thankfully, the thick of the fight still had not reached Molotschna, but even Ukrainians were not immune to conscription of men or confiscation of horses or foodstuffs for the military efforts of either side. She half-expected them to sweep through Alexanderwohl any day and—her greatest fear of late—take Anton with them despite his assurances that the Mennonites wouldn't be touched. She did agree, however, that they needed to wait until after the trial to join the family. What if they were exiled to the west—England or France—and she could join them there? It made sense to bide her time. . .and in the meantime give her father one less reason to worry.

And it gave her time to devise the words to tell them she'd taken a husband. Because in her heart, she couldn't surrender Anton. Not to the real Oksana. Not to an annulment. Not without her heart shattering like one of the mirrors in the winter palace after the rebels' riot. So what if he wasn't royal. He was royal in her heart.

She'd begun to plot her words, her defense to her mother. Certainly, after all Anton had done, her parents would allow them to stay married. Especially if the marriage had been consummated.

The thought terrified her. Not only the intimacy but the risk of telling Anton her feelings. He had not hinted at his feelings even once since that day when he'd asked her to be his wife—his real wife. For all she knew, that had been a ruse to convince her to stay. He'd said he cared for her. But what if he didn't love her? Certainly the way he listened to her read poetry or tell him stories of the family, carefully guarded of course, meant that he enjoyed her company. And she'd seen something appear in his beautiful eyes more than once when he left her at the door to his room after an evening stroll. . .desire? Love?

The thought made her stomach curl with hope.

"Then, because of the holy vows you have declared before these witnesses and the Lord God in heaven, I pronounce you man and wife."

Olga looked up and smiled as Jonas wrapped his wife in a kiss. From his bench, Anton met her gaze and smiled.

She felt a blush burn her cheeks despite the cool air.

The weekend of festivities had kept her and Hilda and Gertruda's family busy for a week. Starting with the meal yesterday evening for the *Pultaovent*, where they had played games and exchanged gifts, they baked for nearly three hundred—the entire village. Since the Klassen barn held more room, the Regier and Klassen families had cleaned it out and swept the threshing floor for the wedding dinner. Anton had moved into the house, sleeping on the floor in the kitchen. It made for raised eyebrows from his step-brother Jonas and reminded her of all he endured for her.

Thankfully, Olga had learned some culinary skills and helped in making the wedding borscht, *kuchen*, *strietzel*, and *pfefferkuchen* cookies. Unlike Orthodox weddings, and especially royal weddings, there would be no dance. But Olga felt celebration in the air all the same as the bride and groom ate together, enjoying the congratulations of their friends and family.

This new life had taken her by surprise. Who thought that she would long for simplicity, for a family with Anton, even life on a farm? She felt a stab of guilt as she watched Jonas and Gertruda, the joy on their faces. She doubted they harbored secrets from each other.

She felt Anton's presence behind her even as she thought of him. He barely could be in the same room without her pulse racing, warmth running through her. She turned and saw his gaze on her, a lazy smile on his face as he leaned against the door frame of the giant double doors to the barn. Beyond him, the starry sky twinkled, a glistening chandelier to this rustic ballroom.

"You look beautiful tonight," he said softly. Although laughter and conversation filled the room, she could hear him perfectly. She swallowed the heat in her throat, glad she had chosen the green ball gown, the one she had worn to the New Year's Eve ball at Tsarskoe Selo, however meager it had been out of respect for the sacrifices all Russians should make to the war effort. Simple yet elegant with velvet sleeves and a silk bodice, she worried now it would look overdone among the Alexanderwohl farmwives. Thankfully, Hilda had sewn herself a new frock, with a ruffled blouse and deep blue velvet skirt, although Olga felt sure that the diamonds Hilda wore at her neck weren't real like the ones that beaded Olga's neck and bodice. The secret made her smile.

"Thank you," Olga said, edging over to him. "You, too," she said and felt another blush. Dressed in the finery he had worn during the days when they first met—wool suit, ascot at his neck, silk shirt, and cuff links—he looked like a different man, although he still bore the ruddy kiss of sunshine in his wavy hair and high cheekbones. He reached out his hand to her. "Walk with me?"

She felt like singing as they exited the barn, strolled out to the swing. She sat on it while he pushed her. The cool air felt fresh and wholesome after the heat and odors of the barn. "They make a lovely couple," she said. "I am sure they will be happy."

Anton said nothing.

"I have observed the matchmaking wrangling and maneuvering of numerous royals these past few years—all for the sake of forming a beneficial marriage union between nobility. In all those arranged marriages, the bride and groom hardly knew one another. Sometimes after the wedding, the newlyweds would go their separate ways.

"People marry for all kinds of reasons. Comfort. Companionship. Political reasons," Anton said.

"Protection." Olga looked over her shoulder at Anton.

"Love," he said. His eyes were in hers, his face unsmiling. She swallowed and nodded.

"Love," she repeated. She thought her heart might alight and burst right through her. She scraped her feet on the ground to stop her swing. Anton stopped pushing and stared at her. His arms fell to his sides. He simply stood, quiet in the moonlight.

She rose from the swing, hanging on to the rope with her right hand and turning toward him. Her mouth felt unusually dry, and she licked her lips.

His gaze fell to her mouth, his expression troubled. Then he closed his eyes, turned away from her.

Panic rushed through her. "Anton, what is it?"

He sighed and rubbed his forehead with his hand. "Nothing. I'm sorry, Oksana."

But she took a step toward him, put her hand on the small of his back. "Anton, please look at me."

He sighed again, then turned, running his hand through his hair. His gaze met hers. "We should go back to the barn."

No. She looked up at him, willing him to see her heart, see the love she poured into her eyes. She took a step toward him, opening her mouth, touching his lapel. "Anton."

He frowned; then, his gaze holding hers, he leaned down, cupped his hand against her cheek, and kissed her. Softly. Tenderly. Perfectly.

She closed her eyes and leaned into his kiss. He tasted spicy, like the apple cider, and strong, like the man she'd learned to trust. She moved her lips, kissed him back, now clutching his jacket with both hands, pulling him tighter to herself.

He wrapped his other arm around her, hugging her against him, deepening his kiss. Yes. He did love her; she knew it. And she kissed him with every hope she had for them, every feeling of gratefulness over the past six months, all the love that had been building in her heart for her husband.

Her husband.

"Anton," she whispered against his lips. "I want to be your wife. Your real wife, the one who. . .who loves you."

He lifted his head, stared at her, breathing hard. She watched his Adam's apple bob in his throat. Saw the indecision on his face.

"Oh, Oksana. You have no idea how I've longed to hear you say that. I love you. So much."

He loved her. She wanted to sing. Instead, idiotic tears filled her eyes.

He touched her forehead to his. "Yes, be my wife. My beautiful, wonderful wife. And I'll be your husband. And I promise to keep every vow I made to you on our wedding day."

She reached up and wrapped her arms around his neck. Then laughed as he swooped her up into his arms.

"I want to show you something. A secret I've been hiding from you."

She tried to ignore the guilt that wrapped around her soul as he carried her toward the house.

"Where are you taking me, Anton?"

Anton pushed open the door to his room with his foot. "Just wait." *Just wait.* He should tell that to his heart. Everything inside him told him to pinch himself, wake up before he found himself unable to breathe with the pain. But miraculously, he wasn't dreaming. Oksana had put her arms around his neck and spoken the words he'd been dreaming of nearly every day and night since they married. *"I want to be your wife."*

He wanted that so much he nearly started crying right there. Instead, he swooped her into his arms and nearly ran toward the house. All the same, he wasn't unaware of the fear on her face despite her words or the way she clung to him. He forced himself to slow down, to keep his heartbeat in control. He put her down. "Wait here."

Moving over to the wardrobe, he shoved it aside. He could nearly feel her eyes grow wide as a door was revealed. He opened it and pulled down the stairs folded inside. "When I was young, before we built the addition, these stairs accessed a storage room. After Hilda and the boys moved in, sometimes I would escape here." He smelled the wooden rafters, the dust. "Come, just for a moment."

She smiled as he strode past her and swept the cover from his bed. Leading the way, he took her hand and helped her up the stairs. He'd once pretended long ago that he ruled everything he saw from this perch that over-looked the barn and the Klassen estate. The room wasn't large enough to stand in, and memory brought him back to the time he'd made a bed up here, opening the window and sneaking up every night, watching the stars and reading by candlelight.

He laid the blanket on the floor, stirring up dust balls.

Then he opened the window. The November air felt cool on his sweaty brow, and he untied his stiff collar and ascot.

"Candles?" Oksana asked.

"Yes." Anton took the box of matches he'd stored on the windowsill so long ago and lit a well-worn row of candles. They sent flickering light across the room and chased the shadows from Oksana's face. She smiled at him a moment before she turned onto her stomach and stared out the window.

"You can see the barn from here."

"Yes. When I was young, I used to pretend I was the tsar watching my people."

"You think the tsar so sneaky?"

Anton laughed, settling next to her. "No. I just wanted to be lord over the manor. The tsar seemed a good aspiration."

Oksana rolled onto her side, propping her head up on her elbow. Her hair had grown out to chin length, and he didn't stop himself from reaching out to touch it, running his fingers through it. Then he bent and kissed her.

He often imagined what it might be like to hold Oksana in his arms, to kiss her with the emotions that had piled in his chest since that day on the road when she'd tried to leave him. That day had sparked new beginnings for them, and he looked forward to her smile at the end of the day like a hungry man. Still, he'd held inside his longing to be truly husband and wife, to make their marriage permanent, afraid that should he mention it, she would reject him again.

Never, however, had he imagined her now, kissing him back, whispering his name. Letting him love her.

"Are you sure, Oksana?" he asked, cradling her head in his arm, running his thumb down her cheek. It was wet, and that scared him a little, because he had tasted her tears before, and the very last thing he wanted to do was hurt her now. Ever.

"I'm sure, Anton. I want to spend the rest of my life with you. I want to have children and make a life with you." She lifted her face to his, weaving her hand into his hair, kissing him, then whispering in his ear. "I want to be your wife."

His throat felt thick, and he did not care that he cried, that she wiped away his tears with her thumbs, that she might think him weak. Because in her arms he felt strong. Complete.

Perhaps the world was his indeed.

He didn't intend for them to spend their wedding night in the attic, but neither did he expect his feelings to overwhelm him so, for Oksana to give so much of herself, and for him to find in that a new kind of love. Of trust. He could learn so much from this woman who caught his heart—bravery and loyalty and surrender and generosity.

For the first time, he knew what it felt like to be accepted. And loved.

She lay in his arms, breathing softly, running her fingers over the Crest of St. Basil that still hung around his neck. "I can't believe the tsar gave this to you. It never left his neck."

"He told me to guard it with my life. That people would be after it once they discovered it missing."

She nodded, her expression solemn as she ran her thumb over the jewels. "If he only knew," she said softly.

The sounds of the celebration below drifted in through the window. Raucous sounds of laughter and horses.

"What is that?" she asked, not moving to look. He didn't look either, just held her, inhaling the scent of her hair, the feel of her in his arms.

"Charivari. It's a Mennonite tradition." He kissed her behind her ear, and she giggled. "Be glad we were far away from here when we wed."

She pushed at him. "Tell me."

He shrugged, pushing her hair behind her ear with his fingers. "A group of the groom's friends publicly embarrass the bride and groom. Like making a horrible din until they're paid with food to leave or setting loose a flock of geese into the wedding celebration."

"That's horrible."

"I put my cousin's buggy on the roof of their house."

Her mouth dropped open, and appropriately, she swatted him. He laughed, kissing her again.

A gunshot yanked his head up, made him frown.

"That doesn't sound like a prank."

He shook his head, peering out the window. *No, no prank.* His chest tightened. "Stay down, Oksana."

"What?" She slid up on her elbow and moved toward the window. "Who are they?"

"Hard to say. Bolsheviks or the imperial forces. Maybe Makhno's bandits." He got up, reached for his clothing.

"Where are you going?" Oksana grabbed his arm, her fingers digging into his forearm. "Don't leave me here."

"I'll be fine—"

"No! What if they take you! Anton, you promised my father you'd look after me. You said you would. You can't leave!"

Her father? His heart thumped, something not quite right stirring inside him. Another shot, then screams outside yanked his attention to the window. He saw the women gathered outside held back by the troops and screaming. Two men lay bloodied on the ground.

"Oksana, I have to get out there."

"No! You can't leave me. You have to stay—to protect me!"

He cupped his hands around her face. "I'll return, I promise."

She clenched her jaw, her beautiful eyes fierce. "Anton Klassen, you are now married to the grand duchess Olga Nikolaevna Romanova, and I demand that you stay with me."

He stared at her, everything inside him going weak, his breath in hot gusts. What? Was she ill? Had she lost her mind?

The bang of the door and footsteps inside the house made him jump. He yanked out of her grip, backing away.

"I'll be right back."

Tears ran down her face as she shook her head in disbelief.

CHAPTER FOURTEEN

Olga sat on the railroad car, squeezed next to a smelly babushka and her lamb, feeling numb to her toes. And it wasn't the gale of the November wind snaking through the cracked windows and freezing the passengers of the *obshye* class.

No, grief had cut off all blood supply to anything but her heart, which ached with every pulse.

Nearby, a chicken squawked, and she put her hands over her ears to silence the screaming. So much screaming.

She could not close her eyes, or she would see them all, the women fighting to free their husbands, the attackers bayoneting or shooting those who broke ranks and threw themselves toward the burning barn. She had watched in horror as Hilda had perished, screaming as the soldiers ended her life. In her sleep, Olga still smelled the stench of the burning barn filling her nose, stinging her eyes, still saw the man she loved race down the stairs.

She would have shattered completely had he not returned moments later breathing hard, her clothing and all easily seen remnants of her existence tossed into her valise. He had then pulled up the stairs behind him and sat there with the kitchen ax in his hand, glancing over at her like maybe he had seen a ghost.

Something inside him had died that night. She saw it go out with a snuff as the sum total of his family, his step-brothers, his father, died in the barn on the Klassen farm. The assailants ransacked their house, and only his quick thinking in gathering her possessions left them anything of value. He had snuffed the candles and stayed at the top of the stairs through the night and into the early morning hours until they were sure the attackers were gone.

The barn, burned to the dirt, left only char and a sickly smell in the air. The women, spent with wailing and horror, sifted through the ash.

Inside the attic, Olga felt sick and had retched until she was raw.

Anton watched her from a distance as if afraid to touch her. He looked spent, the life gone from his beautiful eyes.

"Are you all right?" he'd finally asked when he felt it safe to speak. She shook her head. She might never be all right again.

It was supposed to be glorious, the moment when they finally declared their love, became as man and wife before God. Instead, she felt nauseated, as if hollowed out, their love stolen from them by the dissident throng now holding hostage their land.

So much stolen.

Anton had lifted her, gently carrying her and her valise out of the attic. He had not stopped for the grieving widows and daughters but wore a grim expression as he loaded her into a carriage. Then, with the women spitting at him, wailing and screaming, he had driven away from the smoking remains of the Klassen farm to the Halbstadt station.

They had been aboard the train to Pskov for two days. Olga felt grimy and disheveled, achy and spent.

Anton stood near the window, his gaze falling on her protectively now and again. He, too, looked rough, his suit grimy and mussed, his hair tousled and on end. Bags hung under his eyes. While she had slept little, she doubted if he had slept at all.

Plagued, perhaps, by the lie she had propagated. She didn't know if he believed her or thought her crazy. He had spoken not a word of her announcement.

She leaned her head back, trying to shut out the odor of coal smoke, the stench of bodies and animals and cigarette smoke. Her head bobbed against the hard wooden seat, grateful that Anton had fought for even this much space. And to think, at one time she would have considered this beneath her. Now she was simply grateful to be alive.

The train had a rhythm, and she moved with it, losing herself in the motion, in lost dreams of happy times. Of being in Anton's arms. They traveled north through other towns, some of which bore evidence of their own attacks—smoldering ruins or barren as if emptied. She wondered what would happen to Alexanderwohl and if the whole of the Molotschna Colony would be deserted.

Anton bought her a boiled egg through the open window of the train as they pulled into a station, then a cup of yogurt. Neither did much for her stomach. When night fell, he picked her up and settled her on his lap, wrapping his arms around her so her head fell against his chest. "Thank you, Anton," she said quietly.

He said nothing as he smoothed her hair. She fell asleep with his hand on her head.

The morning sun found her as it filtered across her face and stirred her awake. Olga blinked against the wash of light, trying to orient herself. Wooden ceiling and walls, drab lace curtains hanging at the windows, the smell of fatback frying in sunflower oil. A rough woolen blanket was drawn up to her nose, and every muscle in her body ached.

Alarm made her sit up. The blanket dropped to her waist, and she noticed she wore her undergarments, her slip and shirtwaist. She quickly pulled the blanket back up to her armpits, cold, prickling gooseflesh across her arms.

Where was she? Across from her stood a table with a pitcher and washbowl atop, a stool pushed underneath. Wallpaper printed with tiny roses adorned the walls, and recognition swept through her. Uncle Maxim's home. Anton had brought her back to Yulia. Or at least she hoped her old chambermaid still lived here with her uncle and aunt.

To her right, hung over a chair, she saw her green dress laundered and clean. She slipped from the bed, gathered the blanket around her, and searched for her valise. She found it next to the sagging bureau. Pulling out the work dress given her by Vera Petrovna, she fitted it on, buttoning the blouse over her shirtwaist, then laced up her shoes. She felt grimy and longed for a bath, but not before she found Anton.

She tried the door, and to her great relief, it gave. Creaking it open, she stopped at the sight of Anton sitting on a stool outside her door. His arms akimbo over his chest, his chin nodded down, as if he'd fallen asleep. His hair still stood on all ends, and he wore a scruff of beard growth. She pushed the door farther, wincing as a squeal jerked him awake. He raised his head, startled, then stared at her hard as if also trying to ascertain their whereabouts. She offered him a slim smile.

"You're awake."

"Is Yulia here?"

He met her gaze a long moment before he answered. "No. She's working at a nearby orphanage."

Oh. She nodded and moved out into the hall. He looked horrible. Days of travel had taken their toll on him: Bags hung under his eyes, and he still wore his untidy clothing. "Are we safe here?"

"Yes." He stood, then frowned at her. "I'm not sure— am I supposed to bow?"

She jerked, shocked at his words. "I, uh. . ."

"Because the thing is. . . Well, now that we're here, and yes, safe, I have to know."

She cringed, waiting for the question she knew was to come.

"Just exactly who are you?"

She put a hand to her head. "I need some water."

"There's some in your room." He moved toward her, his hand out as if to catch her.

"And I'd like a bath."

"Of course. In fact, Uncle Maxim has already gone to stoke the banya."

She closed her eyes. A banya. It seemed a year since she'd bathed properly.

"Thank you, Anton."

He stood in the hall, his chest rising and falling, the silence thick, his expression fierce.

How could she tell him the truth? Would it change them forever? Would he refuse her? He couldn't—not after what they'd done.

What they had done. They were man and wife. Truly. That thought staggered her.

He reached out his hand, touching her elbow. "Oksana?"

"I'm okay. Just tired."

He nodded, opening the door to the chamber. "Let's get you that drink." He pulled her inside, setting her down again on the bed. Then he poured her a cup of water from the pitcher and handed it to her. It was cool but fresh. She drank it greedily, her stomach roaring to life. "When did we get here?"

"Early this morning. You were so tired you barely stirred as I carried you off the train. Timofea met us with the carriage. I had telegraphed him from the train station. He suggested we stay at Maxim's until we decide our future."

"No one followed us, did they?"

He gave her an odd look, crouching down against the wall. Kneading his forehead with both hands, he considered her, those gray eyes stormy and troubled. "I've pushed it around in my head a thousand times, and I have to say, you had me believing you. The way you are tied to the Romanov family so closely that you call the tsarina 'Mother' and the tsar 'Father.' And you've never had a family, so it makes sense. I can even see you fantasizing about being one of the grand duchesses, having lived a life in such proximity." He shook his head. "Frankly, I probably would have done the same thing—created a life for myself." He folded his hands on his knees. "And then there's the clothing and the way you treated me when we first met." He gave a huff of indignation. "I believed you, Oksana; I really did. For three days."

She went still, feeling hollow, not sure how she should react. A part of her ached to tell him the truth, to have the honesty between them he deserved. But the other part—the part that had longed to be loved as Oksana, the simple servant girl, without the enticements of wealth and title—wanted to deny her words. Laugh them off and attribute them to panic.

She rubbed her arms and gave him a wan smile. "What happened?"

He shrugged and shook his head. "I asked Yulia. I sent her a note through Timofea asking her the very question, and she told me the truth."

Olga went still.

"She told me that you two were servants, chambermaids. And sometimes you played at being princesses." He gave a harsh smile. "You really scared me, however. To think I thought I was protecting not just the Crest of St. Basil but one of the royal Romanovs." His smile vanished, and his eyes grew dark. "No, not just protecting her. . ."

Olga's mouth dried, thinking of their intimacy. She swallowed, aware of the relief in his eyes, and knew the truth. He loved her as Oksana. But as the grand duchess. . .perhaps for both of them, for their safety as well as their future, her secret should stay just that—a secret. "Sorry. I guess I—I didn't know what to say. You were going to leave me."

Anton's expression turned soft, gentle. He crawled over to her, knelt, and took her in his arms, holding her against himself. She breathed in his strength, despite his unwashed body. "I'll never leave you, Oksana. I promise."

***

Untold sorrow fills my soul on this day, which should have been my most joyous ever. No sooner had I found myself adrift in Oksana's sweet love than our world came crashing in. They died as my wife and I looked helplessly on from our secret place. Their screams echo in my heart, torment my every thought, even my soul. What kind of man am I that my stepbrothers should die while I live? How can my faith survive such horror?

The shrieks filled his brain and jerked him out of slumber with a hot flash of panic. Oksana!

He sat up, the bedclothes falling to his waist, sweat prickling his flesh before he realized the screeching had stopped. Quietness flooded the bedroom. Beside him, Oksana lay curled in quiet slumber, her tawny blond hair fanned out over her face. She looked so young, so vulnerable. Anton closed his eyes and scrubbed his face with his hands, his heartbeat hammering against the walls of his chest. He breathed in and out, slowly, trying to sort through his thoughts.

They couldn't stay at Maxim's forever. Already Oksana jerked at every slammed door, her face drawn in fear when hooves galloped into the yard. That they were vulnerable here seemed glaringly apparent every time Uncle Maxim received a visitor, which seemed increasingly often these days. Anton feared not only for her safety but for her future if the Red or White armies made another conscription sweep through Pskov.

Timofea had suggested they move to the monastery. Oksana would be safe, allowed refuge in the visitors' quarters, while Anton slept in the cells and worked in the forge. For now, it would offer them seclusion, anonymity, and safety.

However, the thought of being even that far away from Oksana sent a searing pain through his chest. He'd miss her warmth beside him, helping them both silence the demons.

And they both had plenty of demons. Seared into his brain forevermore would be the screams and violent deaths of his stepmother, his father, and his stepbrothers—especially Jonas. The thought staggered him, and he slipped out of bed and fell to his knees, his stomach wanting to empty.

He buried his head in his hands. "O God, what have I done?" he whispered. He'd sat in the attic like a frightened child, watching with his bride while the attackers had massacred his entire family. He made himself sick.

"Anton Klassen, you are now married to the grand duchess Olga Nikolaevna Romanova, and I demand that you stay with me." Oksana's words rang in his head. He'd clung to them like some sort of righteous vindication even as in the back of his mind he knew she had to be lying. Grand duchess? The tsar would never surrender the protection of his oldest daughter into the hands of some Mennonite stranger.

Then again, if he were looking for someone to hide his most precious belonging—even more precious than the Crest of St. Basil—he'd also pick the most unlikely of disguises. The most unlikely of heroes.

No, she couldn't be the princess. Oksana had herself denied it when he'd confronted her.

Still, doubts lingered. Like her intimate knowledge of the royal family's activities, her relaxed familiarity with their names, her commanding attitude, especially when he'd first met her. All the same, no grand duchess would surrender herself in the hands of a Mennonite farmwife, would lower herself to weeding gardens and milking cows.

Nor would she marry and love a commoner, a Mennonite, like himself. The idea of his cradling the grand duchess of all of Russia in his arms made him queasy with panic. If the tsar found out. . .he might as well have burned in the flames with his family.

Anton combed his hand through his hair. No, Oksana had simply reacted out of panic and assumed a role she'd always dreamed of.

Just like he'd assumed the role of her husband. Only he hadn't acted out of panic.

And it hadn't been panic, either, that had made him take her in his arms and warm the place beside her in their narrow bed. He could admit that being in her arms erased, briefly, the horror of that night. Allowed him to unlatch the feelings of grief gated in his heart and find comfort for the searing pain that lined his chest.

Oksana had become, truly, his helpmate and comforter.

And he prayed that in his arms she also found sanctuary. Healing. Even hope. Rising quietly, so as not to wake her, Anton pulled on a clean shirt. He poured water into the basin and washed his face. Easing out of the room, he made his way to the kitchen, hoping to find some milk or porridge to bring to Oksana.

He startled when he saw Timofea sitting at the table, nursing a cup of tea. His long curly hair tangled on his robe, and a smile emerged from his scruffy beard, matching the kindness in his eyes. *"Dobra ootra,"* he said, coming toward

Anton. "Are you in search of breakfast?"

"I hoped to find something for Oksana," Anton said, but the smell of porridge made his stomach leap in greed. Aunt Vera was nowhere to be found.

"She left with Uncle Maxim," Timofea said, as if reading Anton's thoughts. "I came to check on you both. Would you like some porridge?"

Anton nodded and waited while Timofea poured him a bowl. He handed it to Anton with a spoon.

"I trust you're well?"

Anton cupped the bowl in his hands, the warmth and smell comforting. "We're getting better." He sat at the table and picked up his spoon, stirring the porridge, sorting his thoughts. "I have been contemplating your suggestion, and I also fear for Oksana's safety." He took a deep breath. "Yes, I would like to take refuge at the monastery if that offer is still available."

"I think staying at the monastery might be the best place for you both right now. Oksana looks fatigued, as do you. Allow us to serve you."

Anton nodded, surprised at the rush of gratefulness he felt at Timofea's offer. "Thank you."

Timofea took a sip of his tea, his eyes on Anton. "What happened, Anton?"

Anton had told them little about the attack at his farm, the death of his family. Mostly, the words had clogged in his throat, horror turning them to clay. But now, sitting in the sun-dappled kitchen, the world of Alexanderwohl seeming so far away, he let the story spill out—the wedding, the Red Army attack, and their escape to Pechory. "I didn't know where else to go."

"You were wise to come here. We can offer you both protection." Timofea said. "But I'm curious—why did you not join your brothers in their fate?"

Anton breathed deeply, swallowing through a tight jaw. He looked away from Timofea to the monastery in the far-off distance, the golden cupolas, the blue-painted chapels, the white-capped cliffs beyond the walls. "Oksana and I are truly married by the standards of the church."

Anton expected a quick intake of breath evidencing Timofea's shock. Instead, the young man nodded. "I wondered as much. But I'm curious. You both said that you wanted the marriage annulled."

"Things changed between us." Anton let a smile crease his face. "I love her."

Timofea matched his smile, his eyes kind. "I imagined this would happen." He ran the teacup handle between two work-worn fingers. "Is Oksana still asking to see Yulia?"

"Yes. Where is she? When you delivered the note, you mentioned an orphanage?"

Timofea nodded. "She works as a wet nurse."

Anton looked up from his porridge, the words rooting into his heart. "A wet nurse? How?"

Timofea looked away, and Anton noticed tears in the young man's eyes. "She gave birth to a son not more than one month ago. He's weak and sickly, and my uncle arranged work for her that might provide for both of them."

Sorrow washed over him for what Yulia had endured. "I'm sorry to hear that."

Timofea stared out the window into the sunshine, the farmyard. "She told me something, Anton, that I believe is of importance. Yulia knew her attacker."

What? Anton caught up to him. "Who was it?"

Timofea shook his head. "She won't name him. Only that he was a man with whom she had become acquainted while at the palace. She believes he followed her to Borovsky's home, and when she repelled him, he overpowered her."

Anton remembered the way Oksana had so freely given of herself to him, and the thought of any man demanding such a surrender sickened him. "Is he still a danger to her?"

"I don't think so. But from what she says, I believe he might have also been after Oksana. Yulia won't tell me why, but I suspect he believes Oksana carried away with her something of value from the palace."

The Crest of St. Basil? But how would an acquaintance of Yulia's know that he had it? His hand nearly went to the object hanging from his neck. Unless they discovered it missing when the tsar returned to the palace and assumed it had somehow been passed to Oksana. Or Yulia. Another wave of sickness followed at the realization that perhaps he'd been the reason for Yulia's attack.

Timofea finished the last of his tea. "Anton, have you thought further of your future? Of course, you're welcome to stay at the monastery as long as you like. But when the tsar's family is tried, well, I am not sure any of their household servants will be safe, especially if they are suspected of transporting the royal fortune."

Anton nodded, scraping the last of his porridge. "I've been thinking of an idea for some time. Years perhaps. It is probably our best option."

Anton paused and took a breath. "I think I should go to America—and take her with me."

CHAPTER FIFTEEN

He watched his uncle Oleg and cousin Felip as they exited the ministry of transportation. He'd been watching them for weeks, sensing in their cool demeanor their plans. The fact that they hadn't mentioned to him or his mother their intentions told him just how shallow their loyalties ran.

Now that the royal family had been exiled to Siberia, it was every Romanov for himself. Oleg couldn't escape the country fast enough.

As for Felip, well, Gleb knew his secrets. Knew that he had a secret romance with the daughter of a former merchant who now languished in jail, his produce confiscated for the masses. Gleb knew that Felip would not leave without her.

Nor without the cache of family jewels Tsar Nikolai had parceled out to members of the family, one by one. Not a large cache, especially by Romanov standards. But enough to get them out of the country, settle them in new finery in Europe.

It was the least he could do after turning the country against them.

Sadly, Gleb's portion remained with his mother under lock and key. And really, he didn't want to steal from her the things he might, some later day, need.

But Felip had goals that matched his own. Steal the family treasure and escape the country with the woman he loved. Gleb planned to meet them at the train with a little surprise of his own.

His stomach growled as he watched them cross the street, climb into their carriage. A marked target for protestors. He even saw a crowd begin to gather and held his breath until they were away. Then he sank into the shadows, gripping the neck of his vodka bottle.

Nothing had gone like he had planned. How Yulia and Olga had slipped away without his noticing—that took him by surprise. But he would find them. And Yulia's family in Pechory would be a good place to start.

But first he needed the money. He drank the last of the vodka, letting it heat his insides, giving him courage. Then he staggered out into the street and followed the crowd toward the house of Felip Aleksander Romanov.

<hr />

The Anton who chopped wood just outside the monastery's walls and fed the smithy's fires, who pounded horseshoes and formed bridles, was not the same man she'd held in her arms in the attic overlooking the Klassen estate.

He was broader for one, his chest and arms thick and muscular. His face rarely wore the smile she'd come to rely on; instead, a grim set of his mouth became his standard expression, except, of course, for the times when he saw her staring at him over dinner perhaps from two tables away. He offered a sad, patient smile, the kind one might give to reassure a child.

He spoke few words to her, especially now that they slept and lived in different sections of the monastery. She made a habit of looking for him as she went to prayers or helped in the kitchen, although lately being around the smells of food made her nauseous. Most of all, she missed curling beside him at night, his warm body calming her fears, reminding her that she was safe. She knew that moving to the monastery had been his way of protecting her, but she would have lived in a cave if only she might have his arms around her.

The crisp winter air felt cleansing as she rode beside Timofea through Pechory. The hard wooden seat and the creak of the carriage reminded her of so many trips to Gross Tokmak, when their English lessons gave way to the comfortable silence of sitting beside Anton. Tears glazed her eyes a moment before she blinked them back. The smell of wood smoke and curls of black from chimneys of simple wooden homes fed her spirit. Laundry snapped in the cold wind, and dogs ran out from behind tall painted fences, barking at the horses as they passed. Timofea rested his forearms on his knees, holding the reins as they rode.

"Thank you for bringing me to see Yulia," Olga said in an effort to fill the silence. Timofea had been tight-lipped about Yulia since their arrival at the monastery nearly a month ago. Aside from his courteous deliveries of food, she'd seen him rarely and usually as he huddled with Anton in conversation.

Those conversations had sparked her imagination for nearly a week; Anton's concerns seemed to have elevated after news reached them that in late October the Bolsheviks had taken over full control of the government. She wondered if Anton and Timofea might be plotting to send her away. Maybe to a convent.

She wasn't going anywhere but back to her family. Ever.

Timofea sat up, glanced at her with a tight smile. "There is something I have to tell you about Yulia." He sighed. "She has a child, conceived from her attack. She calls him Boris, refusing to give us a patronymic name. He isn't well."

Olga sat in stunned silence. Yulia had a child? She pressed a hand to her queasy stomach. "Why didn't she send me a letter or a telegraph? I would have come, assisted her in the delivery, helped her care for her child."

"My uncle arranged for her employment at an orphanage. She was ashamed, Oksana. She didn't want to tell you. I've only now convinced her to see you."

Timofea's face betrayed his grief over his sister's misfortunes. "She's not the same woman you left, Oksana. Although Boris has brought her a measure of renewed joy, she still seems broken inside. As if she's lost her purpose for living."

Olga wiped at a tear that escaped. "Thank you, Timofea. I will do my best to encourage her." She knew just how Yulia might feel.

The orphanage seemed forlorn as they pulled up. A mustard-yellow, two-story wooden building with a weedy yard and broken fence bordering the grounds, it gave no indication of cheer. Timofea helped Olga from the carriage and opened the door for her, then led her inside. Bright pictures drawn by the children lined the shadowed corridor. Olga heard singing, slightly muffled, coming from a room at the end of the hall.

Timofea stopped at a wooden door and knocked while Olga wrung her hands. Poor Yulia. First the attack, then the child, and then Anton's demanding the truth. Her heart twisted at Yulia's loyalty.

The door opened, and to Olga's surprise, the face that met her seemed older, wiser. Her long hair she'd tied back into a bun and covered it with a head scarf; she wore a white linen coat. Yulia smiled, real warmth in her eyes despite a definite etching of sadness. "My lady," she said and bowed her head.

Timofea frowned, looking between them. Olga reached out and pulled Yulia into a tight embrace. "Yulia. I'm so happy to see you."

Yulia seemed hesitant to hug her back, but Olga held her until the woman leaned into her. "I was worried," Yulia said in her ear.

Olga smiled at her. "Me, too. I hear you're a mother."

A shadow washed over Yulia's expression, but she nodded. "I have a son. Boris." She opened the door to the room, and Olga saw a small nursery with swaddled infants placed on their sides in one large bassinet, their chubby heads poking out of cocoons of cloth. Wrapped tightly, they nearly all looked alike. She wondered how Yulia told them apart. Yulia picked one up and held the package out to Olga.

Olga took the wrapped bundle, saw the puckered lips, the eyes closed in peaceful slumber, and a wave of longing swept over her. "He's beautiful, Yulia."

She smiled, her dark eyes lightening a bit. "Thank you."

"I'll fetch you in an hour, Oksana. I have errands in the village." Timofea closed the door behind him.

Yulia offered Olga a seat. Olga sat, aware of another wave of nausea at the smells of antiseptic that embedded the walls. She rocked little Boris in her arms. "He's so small."

"He was much larger a month ago, it seemed. He's not growing well." Yulia wore worry in her expression. "The doctors don't know what is wrong. I feed him nearly every two hours."

Boris opened his mouth in a yawn.

"You look tired, Your Highness."

Olga looked up and gave her a sharp look. "Yulia—"

"I'm sorry. It's just that. . .I miss my life at the palace and with you. Everything seems so different."

"It is different. The royal family is under house arrest, and my father is going to be tried as a criminal." Olga kept her attention on Boris, blinking back tears. "And I am married to a man who doesn't believe I'm the grand duchess."

"You told him?"

Olga closed her eyes. Nodded. "Only he didn't believe me, especially after you denied it. I know I should thank you—you only did as you were instructed. Still, this lie becomes more crushing with each day."

"I'm sorry. I didn't know what to do. His note seemed so earnest, but I feared for your safety. He seems to truly care for you."

Olga let those words minister to her frayed nerves. He had told her he loved her, but since they had moved into the monastery. . .

"I don't know what to think about Anton, Yulia." She stroked Boris's cheek with the back of her finger. "He's a good man, and he's only trying to protect me, I know. But what if. . .what if I admitted the truth and he didn't. . . Well, I mean it's not like it's exactly forbidden for a commoner to marry royalty, but certainly my parents—"

"Your parents are in captivity. The tsar entrusted you to his care."

"They didn't expect me to marry him. Or for us to. . ." She looked up at Yulia, who stepped back, a hand over her mouth, her eyes wide.

Olga nodded, feeling a blush.

Yulia crouched at her feet, kneeling over Boris, touching her hand. "You're afraid that if he finds out you're the grand duchess, everything will change."

"I admit I've enjoyed knowing he loves Oksana the chambermaid."

"That's not going to change if you tell him, mistress. He loves you. And you being the grand duchess won't make his feelings any different."

"Won't it?" Olga looked at Boris, a deep longing welling up inside her. "I've lied to him all this time. You don't think he would forgive me, do you?"

"You really love him, don't you?"

Olga looked up, surprised at Yulia's forwardness. Then, quietly, she nodded. "I love him more with each breath. He's a good man, and truthfully, I'm hoping that when I rejoin my family, my parents will be forced to accept him for all he's done for me."

"Your Highness, you can't actually be thinking of rejoining them! There is talk of. . .of. . . ." She shook her head, her eyes wide.

Olga felt a chill brush up her spine. "What?"

Yulia swallowed, looking away. "Execution."

Olga went completely still, the blood draining from her body. She breathed, just breathed, in and out, her world spinning.

Yulia stood up and took her baby from Olga's arms, then knelt next to her. "I'm sorry. Probably they will simply be exiled. But you must know the truth."

Olga shook her head and stood. A wave of dizziness washed over her, and her knees buckled. She landed hard in the chair, caught by Yulia's hand on her arm. "Are you okay?"

Olga pressed one hand to her head, the other to her abdomen. "I don't know. Lately I have been feeling weak, even nauseous. I don't know what is wrong with me. Probably it's stress." Hot tears washed her eyes. "I need to join my family."

"You need to stay hidden." Yulia put Boris back into his bassinet beside the other babies, then crouched beside Olga's chair. Her voice gentled. "Accept Anton as your groom and leave Russia before you join your family in their fate. Perhaps it is what your father intended all along."

"I'll never leave the country as long as my family is here!"

Yulia's eyes widened, clearly taken aback at Olga's tone. Olga wrapped her arms around her waist. "I think I'm going to be ill."

Her chambermaid wasted no time in grabbing a bucket for Olga. She shoved it into Olga's hands. But the wave of nausea passed, and she leaned back in the chair, a prickle of sweat across her brow. She drew a deep breath.

Yulia wet a rag, placed it over Olga's forehead. She stepped back and surveyed her, her hands on her ample hips. "Olga," she said finally. "Is there any way you could be. . .pregnant?"

<hr />

"I believe I have our passage arranged," Anton said to

Timofea as the monk returned with the carriage. He had watched as Timofea helped Oksana down in front of the visitors' quarters and then led the vehicle to the livery. She seemed unsteady on her feet for a moment, leaning on the monk before she entered the building.

She'd looked especially pale of late. It worried him, especially since he'd seen her health improve over time on the farm. The trauma of last month's events seemed to have caused her to relapse.

Timofea handed him the reins of the animals, and Anton moved to unhook the carriage.

"When do you leave?" Timofea said, working the buckles on the other side of the team.

"Early March. They don't like to sail during January, saying the ocean is too rough. But I have found us a steamer leaving from Petrograd on March first. We'll charter a fishing vessel to take us up the Velikaya River and bring us to port. Surely she'll be well enough to travel by the first part of March?"

Timofea shrugged, his face cast in worry beneath his hood. "This is her third visit to Yulia, and she seems weaker each time. I wonder if it is Yulia's worry that affects her." He shook his head. "Boris continues to become more lethargic. And he's not gaining weight. I believe the baby may not live."

Anton felt a fresh stab of pain for Yulia. "Perhaps we should ask her to accompany us."

Timofea nodded. "Perhaps. When will you tell Oksana?"

Anton lowered the tongue of the carriage and began unhooking the harnesses. "I need to catch her alone, to talk to her outside the confines of the monastery. Our current living arrangement offers no opportunity to be alone."

Timofea led one of the horses to a stall. "I know this isn't the most suitable situation for a married couple. However, in Oksana's present state, I fear she needs rest, not companionship."

Anton gave him a dark look. "Timofea, please give me some credit for being a husband who cares for her, not a brute."

Timofea turned, a smile on his face. "Calm down, Anton. I'm just saying that I see the way she looks at you. I believe she misses you. And worries for you. I don't want her more burdened by the plans you've made for yourselves."

"She needs to know. To say good-bye and gather supplies. With Orthodox Christmas and New Year's only days away, time is passing quickly."

Timofea worked off the bridle and hung it on a nearby hook. "How about if I arrange for her to meet you at the chapel in the caves? Tomorrow, after evening prayers."

The next day stretched to eternity as Anton oiled the leather tack and worked with the smithy to fashion gear, his mind on meeting with Oksana. He excused himself early to bathe then changed into his wool pants and a clean tunic. He felt like he did the day of his wedding, his stomach in knots, sweat down his spine. He hadn't had a quiet, secluded conversation with Oksana since the day they'd arrived at the monastery. He could admit he had hopes of taking her in his arms and reminding her of the promises he'd made the night they became man and wife.

Snow peeled from the sky in soft flakes as he made

his way across the compound and through the back gate, skirting the fields to the caves that had served as monastery headquarters in the early 1500s. Even now, they used some of the caves for prayer retreats, a banya, and a traveler's chapel. He held a lantern, and it cast an eerie yellow glow over his footsteps crunching in the snow.

He eased the door of the chapel open, his eyes adjusting to the shadows in the whitewashed room. His pulse jumped when he saw a slight figure kneeling before the crucifix at the front of the room. Light flickered from thin orange candles set before frames of golden icons.

"Oksana?"

She turned, and something inside him gave at the sight of her smile, her thin face. She rose, and he crossed the room in two strides and swept her into his arms. "Oksana." He'd missed her so much that for a moment he thought his chest might explode. He pulled back her hood and buried his face in her hair. "*Dorogaya*, I've missed you."

She leaned back, and he saw her eyes glisten. "Me, too."

He kissed her. Sweetly, holding back his desire, remembering how weak she seemed lately. She wrapped her hands around his upper arms, kissed him back. Then he lowered his forehead to hers. "How have you been?"

She shrugged, took a step back. "Lonely. Tired. I've visited Yulia a few times."

"I saw that. Timofea keeps me informed, mostly. I apologize for our living situation. Believe me, it's not what I'd hoped for." He gave her a sad smile. "But I think because of the situation we fled, we are safer within the walls of the monastery for now."

She gave a small nod. "I understand, Anton. I trust you."

She trusted him. Oh, how he didn't deserve her. "Good. Because I have a plan." He took her hands, so small and fragile, in his work-roughened grip. He wanted to cringe. She looked up at him expectantly. "Remember how I told you I wanted to move to America someday? How I envied you that you spoke English?"

She frowned and gave him what seemed a wary nod.

"I've booked us passage on a steamer out of Petrograd the first of March. We need to start a new life, Oksana. A new beginning, and I believe it's in America." He gave her a smile, expecting hers.

But her face screwed up in a sort of horror as the news sunk in. He saw her withdraw, and from deep inside that broken person she'd become, the other Oksana, the one who'd silently endured with determination his stepmother's berating, or scolded him nearly a year ago in Petrograd, rose from her frail figure. "Absolutely not!"

He jerked at her words, feeling them almost as a slap. She yanked her hands from his, stepped back from him. "I am not leaving Russia! Have you lost your mind? I can't leave."

Anton put a hand to his head, furrowing it through his clean hair. "What? Why ever not? This is. . .this is the best thing for us. For our future. We won't have anyone after you or. . .me. We can live free and start over again."

"I don't want to start over again! Don't you understand, Anton—I want to join my family!"

"They aren't your family! Can't you get that through your head? You don't owe them anything! Your service to them is *over*." He hated to be harsh, but didn't she see? He ached for her to see. He was her family. They were each other's only family, especially now. His eyes burned with frustration, and he whirled, stalking away from her, nearly shaking.

She went silent behind him. He closed his eyes, tightening his jaw, willing his tone back to civility. "Doesn't what happened between us matter? Doesn't it change things?"

At her silence, he turned. She stood, hands clasped before her, tears running down her cheeks. Quietly she nodded. "It does change things. One thing. We can't go to America, Anton. But you can't leave me, either."

What? He would never leave—

"I'm pregnant."

His world stopped. Just stopped spinning as all time congealed into one moment of shock. And joy.

"Pregnant?" He shook his head, not knowing what else to say.

She smiled and blushed. Nodded.

"Oh, Oksana." He closed the distance between them, dropped to his knees, and hugged her around the waist, laying his head against her soft stomach. Inside there was a baby. His baby. He closed his eyes and felt tears gather at the corners. "A baby."

She giggled, her hands on his head, weaving through his hair. "You're happy?"

He nodded, leaning back, grinning. "I'm happy."

Her smile dimmed, and she sighed. "Now you see why we can't travel."

"Not yet. But after the baby is born, I don't see— "

"Don't you understand, Anton?" Oksana put her hands to her face, shaking her head. "There's no other way to tell you this but just to say it." She took a deep breath, her eyes finding his, and the expression in them scared him just a little. Slowly he rose.

"I lied to you." She swallowed. "Twice. And I'm sorry." Her face grew pale. "I even instructed Yulia to lie to you for the sake of our country."

His chest started to tighten, and he took a step away from her.

She nodded. "Think about it, Anton. The crest, the clothing, the way I treated you. You know it in your heart already. I know I should have confessed when we arrived here. . .but I was afraid, and I didn't know if you could— you would— "

She swallowed and swiped a tear from her cheek. "From the time I was a child, the real Oksana was raised to take my place should I need a decoy. And she serves me now as my surrogate in exile with the Romanov family." She lifted her chin, as if truly royal.

He shook his head to clear it, but she advanced on him, took his hand. "I am who I say I am. I promise you in this holy place that I am the grand duchess Olga." She placed a hand over her womb. "And this child could very well be the rightful heir to the throne when the throne is returned to the Romanovs." She tightened her grip on his hand, realizing, probably, that he had stepped away from her. "Now you see why we can't leave the royal family and go to America."

He stared at her, shock taking hold of him, filling him with the magnitude of what he'd done.

He had married the grand duchess. He had been intimate with her. They were going to have a child.

The weight of the crest and his mission radiated cold through him as he turned and stalked out into the night.

CHAPTER SIXTEEN

She felt like royalty again. Distanced from everyday life, waited upon hand and foot. Separated. Pampered.

Alone.

Olga walked to the window overlooking the fields. Although winter clung tenaciously to the rim of the fields, the last of the blackened snow melted as the June sun climbed the sky. She stood in the open window, watching the nuns bent over to spade the earth and plant potatoes and other vegetables. New life. She could smell the breezes, nearly taste the tomatoes exploding in her mouth. To think that last year at this time, she'd been trying to learn how to milk a cow and planting beans next to Anton.

It felt like a lifetime away. She had found a measure of happiness then—somewhere deep inside, despite her separation from her family.

She spread her hands over the new life growing inside her, trying to imagine what this little royal prince might look like. When he'd begun to move, the feather touches inside her had reached right into her soul, healing, strengthening.

She'd seen nothing of Anton since the night after he'd left her and marched out into the cold. He'd returned awhile later, again changed. He acted aloof, as if she might be made of china. She didn't miss the red rim of his eyes as if he'd been crying or berating himself, probably for marrying such a deceiver as she. Even his polite smile didn't touch his eyes. He'd wrapped a blanket around her, brought her back to her cell, and the next day, he had returned and, to her horror, driven her to a convent not far from the monastery.

She'd sat numbly beside him, seeing his hands hold the reins, feeling his strong arms around her as he lifted her out of the carriage and nearly carried her inside the Sts. Mary and Martha Convent. He'd left her at the door, kissing her hands, first one, then the other, before assuring her everything would work out and leaving her in the hands of the mother superior. Olga remembered the sky as dark as the Volga on a cold day, mirroring her heart as she watched him ride away.

She wanted to hate him. But deep inside her heart, she knew he had left her here for her protection. He had told the mother superior that she was his wife and that he had taken employment at the monastery and was unable to care for her. Indeed, the sisters in the convent amply cared for her. She missed Yulia, Timofea, and especially Anton, but time to write in her journal and read soothed the ragged edges of her soul. In a way, she felt as if she shared in her family's captivity, bearing the weight of the unforgiveness of all of Russia on her heart.

A knock came at her door. She turned and smiled at the nun who entered, carrying her lunch on a tray: *shee*—cabbage borscht made from sauerkraut—and a glass of thick milk. "Thank you," she said. The nun bowed and exited.

Olga sat at the table, bowing her head, when another knock came. "Enter."

The mother superior came in, smiling, her hands tucked in her habit. She was an elderly woman with a wide, wrinkled face and kind eyes. They'd spoken on occasion after vespers, usually about Olga's health. "I have a visitor for you," she said. Olga's heart did a traitorous leap as the nun stepped aside.

Yulia stood at the door, her hands holding a wrapped parcel. "Hello. . .Oksana."

Olga hid her disappointment, stood, and held out her arms to her friend. The nun left them, closing the door behind her as Yulia embraced her. "Your Highness. I'm sorry I haven't visited earlier."

Olga held her at arm's length, surveying her. She looked thinner, her long brown hair lackluster, bags under her eyes. Sorrow etched her expression and filled Olga with dread. "What is it?"

Tears immediately filled Yulia's eyes, and she angrily whipped them away. "I'm sorry." But Olga brought her to the bed and made her sit. She laid the package on her lap and pressed her hands over it. "My Boris died shortly after you went into seclusion."

Oh, Yulia. Hot tears filled Olga's eyes, and she drew Yulia close, held her. Her chambermaid composed herself quickly, smiling through her tears. "He was truly a gift to me, however. And with my job as a wet nurse at the orphanage, I am now the mother to many, perhaps."

Olga couldn't help but admire her for the courage it took to serve the babies after losing her own.

"I brought you something." She held out the package to Olga.

Olga untied it. "A blanket! Thank you." Made of scraps

Olga recognized from Yulia's own clothing, the blanket seemed somehow a piece of Yulia offered to Olga.

"Timofea kept me updated on your pregnancy, and since I couldn't attend you, I made you something of the things I made Boris."

Olga wrapped her in a hug. "You are a treasure to me. I don't deserve your kindness."

Yulia considered her with steady eyes. "I also come with some bad news." She took Olga's hand. "Your cousin Felip was found murdered in Moscow."

Olga's mouth dropped open, sorrow in her throat. She didn't know Felip well, but she remembered the few times she'd played with her distant cousin.

"How?"

"We don't know. Lenin's fiends, probably. It is said he has formed a squad of assassins called the Cheka, whose job it is to root out loyalists and murder them." Yulia beseeched her with her gaze. "You and Anton need to leave Russia as soon as this baby is born."

Olga yanked her hands away. "Did he send you?" She stood and stalked away from her.

"Who?"

"Anton! This was his idea, wasn't it?" She turned, accusation in her tone.

Yulia shook her head, eyes wide. "My lady, I haven't spoken to Anton."

At the mention of his name, Olga closed her eyes, rubbing her hands over her bulging stomach. "I'm sorry. I'm just. . . Have you seen him?"

Yulia stayed quiet so long that Olga turned back to her. Yulia wore a sad expression. "I have."

Alarm shot through Olga. "Is he okay?"

"Yes, yes. Of course. He still works at the monastery. But Timofea is worried for him. He seems so despondent, spending all his free hours in prayer. For a long while, Timofea thought he'd taken a vow of silence." Yulia gave her a smile. "I think he must miss you."

As I miss him. The ache felt alive and ready to swallow her whole.

Yulia stood, came to her, and took Olga's hands in hers. She let out a sigh. "It is entirely possible that a dark fate is in store for your family, Olga. I fear it." She looked beyond her and out the window. "You are carrying a future king or queen. And you need to protect that heir of Russia."

And Anton's heir. The child, the family he'd always longed for. That thought had found her too many times. He would be a hero like his father.

Or like she had thought he was. Her heart turned cold, pushing him from her mind. He had abandoned her. Turned his back on her. His prayers were probably for absolution.

She raised her chin. "I am Russian. And I will stay in Russia."

Yulia dropped Olga's hands, shaking her head. "Pardon my rudeness, Your Highness, but such thinking is foolishness."

Then she turned, opened the door, and left, her footsteps echoing down the hall and through the chambers of Olga's heart. Anger and shock mixed with fear. Foolishness? Yulia took her for a fool?

She slumped on the bed, her hands over her stomach, feeling the baby move inside her. How could she be wrong to want to join her family? Wasn't that her duty?

As if in answer, the baby kicked inside her. Such a small person, yet he took up so much room in her body, in her heart. She had begun to talk to him, to share with him her dreams, her hopes.

She lay down, her hands under her head, twisting on her finger the ring Anton had given her on their wedding day. She took it off, staring at the symbol that had seemed so empty. Now it felt like her only link to her future. An etching on the inside caught her eye. She peered at it, making out a reference. *Psalm 100:5.* Grabbing her Bible, she flipped open to the verse and read it silently. *"For the LORD is good; his mercy is everlasting; and his truth endureth to all generations."*

She heard Anton's voice in the verse and closed her eyes. *All generations.* The words filled the cracks in her heart, her soul, feeling like a promise. God had been good to her this year—He'd given her Anton to protect her and now a hope for the future, a new life inside her.

Maybe she was a fool. She'd been clinging to the person she was—Olga Nikolaevna Romanova. But she hadn't been that princess for more than a year now and had found peace in becoming Oksana, a chambermaid loved by a farmer. Not just peace but love.

And in the end, wasn't that what she had always longed for? Just to be loved for who she was. . .not because of her title or her wealth? Tears gathered and filled her ears as they ran down her cheeks. "God," she said, feeling naked without her prayer shawl, her candles. Was she even allowed to pray like this? She got up and knelt beside her bed, crossing herself and wishing she had a candle. "God, show me what you want me to do." She crossed herself again. Perhaps she should go to the chapel. Commit her ways to God.

And then she would ask to go to the monastery. Because in her heart, she knew Yulia was correct. Her words, her thoughts had been foolishness. She was a fool.

A fool in love. "Baby," she said as she watched her stomach move, "we're going to America."

❦

The June sun beaded sweat on his neck and back. Anton stood, leaning on his spade, stretching his back, aching to his toes. For monks, he'd never met any group of harder-working men. The potato fields stretched for a hectare, and he'd be here until next November covering them over with dirt if he didn't focus. But thoughts of Oksana, no, Olga—he still couldn't think of her as the grand duchess—invaded his mind, slowed his efforts, sometimes standing him still.

He worried about her. Thankfully, the mother superior kept him updated on her condition, sending notes to Timofea.

He hated himself for what he'd done, putting her into seclusion. But in her condition and position, he could not think of an alternative. Not a safe one, at least. Nor one that might live up to her expectations as royalty.

Royalty. He'd married the woman who could provide the next heir to the throne. Even though Tsar Nikolai had abdicated, his brother Mikhail refused to take the throne without an edict from the people, which left the royal title open to the ailing tsarevich Alexei or the offspring of the oldest daughter, Olga.

Then again, maybe she wouldn't be considered royal after a marriage to a commoner like him. What had he done to her? Anton took off his straw hat, wiping his brow with the sleeve of his grimy shirt. He smelled like he hadn't bathed in weeks, although he'd taken a banya with Timofea only last night.

The young monk couldn't understand why Anton had sent away his pregnant bride. And for now, he would stay in confusion.

"Do you still have tickets for your passage to America?" Timofea had asked, sweat dripping off his brow, curling his hair.

"Yes. But I'm not sure we'll use them." He'd been weighing his options for seven months as winter turned into spring and finally summer. And every thought ended with one: What could he ever give her that she didn't already have? He was no one, a commoner. A farmer, a Mennonite from Ukraine.

"Why not? With the Bolsheviks searching for loyalists, stamping out the last of the Royal Army, I beseech you to think again, Anton. You may well hide her in a convent for now, but when the child is born, you'll need to provide a home. And as long as Lenin and his Cheka minions are in control, you will always look over your shoulder for trouble."

Anton said nothing as he added more water to the fire, letting the steam stifle their conversation.

Even now, it seemed his brain felt gnarled, tired. He closed his eyes, letting a tepid summer wind cool him.

"Anton! Master Anton!"

The voice turned him toward a novice running out from the monastery gates. Breathing hard, he bent, gripping his knees.

"What is it?"

"Your wife. She's here. She asks to speak to you. She waits for you in the cave chapel."

Olga was here? Alarm speared him through, and he dropped the spade. "Is she hurt? Is it her time?"

The boy shook his head. "No, she comes accompanied by two nuns and seems fit, if not. . ." He made a face and shrugged. "If not great with child."

His child. "Thank you," Anton said and strode across the fields toward the grounds. Probably he should clean up, but he hadn't time to take a banya or draw a bath. Instead, he stopped in at the washroom and scrubbed his face. Tanned and whiskered, he hadn't paid much attention to his appearance lately. He changed into a clean tunic and pants and made his way to the caves.

He didn't expect the woman of grace and beauty who turned toward him when he entered the chapel. Her hair had grown, yet she wore it pulled back in a shapely bun, her head encircled with a silken white headband like a crown. It made her eyes even more beautiful, and her face radiated a healthy glow. Dressed in a simple white gown with the waist let out to accommodate her new shape, she looked exactly how he'd expect her to look. Regal. Refined.

Royal.

He took one look at her and bowed. "Your Highness."

"Oh, Anton, don't—"

"I hope you're well." He stood, tearing his gaze off her, off the obvious evidence of his child inside her. He couldn't look at her. Not without aching inside at all that had passed between them, all they'd lost. "Is there something I can do for you?"

"You can stop acting like this and kiss me."

He stared at her, taken aback by her boldness. She lifted her chin, but he noticed nervousness in the way she fingered the cross she always wore at her neck.

"I don't think I can do that, uh, Your Highness."

"Olga."

He swallowed, again looked away. Shook his head. "I owe you so many apologies, I don't know where to start."

"No, you don't, Anton. I am the one who owes you."

He closed his eyes. His body tensed as he felt her take a step toward him.

"I lied to you. My father lied to you."

She put her hand on his arm, and instantly his mind went to the time when he had held her—that night so long ago, the night when his world shattered. He took a deep breath.

"I know you sent me to the convent for my health. And I've had a lot of time to think."

That wasn't the only reason he had sent her away. He opened his eyes, met her gaze, saw the acceptance there, and felt sick. He started to shake his head, but she continued.

"I have been a fool to think that I will return to my life at Tsarskoe Selo. I know that my family may be exiled. . .or worse." She tightened her jaw as if reining in emotions. "We have to think of our child now. And our future." She took a deep breath. "I will go to America with you, Anton."

He stared at her, stirred by her courage yet wanting to cry. He could not stop himself from cupping his hand to her cheek, running his thumb over her soft skin. She leaned into his touch, her eyes on him.

"Oh, Olga, I have missed you."

Her eyes glistened.

He sighed and dropped his hand. "But I cannot take you to America."

A beat of pain passed between them while he watched her expression change, tighten into a frown. "Why not? Of course we will wait until the baby is born, but we can leave immediately after. It is a wise idea—"

"It is a wise idea, I agree. But I've been thinking also, Olga. And the truth is, we should go through with our annulment."

He watched as confusion turned to shock. She stepped back from him. "We can't do that!"

"We can. You were under stress when you married me. You took on another's name—"

"You are going to annul our marriage because I used a different name?"

"And you know, as well as I, the church would never allow our marriage—"

"But I'm carrying your child! What do you think they would say about that?" Her eyes fired, and he saw again the woman who had stood up to him in Petrograd, the woman who spoke what she believed. His words felt like razors in his throat.

"I think they'd say you were coerced. That under trauma, you acted in a way to protect yourself—"

"You didn't force me, Anton. I love you!" She turned away from him, shaking, her hands balled at her sides.

Oh, Olga. He was shaking, too, just a little, as he put

his hands on her shoulders. She flinched but did not move away.

"*Dorogaya*. I love you, too." He sighed. "But I am no one. Nothing. I have nothing to offer you. No home, no business. No position. Nothing. I am not worthy of your love. This is why I sent you away, so you would see this. I am not the man you should have for your husband, and we both know that."

She shook her head, turning, but he put his finger over her mouth.

"I will talk to Timofea and tell him the truth. I will ask him to annul our marriage."

"No!" She slapped at his hand, backed away from him. "I can't believe you would do this to me."

He fought to keep his voice steady. "If anyone ever finds out that you're the grand duchess, you won't be safe. And I don't have the first idea how to protect you. I'm not a man trained to bear arms or fight." He gave her a hard look. "Once the baby is born, I will pay for passage to your relatives in England with the ticket I purchased. You and he. . .or she. . .will be safe." He hated how she curled her arms over her stomach, protecting herself—protecting their child—from him.

He swallowed, fighting through his emotions. "Go back to the convent, Olga. And may God watch over you." Then he turned and again stalked out of the chapel before she could see him cry.

CHAPTER SEVENTEEN

H e watched from his perch in the tree as she rode out from the monastery, fattened probably from her new life as a peasant. She rode with a robed monk, younger than himself, who handled himself and his two-horse team with ease. Gleb lowered his spyglass, congratulating himself for tracking her down.

It hadn't been easy. He'd grown his hair long, affected the look of the rebels. Angry. Dangerous. Blood on his hands.

Blood on his soul. He needed the money to start a new life. The right life, the one he'd been born into. Royalty.

Princess Olga thought she could hide inside a linen frock or under a nun's habit, but he recognized her sharp eyes, her regal posture. She couldn't deny the life she'd been born into, either.

Some disguise. She would never be a commoner. He could hardly believe that no one else noticed, no one recognized her.

He almost felt sorry for the woman who had taken her place. Who would, in all probability, die in the exchange. With the tsar's authority stripped, it would be only a matter of time before Lenin executed them.

And he hoped to be long away to France or Spain by then. The death of one lowly peasant girl who happened to bear the resemblance of a princess would be eclipsed by the crime against the royal family.

He watched them pass, nearly tasting his escape. Surely she still had the jewels. He just needed to get near her, convince her to surrender them to him. Maybe if she was lucky, he'd even take her with him.

Once upon a time, he'd made her laugh. Charmed her with his antics, played with her and all the girls at the Black Sea in Livadiya.

He could charm her again. Become the next tsar of Russia.

They would need a new tsar someday. And he'd be happy to oblige.

"Come home, sweet Olishka. Time to come home."

⁂

"Timofea, I have a hard question to ask you." Anton closed the banya door behind him. The steam prickled his skin, sweat already beading. After working all day in the livery and weeding the fields, he probably didn't need the extra sweat leeched from his body. But being in this cave, with the dim light from the lantern providing a measure of privacy, drew secrets from him as easily as the heat drew out the grime from the day.

He climbed onto the bench and sat next to Timofea. "What is it, Anton? Is it about Oksana?"

"It is." But not what he thought. Timofea had delivered messages from the mother superior twice over the past few weeks—messages he hoped included the news of Olga's delivery. And the end to their life together, although in reality that had ended the day he sent her to the convent.

"But first I must tell you something in the strictest of confidence." He turned to Timofea, his eyes hard, his tone quiet. "You must agree to never, ever reveal this secret. So help you God."

Timofea's eyes widened, taken aback. "Are you okay?"

No. He'd probably never be okay again. But he nodded. "I've thought long and hard about my next words, and I believe it's in my wife's best interest to reveal the truth to you. You alone."

Timofea fell silent, staring at his feet. "Okay, Anton. I promise to keep your secret. Upon my word as a servant of the Lord."

Anton sighed, feeling already the heat of the room slicking his skin. "The chambermaid I married, the woman you know as Oksana, is in fact Olga Nikolaevna Romanova, grand duchess of all Russia."

Timofea stilled beside him. Sat upright. Stared at Anton.

Anton nodded.

Timofea's mouth opened in appropriate shock. "Oh. . . and. . .you. . ."

"Yes," Anton said, not exactly sure what error in judgment Timofea might be referring to but agreeing to them all. "I didn't know Oksana was the princess until. . .well, until after we'd conceived our child. I thought I had married a chambermaid."

Timofea shook his head, his stare hard on Anton. "This is a dangerous secret you've been holding from me."

"I know. And it couldn't be helped. My first responsibility was to the tsar and his charge to protect Oksana, or Olga, as it were."

Timofea pursed his lips. "I doubt the Church, even

with the royal family now in disgrace, will bless to your union."

Anton hung his head, sweat beading between his shoulder blades. "I know. I have wrestled with this for nine months, knowing I have stolen from Olga so much of her future. But I have a plan. I am going to send Olga and her child away to their family in Europe. You'll annul the marriage on the grounds that she bore false witness. . .or if need be, on charges against me."

Timofea frowned at him, horror on his shadowed face.

"Olga will be safe and raise her child in obscurity. She'll find a suitable husband, and when this revolution is quenched, her family will welcome her back."

"And if the Bolsheviks should maintain power?"

"Then Olga will live. In exile. But she'll live."

Timofea shook his head. "Anton. Just because the Church won't bless your union doesn't mean it isn't in God's plan. You can't abandon her."

"Do you think I want that?" He felt his emotions build, heated as they were with the agony of his decision, the waiting, the betrayal of their secret. "Do you not think that every day that goes by I long to be her husband, the father to that child? Do you not think that I feel sick inside when I think of leaving her, knowing the pain I am causing her?" He shook his head, looked away, trembling. "I love her, Timofea. But I am nothing. No one. And she is a princess."

Timofea considered him, his jaw tight. " 'For the foolishness of God is wiser than man's wisdom, and the weakness of God is stronger than man's strength.' "

Anton stayed silent, confusion knotting his brow.

"Oddly enough, that was my reading today in chapel. But I think it was for you."

"I don't understand."

"Do you remember when you came to me on the day of your marriage with a verse you said God had given you?"

Anton nodded, his chest thick. "Psalm 100:5. 'For the Lord is good; his mercy is everlasting; and his truth endureth to all generations.'"

"Do you think that God didn't know Oksana's true identity? Of course He did. And yet He spoke to you through this verse, assuring you of His love for this generation and the next. This child is yours, Anton. Your child of promise from God to fulfill your longings to have an heir. Yes, to my eyes, it seems foolish. And it will take God's strength to complete this task He's given you. But He never intended for your marriage before Him to be in name only. I knew this even as I married you." Timofea got down from the bench, pouring water over the fire. Steam hissed, filling the cave. "Go to Olga. Tell her that you will love and protect her as you promised, by God's strength. Then go to America and start a new life. When it is safe, you can return to Russia. With the heir to the throne." He climbed back onto the bench. "Until then, your secret is safe with me."

Anton leaned back, feeling stress run off him in rivulets. "I don't know, Timofea. It's not that easy. I also have the crest to worry about. I can't take that to America."

"Leave that here. With me. I will take care of it."

Anton considered him, the youthful face that held so much wisdom. "The tsar made me promise to take care of it."

"He asked you to guard it, yes. But if I recall your words, didn't he tell you to protect Oksana—Olga—above all cost? Do you truly believe that the crest is more important to him than his own daughter?"

Anton thought back to that night, to the kneeling form of the tsar and to his words. *I can't help but believe that the Lord, in His mercy, saw fit to answer my prayer for aid by uniting our paths in these woods. Some would say it is fate or happenstance, but I personally believe it is Providence that brought you to me.*

He remembered wondering why the tsar would choose him, a Mennonite who adhered to a creed of nonviolence, to protect his most sacred belonging. His daughter. Perhaps it wasn't protection the tsar sought. . .but a man who might trust in the Lord's protection. Because as a Mennonite, he'd been taught to look upward, to put his life into God's hands.

Perhaps that took the most courage of all.

He looked at Timofea, feeling suddenly as if the confusion that had darkened his path for so long had cleared. "Together we'll hide the crest. And then I'll fetch Olga, my wife."

Timofea smiled, sweat dripping off his beard. "Fear not, Anton. God will keep his promises to the heirs of Anton."

Olga rose from her bed, an ache pressing all the way down her back and tightening her legs. She felt like an elephant or a whale, cumbersome and heavy, the baby commandeering not only her entire body but also her strength. And it was only morning.

She flopped back down, her hands over her belly, feeling the child move inside her. "Hello, little one," she said softly. She rubbed her stomach, amazed at the love she had come to feel for this unnamed child. Anton's child. She wondered if he might have his straight blond hair or her curls. Would he have Anton's strength, his sense of honor? Would he have her stubbornness?

The same stubbornness that told her she would not allow Anton to annul their marriage. Never. He might have sent her away, but she had seen him stride through the ancient cemetery on the outside of the monastery, sit among the graves, bow his head, and sob.

She'd stood there watching him unravel, aching for him. If only she'd kept her secret, never told him her true identity. His words traveled back to the convent with her. *I am no one. Nothing.*

Hardly. "Anton, you're my friend. My protector. The one I love." She said it aloud, wishing she wasn't so pregnant the mother superior wouldn't allow her to leave the grounds. If she had her way, she would have returned to the monastery and told him that no one had ever made her feel more royal, more cherished than he. She might have lived in comfort at the palace, but with Anton, she had found a man who loved her without the trappings of wealth. A man who saw the real Olga. . .the one behind the finery.

The Olga she longed to be.

The baby moved, and she felt an elbow or perhaps a knee under her rib cage. Her stomach growled.

She pushed herself up again and noticed that the morning had progressed without her attention—dawn long since merged into the full sunshine of the late morning.

She stood at the window for a moment, breathing in the smells of summer, watching the nuns at work as they fed the animals and tended the kitchen garden. She completed her morning toiletries and padded down to the kitchen, hoping for some leftover porridge or bread.

The mother superior gave her a smile and greeted her with a nod. Around the convent, words weren't spoken until after morning prayers at ten o'clock. Olga felt it a challenge to keep everything bottled inside and had taken to speaking to her child. She nodded in return, took a glass of milk and a slice of rye bread, and exited to the dining room.

The bells for morning prayers chimed, and Olga made her way to the chapel. On her way, a novice caught her, handing her a note.

She had a visitor. Her heart leapt, but she fought against hope, knowing it was probably Yulia. Her former chambermaid made regular visits to the convent to keep her company and make sure she was abreast of the news of her family, although lately they had heard nothing.

She eased herself down the corridor, stopping once to rest, bracing her hand on the plaster hallway leading to the visitors' chambers. Probably her labor would be soon. She couldn't deny the feeling of dread, wishing her mother might be with her.

Wishing her mother even knew her oldest daughter was about to be a mother.

Olga opened the door to the visitors' quarters and froze.

Anton. He stood handsome and tan, his hands holding a straw hat, dressed in an overcloak like the monks wore. The humble attire did nothing to diminish the effect on her heartbeat—his strong shoulders, his golden forearms, the smile on his face. "Hello, Olga."

He gave a slight bow. She sighed as she eased into the room and clasped her hands in front of her. "Please, Anton. I don't want you to bow to me."

"I can't help it." He smiled, and it seemed so warm she felt sweat break out across her brow. "You're so beautiful, I have to bow."

She gave a huff of disbelief. "I'm as large as a milking cow. Don't try to flatter me."

"I think you're breathtaking." He stepped forward, taking her hand. "I have a picnic for us. Like the time we went to the Begim Tchokrak River." She saw memory in his beautiful blue eyes, and her heart dared to skip again. "Are you well enough to join me?"

She smiled and felt a blush press her cheeks, although she did not know why. "Yes, I think so."

"Good." He replaced his hat. "Shall I carry you?"

She giggled. "I don't think you can. But I will lean on your arm."

"I can carry you, Olga." The tone of his voice left no question. Still, she shook her head, looped her arm through his.

A carriage awaited them outside. He lifted her to the bench, then came around and climbed up beside her. It reminded her of so many trips to the church and back only the summer before. His shadow fell over her like a protective shield.

Outside the walls of the convent, the countryside felt lush and full, the leaves of poplar trees rustling in the breeze, the green tufts of potato plants like jewels in the dark earth. She smelled flowers and the scent of tomatoes as they rode past the vegetable gardens and out to the main road.

"Where are we going?"

"To the river near the monastery. I found the perfect place for you to cool your feet."

She would like to cool her entire body, but that would probably not be appropriate, even if he was her husband.

"How are you feeling?"

She gave a small laugh. "Uncomfortable. I wonder if my mother felt this way with me."

"No doubt you were a perfect baby."

"I think our son is a perfect baby." She laid her hand over her belly. "Quiet, except at night, of course. And active enough for me to know he is listening."

Anton looked over at her. "What if it is a girl?"

She giggled. "Then she is strong and healthy, brave like her father."

"Her father isn't brave, Olga." Anton's smile dimmed.

"I think he is. He's brave enough to sacrifice everything he has for me. I find that courageous." She touched his arm, feeling him tense. When he looked at her, he wore the slightest smile.

The baby kicked, and she jumped, then laughed. "Your son—or daughter—agrees with me."

His gaze went to her stomach under her simple tunic overgown. "May I?"

Puzzled, she nodded all the same, something inside her going soft when he stopped the horses, turned, and placed his hand upon her stomach. She moved his hand so he might feel the little lump.

She waited, the heat from his hand radiating through her, the memory of being in his arms so fresh she wanted to reach up and put her arms around him. But she wasn't going to wreck this moment with hopes too brash. By God's grace, He had brought Anton to her today. While she knew not why, she would embrace this time and by the end of the day convince him not to leave her.

"Wait," she said as she felt the baby shift. She met Anton's gaze, stilled in expectation. Then, suddenly, the baby kicked.

Anton's face betrayed an expression of wonder, his gray eyes alight. His mouth opened in a smile. "That's. . .that's amazing. Does he do that often?"

"Midnight is his favorite hour."

Anton laughed, feeling her stomach for more movement. "This is a miracle."

"Wait until he is born. That will be the true miracle."

Anton looked at her, cupping her face in his hand. "No, you are the miracle, Olga." He took a deep breath, swallowed. "I never thought I would be fortunate enough to fall in love, to find that one person who looked past my childhood and believed in me. But you did." He sighed. "I am so sorry I failed you."

She opened her mouth to speak, but he held up his hand.

"Let me finish. I never should have sent you to the convent for your pregnancy. I should have found a way to be beside you. I simply didn't know how to take care of you—"

"They took good care of me here, Anton. This was the right decision."

He shook his head. "Even so, I should have visited you more. I know you've been lonely." He gave a small smile. "I've been lonely. And I know our last conversation was not. . . Well, I said things I didn't mean."

"Like you being nobody?"

His smile turned wry. "Actually, I meant that part. But God in His grace has made me somebody. Your husband."

She touched his hand on her cheek, feeling her pulse quicken. *Yes, Anton, you are my husband.*

"And after prayer and talking with Timofea. . .well, I think we should go to America. . .together. The three of us."

She blinked at his words, digesting them, not only his decision to go to America but. . .

"You told Timofea?"

He nodded, his eyes holding hers. "He is sworn to secrecy. I had to tell him to give him reason to annul our marriage. But he helped me see the truth." He swallowed, clearing his throat. "I have to agree that perhaps God put us together. And I pledged to your father to protect you above all. I may not know how to fight, but I can choose to trust God and protect you as best I can. I love you, Olga. And by God's grace, I will be your husband." His tone turned somber. " 'Grow old along with me! The best is yet to be. . . .' "

Her heart swelled inside her. "You remembered."

He nodded. "Of course. Robert Browning."

She laughed as he urged the horses forward, and she leaned into him, his strength and protection. This was the man with whom she had fallen in love, the man who made her feel safe and whole, protected and cherished. The man who loved her not because of her royalty but in spite of it.

She closed her eyes, wearing a smile.

Anton said nothing as they drove past the monastery, the cemetery, and finally into a field south of the grounds.

"I saw this place while looking out of the parapets in the chapel." He helped Olga from the carriage, then carried a blanket and a bucket of food across an open field thick with wildflowers. The sound of the rushing river beckoned.

They reached a rocky tumble of boulders. Olga peered over the edge. Ten feet down, the river flowed fresh and inviting. "After we eat, I'll help you down. The water is quite refreshing."

He spread out a blanket and helped her onto it, and she sat, leaning back on her arms, her head thrown back to the sunshine as he pulled out crusty rolls, milk, and farmer's cheese. "Wait here," he said with a twinkle in his beautiful eyes and rose, walking out into the field. As she watched, he began to gather wildflowers, glancing now and again toward her. She watched him work, his wide back, his sure steps, gallant in his efforts to create for her a fine table.

She didn't hear the scuff of feet on the rocks until a body stood over her, a man's long shadow shading her eyes. She blinked at him, shock filling her throat, tightening her chest. Recognition felt like ice over her, chilling her to the bone.

"Gleb? Is that you?" She remembered her cousin as a rascal, a playful man who had captured her heart—and the hearts of many others—with his sly smile, his mysterious dark eyes, his strong arms that could toss the grand duchesses into the Black Sea and make them squeal with delight.

Now he wore an unkempt long beard, his hair also long about his face and neck. Dressed in a pair of wool pants and a grimy blouse, he looked nothing like the man she had once dreamed of marrying.

Certainly not the hero Anton had become.

"Hello, Your Highness," Gleb said. One side of his mouth cranked up. "You're a difficult lady to track down."

Olga drew in a breath, frowning. "I—I'm not sure what you're talking about. I'm Oksana. . .Mistress Olga's chambermaid."

He laughed. Harsh and sharp, it cut through the facade and spiked fear through her. "Hardly. I don't think any chambermaid would escape the palace with a million rubles' worth of jewels sewn into her corset, do you?"

She swallowed hard, her breath escaping.

He crouched next to her, his breath hot and ugly on her face. "It is so, so very good to see you."

CHAPTER EIGHTEEN

This must be what heaven felt like. Anton moved among the strawflowers and the honeysuckle, picking handfuls for his princess.

Really, his princess. He'd married a princess, and they were going to live happily ever after. He laughed to himself.

Olga screamed. The sound went through him like a spear. He whirled. His breath left him at the sight of a man standing over her. Sunlight glinted off something in his hand.

A knife?

No! After all this time, someone had tracked them down? Questions blinded him as he dropped the flowers. "Olga!"

The man who stood over her looked like one of the out-of-work Bolsheviks hanging around the Soviet buildings or protesting. Disheveled, with long scraggly hair and the demeanor of too many nights on the street, he grabbed Olga and yanked her to her feet.

Even from twenty paces away, Anton could see pain flash across her face. "Leave her alone!"

"Stay back!" The assailant put his hand around Olga's pretty neck, pulling her toward himself. He aimed the knife at her stomach. "Stay back!"

Anton stopped, nearly tripping, holding up his hands

in surrender. "Just let her go. Whatever you want, you can have it."

"I want the grand duchess, Monk. And her jewels."

Anton went cold. "You're mistaken then, man. This is but a poor woman married to a peasant." He fought to keep his voice steady, honest.

The man huffed, shook his head. He tightened his grip on Olga's neck, and she cried out. "Gleb! That hurts!"

She knew him. Anton's breath caught as Timofea's words flashed through his mind. *Yulia knew her attacker. Someone from the palace.*

"You're the one who raped Yulia."

Gleb narrowed his eyes, the barest hint of truth. "Don't move, or the grand duchess and her baby die."

Anton shook his head, took a step back, his brain whirring. He watched as Gleb pushed Olga forward, not gently, toward the carriage parked at the far end of the field. Gleb eyed Anton, the knife at Olga's belly.

Anton stood there, his adrenaline spiking, barely resisting his nearly animalist urge to lunge at the man. Breathing hard, he balled his hands into fists, every nightmare screaming at him.

Lord, help me! I don't know—

Olga tripped. Crying out, she fell forward.

Anton roared, diving at Gleb. The man turned, shock on his face, a second before Anton took him down, reflexes driving him as he fought to get ahold of the man's wrist. "Run, Olga!"

Gleb swiped at him, cuffing him at the head. The blow centered Anton, bringing him back to wrestling matches with Jonas. He grabbed Gleb around the throat, tightened as he reached for the knife.

Gleb twisted, swearing at him. Anton couldn't hear Olga and hoped she was running to the monastery for safety. "Drop the knife!"

Gleb's face turned red. He kneed Anton. His grip loosened, and Gleb followed with another blow to his temple. His head rang, a black stripe of death across his vision. Then Gleb kneed him again, and he jerked forward.

Gleb rolled, ripping his arm free from Anton's grip. Now on his back, Anton grabbed at him, but Gleb had blood in his eyes. He lunged at Anton. Anton barely deflected the knife as it skimmed his cheek. He sent the heel of his hand into Gleb's jaw, heard a satisfying *ugh*!

Gleb fell back, kicking at him as he landed in the grass. Anton leaped toward him, fury in his veins.

Enraged, Gleb roared and leaped, slicing at him.

White-hot pain dissected Anton's every thought, took his breath as Gleb plunged the knife into his side, scraping across his rib cage. Anton gasped, a sound coming from him like he'd never heard before. He dropped to the ground, breathing hard, clutching his wound. Blackness washed across his gaze.

Gleb climbed to his feet, standing over him, breathing hard.

"Anton!"

Olga's voice jerked Anton's attention. She lay in the grass, one bloody hand over her womb.

Olga!

Gleb turned toward his prey. Took a step.

Anton kicked his feet out from under him.

Gleb hit the ground hard. And didn't move. His eyes

were wide, blinking at Anton as his mouth opened. Then a sick sound leaked out, the sound of despair and horror, not unlike how Anton felt.

Anton got to his feet, forced himself past the pain and to Olga's side. She lay breathing hard, her face white.

"The baby."

Anton bent down and scooped her up, the pain in his side nearly blinding him. Then he ran, without looking behind him, to the monastery.

He began calling for Timofea before he reached the gates. Another monk opened the door, and Anton charged into the compound, gasping. No doubt he'd lost a lot of blood, but not compared to Olga, who lay nearly still in his arms. "I need a doctor. Now!"

The young monk gave Olga one look and raced out of the gate, hopefully toward Uncle Maxim's house. Anton could taste fear in the expressions of the monks who came running from the chapel or the kitchen.

"Lay her down."

"We need bandages."

"What about the baby?"

"Timofea!" Anton waded through the monks straight for his cell, striding down the long hallway with a trail of robed monks behind him.

Timofea met him at the stairs, his face a mask of horror. "What happened?"

"She's been stabbed. I think it was the same man who attacked Yulia." He brushed past Timofea, fighting past a wave of weakness, and kicked open his cell door. "He's in the field. I don't know if he's dead or not." Anton laid her down on a cot. So much blood. It saturated her dress, dropped off his arms, and staggered him. His legs buck-led, and he fell onto the floor. "He knew her, Timofea. He knew it was Olga."

Timofea grabbed him up by the back of his robe. "We'll find him. Are you hurt?"

"I'm fine. But Olga needs a doctor."

Timofea took her hand, closed his eyes.

That's right; pray, Timofea. Because in the end, all we can do is trust the Lord.

Anton crawled to her, near her head. "Olga, please don't die."

She opened her eyes, gave him a pained look. "Save our baby, Anton." Tears ran down her cheeks. "Just save our baby."

No. Please, God, I want Olga. And our child. Our family.

"Where is she?" Uncle Maxim strode into the room, winded, carrying his bag of supplies, followed by the young monk.

Anton stood. The room swayed slightly. "Thank you, Maxim. Help us, please."

Uncle Maxim knelt beside her, and as Timofea closed the door, he opened her dress and examined the wound. "We need to operate. Right now. Get the baby out."

What? Anton felt light-headed. He glanced at Olga, whose breath seemed to hiccup in and out.

"How?" Had he said that? He felt like he could barely breathe, let alone speak. Or maybe Timofea had. He pounced to his feet.

"A cesarean section. It's risky, but otherwise they could both die. I have enough anesthesia, but this is hardly the right—"

"Do it. Now." Anton stood over his wife, watching the blood flow from her. "Save my wife, Doctor."

Maxim gave him a grim look, then nodded.

Anton had helped his father birth horses and the occasional cow. He had seen him pull out the animals by the hooves or by the head. But he felt light-headed and ill watching Maxim sedate Olga, who stared at Anton with wide, scared eyes as Uncle Maxim put a needle the length of his forefinger into his wife's abdomen. "I have ether if you would prefer—"

"No! Just hurry," Olga said, groaning.

The wall held Anton up as Maxim opened Olga's womb. She groaned, sweat dripping off her forehead. She held his hand, crushing his knuckles. He wiped her face with a cloth.

Then Maxim extracted a baby. A girl. Bloodied, perhaps even wounded. Anton couldn't tell, only that she was blue.

She didn't move, didn't breathe, and Maxim placed her on the table, cleaning her throat, then spanking her. Again. Again.

Timofea prayed aloud. Olga wept.

Please, God, please, was all Anton could manage.

And then, crying. A startled shriek of pain that filled his chest with joy.

Olga gasped. "Is she alive?"

"For now." Maxim bundled her in the blanket Anton had slept in. "But she's injured. From what I can see, she's been stabbed. The wound could be close to her heart. We need to take her to the orphanage. They have the closest medical facility equipped to handle a tiny infant like this."

He handed the baby to Timofea, who moved to leave.

Anton blocked the door. "No. I want to see her first. And Olga must see her."

Timofea looked at Maxim, who gave the barest of nods.

Anton took the baby in his arms. The blanket had begun to soak up the blood, and the baby screamed, wriggling in his arms, her face screwed up in agony. His eyes filled, and he didn't care that tears ran down his face. "Oh, little one. Please live." Despite her wounds, she was perfect, with blue eyes and the finest tufting of hair. "A daughter."

"Anton, I must take her."

Anton glanced at Maxim, who was stitching Olga's womb. Then he knelt beside Olga, holding the baby at her head. "See your daughter, Olga."

She turned her head, reaching out, touching the baby's head. "She's beautiful, Anton. She's a princess."

Anton nodded, unable to speak.

"Anton, I must. . ." Timofea came close, holding out his arms. His heart tearing in half, Anton transferred his daughter into the arms of the monk.

"Hurry," he whispered. "Run." Timofea met his eyes, nodding.

Anton leaned against the wall, his head spinning as Timofea left the room. He felt weak, and every breath felt like razors in his chest. Kneeling next to Olga, he couldn't watch as Maxim stitched her up. Instead, he cupped his hands on either side of her face, kissed her forehead. "I'm so proud of you."

She smiled weakly, then closed her eyes. "A daughter. What shall we call her, Anton?"

"We will carry her with us across the sea to a new life. Maybe we should name her Marina, for she will be our little sea maiden. Do you like the name?"

She gave the barest of nods. "Marina Klassen. I like it."

He pressed his lips to her head, feeling the energy run from him. He sat back on the floor, the room spinning. Leaning his head against the wall of the cell, he closed his eyes.

Tired. He felt so tired. And what about Gleb? Had he died? What if he came after—

"You're bleeding!"

Anton opened his eyes, barely able to focus on Maxim, who knelt beside him. A pool of blood at his feet betrayed the truth.

Without preamble, Maxim reached out and examined Anton's cloak, finding the hole, then ripping it open. "You've been stabbed!"

Anton nodded, leaning his head back. "I'm okay."

But the world was already closing in on him. He heard Olga's voice, panicked as she called his name, Maxim yelling for help.

He slumped over into Maxim's arms as the light snuffed out.

❦

Everything inside her ached right down to her toes. Olga came awake to a wash of pain. Daylight streamed through the window, turned the cell walls to amber. She groaned, and someone moved toward her, put a cloth over her forehead.

"Anton?"

A sigh drew her gaze, and she saw Yulia sitting beside

her, fatigue on her face. "No, Your Highness." She gave a wan smile. "How are you feeling?"

Olga searched the room. "Where's Anton?"

"Shh. . .you should be resting." Yulia took the cloth from her head. "You have had a fever. Three days now. But Uncle Maxim gave you some medicine, and your fever is down. You will need to be ready to travel by tomorrow morning."

"Travel?"

Yulia nodded, but Olga noticed she did not meet her eyes. "To America. Like you planned."

She'd planned to be with Anton. Wherever he took her. She tried to push herself up, but pain shot through her body, turning her inside out. "Where is Anton?"

Yulia got up, turned away, walked to the window, and stared out.

Olga felt a rush of panic so sharp she gasped. *No.*

"Where is Anton, Yulia?"

She saw Yulia's shoulders sag. She gave a tiny shake of her head.

No.

Olga's breath came in hiccups, grief smothering her, thick and heavy. *No.* "I don't understand. He was fine. He was here, holding the baby—the baby."

Yulia turned, tears running down her cheeks, off her jaw. "I'm sorry. Maxim took her to the orphanage hospital. They have so few supplies there. . . . Olga, you must listen to me. Timofea has booked your passage, First Class, on a train for France. It's the quickest route out of Russia. You will be on it under a doctor's care, who is traveling under Anton's name." She took Olga's hands, pressing them together. "You must leave, Your Highness."

"Wait. Stop. Listen to me. Anton was here. He was fine."

Yulia shook her head. "Gleb stabbed him, Olga. He lost so much blood bringing you here." She closed her eyes. "Timofea told me just hours ago. They buried him. In the community plot near Pskov."

Disbelief had Olga by the throat. *What? No.* "Anton can't be dead. He promised to protect me." He had promised to love her. Cherish her.

Be her husband. They were going to America together! She couldn't leave Russia without him, without her family. Alone?

"I can't leave." Her voice broken, grief taking her apart in gulps. "I can't leave. . .not without Anton, not without my baby. . . ."

"Anton is not here." Yulia tightened her grip on Olga's hands, her expression strained. "You must be brave now for all of Russia."

Olga's eyes went wide, confusion cutting through her grief. "What? I. . .don't understand."

"I know. But you must trust me. Gleb got away. He's been looking for you since you left the palace." She turned away, her face pale. "He's the one who came after us at Borovsky's. It's my fault, all of it." She wrapped her arms around herself, trembling. "I told him that we were going away, not to worry because the grand duchess would be safe." Her tears fell heavily, crippling her voice. "He and I—I thought he loved me." She swiped at her tears as Olga stared at her, mute with horror. "I'm so sorry, Your Highness. I never thought. . . If there were some way to make it up to you, if I could give my life for yours. . ."

Olga opened her mouth, breathing hard through the knot of emotions in her chest. Barely able to catch her breath. Yulia had betrayed her?

But by the look of grief on her face, Yulia had already paid dearly for her mistake. Olga stared at her, furious, unable to speak. Yulia covered her face and sobbed. "You must leave Russia before Gleb returns. I do not know what will become of you now that. . .that. . ." She looked up and shook her head. "Olga, they killed them. Lenin killed your family."

"What?" Olga whimpered, feeling numb, or just wishing she might be. "Dead?"

"Please, my lady. Listen to me. You must leave Russia."

Olga stared at the wall, shaking. "They killed them? Maria? Alexei? Anastasia?" No. They wouldn't kill her family, would they? But she'd been hearing such rumors in the wind for nearly a year, and something deep inside knew.

She opened her mouth. A moan left her. "What will I do now?"

Yulia's silence spoke volumes, speared her right through the heart. She had no one. No one left to protect her. To love her. Her grief bubbled out into a wail, and she turned to the wall and sobbed.

CHAPTER NINETEEN

I t felt surreal. As if it all might be ending the same way it began. With Yulia packing her bags, dressing her in her travel garments, covering her face and hair with a wig. She felt drained, hopeless, and hollow.

Alone.

Olga let her chambermaid dress her, let her help her from the bed, leaned on her as they shuffled out of the monastery quarters and to a waiting carriage. Outside, the smells of summer still ladened the air, flowers and sunshine, field grass turning deep jade. Chickens clucked in their pens, and sounds of hammer against metal brought to mind Anton's practiced swing. His arms around her.

She thought she might collapse and reached out to catch the carriage. Yulia helped her inside and nodded to the driver. Every creak of the carriage made her ache, and she knew she might never heal. Not really.

They turned toward Pskov. Yulia told her she'd be taking a train. She didn't relish the long hours ahead, alone to ponder all she had lost.

All God had taken from her.

She had been such a fool to trust in Him. Such a fool to believe He had given her a new start. She felt anger like a hot ball inside her, and it seemed it might be the only thing keeping her alive.

"I want to stop by his grave." She had been fighting scenarios all night—the dreams that came to her of Anton alive, his smile finding her soul, sweeping her into his arms, telling her that everything was okay, that they would have more children. In her dreams, she wove her hands into his thick blond hair and let him kiss her. Really kiss her like the night at the farm.

The night she had found out exactly what it felt like to be a princess. A woman charmed by the man who loved her.

"I don't know if that is a good idea."

"I asked to be taken to his grave, Yulia." She used a tone that felt unfamiliar. But if she were to survive alone, perhaps she needed to remember just who she was. Olga Nikolaevna Romanova, the last surviving member of the Romanov family.

She lifted her chin and leveled a commanding look at Yulia. The chambermaid lowered her eyes and nodded.

They'd spoken little about Yulia's betrayal. Olga didn't know what to say, knowing that Yulia felt Olga's grief to her marrow. She had wept bitterly alongside Olga until both seemed wrung dry.

After all, Yulia knew what it felt like to lose a child.

Olga reached out, took Yulia's hand in hers. She didn't look at her. Could not. For now, that would have to be enough.

They rode in silence to the cemetery, Olga finally leaning on Yulia's shoulder as fatigue wore her down. The grounds seemed a quiet place as they pulled in, shaded by a grove of oak and poplar. The trees made the glen cool, sheltering the graves. Their driver pulled up, then helped

Olga down. She leaned on Yulia as they made their way to the freshly dug grave.

Somehow she thought that seeing his grave would give her finality, would help her accept Anton's death. But seeing the marker only made her cover her mouth, holding in a cry.

Klassen. Anton Klassen. She felt the truth slash through her. Her child had been a dream, something alive but ethereal. A hope, perhaps. But Anton had been her breath, the very real example of God's touch in her life. How could she possibly live without him? She walked over to the marker, leaned against it.

"Yulia, please fetch my camera."

Yulia gave her only the slightest frown before she left to find the folding camera. She returned.

"Please give it to the monk. I'd like a picture." She tried a smile, but the grief inside held her fast. Instead, she leaned on the grave, taking off her cloak. She felt as if refinement only made a mockery of the life they'd lived. The short, happy life.

Yulia leaned on the opposite side as the monk fumbled with the camera and finally snapped the picture. So many happy moments inside that lens. Olga wasn't sure if she could bear to look at them, to develop them. But should the day ever come, she wanted to remember this place.

The place where she buried all her happily-ever-afters.

Yet the place where they had all begun. The place where God had invaded her life and told her that even in darkness, she could yet hope. That out of the most unlikely of heroes, she might find a prince. And even if for a short time, she might know what it felt like to love and be loved.

What it felt like to carry inside her the embodiment of that love.

She closed her eyes, clinging to the feelings that had for so long kept her alive. Love. God's love through Anton.

No, maybe she wouldn't live the happily-ever-after she had always dreamed of, hoped for. But without God, who did she have? *"The Lord is good. His love endures forever."*

" *'Now faith is the substance of things hoped for, the evidence of things not seen.' Hold on to your faith, Olga. With it, you have everything. But without it, you'll have nothing."* Her mother's voice, on the eve of Olga's departure from the life at Tsarkoe Selo. She closed her eyes, longing for the faith of her mother, the faith of her husband. She had two choices. To walk into her new life with God. . .or alone. She wiped her cheeks, remembering her prayer not so long ago, her willingness to trust God. With Anton.

And now, without him. But still to trust God.

"We need to look to the future—sometimes to the next generation—but we can believe in Him." Anton's steady voice filled her mind, soothing. Calm.

She might not have Anton, but she had his words and the memories. Even, perhaps, his faith. And she wouldn't surrender them for even one night in her bed at Tsarskoe Selo.

Maybe faith right now wasn't a feeling but a decision. To put one foot ahead of the other. "I'm ready," she said in a voice she barely recognized. Yulia helped her to the carriage. They pulled away, Olga refusing to look back.

The train had already arrived at the station, the creosote and oil bathing her nose in acrid smells, turning her stomach as she drew near. She spied Timofea waiting near the door of the station, and he came out to meet the carriage, his face grim. He said nothing as, ever so slowly, he helped her down. Yulia followed, looping Olga's arm around her shoulders.

Timofea reached for Olga's bags, then led them through the station and to the platform. The line of green coaches with gold lettering made her think of their family's royal coach with the velvet seats, the private dining cars serving smoked salmon and caviar.

Or perhaps the train ride she'd taken with Anton as her husband, when she had vowed to free him to take another woman as his wife.

Or finally riding obshye class with the peasants, Anton's watchful presence only feet away after the aftermath of his family's murder.

Hopefully this would be the last train she'd ever ride. She made that vow to herself as she hugged Yulia.

"I'm so sorry, mistress," Yulia said softly as she clung to Olga.

Olga closed her eyes, willing herself to forgive. "Go in peace, Yulia," she said softly. Yulia's eyes filled, and emotion clogged Olga's throat. "Yulia," she said, "God promised my Anton that He was good and His love would endure forever, that His faithfulness would continue through all generations." She squeezed Yulia's hands. "I have to believe that the Almighty alone knows what plans He has, and He will carry us, you and me, to this future."

Yulia nodded, wiping away her tears. "God be with you, mistress," she said as she gave Olga a final embrace.

Olga turned away, waiting for Timofea, who had already entered the railcar to stow her luggage.

He came down the stairs. Then, with a strength that took her breath away, he swept her into his arms and carried her up the stairs.

He put her down, steadying her, at the top. Then he looked at her and smiled. "I remember when you married Anton. He told me that God had given you a verse."

She nodded, grief fisting her heart. " 'For the Lord is good; his mercy is everlasting; and his truth endureth to all generations.' " Her voice emerged broken despite her efforts to keep it steady. Oh, how she wanted to believe that. *Help me believe, Lord!*

Timofea wrapped his arm around her waist, helping her into the car. She noticed that he'd secured for her a place in the first-class car, probably a private berth, one with only two bunks. At least she'd have privacy as she recuperated. He stopped before the door. "God hasn't left you, Olga. And He never will."

Timofea opened the door.

Olga stood in the hall, everything inside her turning weak.

Anton looked up from his seat on the bunk. He smiled at her, slow and sweet. "Hello, Oksana."

Anton.

She reached out to catch herself on the door frame and instead launched herself into his arms. He caught her up, holding her tight. Anton. Alive, strong, and breathing. "Anton."

Tears washed her eyes as she clung to him.

Anton tucked her close, quieting her. "I know. I'm so sorry."

"As am I." Timofea said. Olga turned and met Timofea's

sad gaze. "I felt that Yulia could not know. For your protection, we had to continue with the ruse." He handed her a passport. "Your new identity. I hope you will consent again to the name Oksana."

She opened the passport, read her new name. Oksana Petrova. Yulia's family name. Timofea's name. It seemed fitting. They both seemed like family now. "I shall bear it with pride for the one who gave her life for mine, and with honor to you and Yulia, who have given this name a heritage of faith."

Timofea gave her the slightest bow, a smile tipping his lips at her words. "May God go with you."

She shook her head, unable to speak. Then she looked at her husband. "Anton. I thought—"

"Shh. I know what you thought. I'm so sorry." He looked it, too, grief in his tear-rimmed eyes. "I felt like a murderer watching Timofea bury Gleb, especially when he erected a headstone with my name. He even devised the plan to deceive you, as much as I hated it. But we both agreed that other members of the royal family or servants who knew about the ruse might track you down and kill you for your jewels or simply because you could bear one last heir to the throne." His expression betrayed his grief. "I am so sorry about your family, Olga. But I can't deny the relief I feel that you weren't with them."

He cupped his hand to her face. "I know I must have scared you when I attacked Gleb. Perhaps, finally, I've figured out what bravery is—putting someone above myself. Perhaps true courage isn't about taking up arms at all. . .but in serving the ones I pledged to love."

Tears filled his eyes. "I gladly would have died if our

little Marina had lived." His jaw tightened, and he pulled her tight. She heard his heartbeat in his chest and clung to him. The thought choked her, burning her throat, filling her eyes. They wouldn't have time to hold her, to say good-bye, having to trust Maxim to find a place to bury her. She tightened her arms around Anton, and she heard him suck in a breath.

She looked up at him. "You're hurt."

"I'll live." He tucked his finger under her chin, tilting her head up. "Will you?"

She nodded, feeling a new hope underlying her sadness. "Now I will."

She heard Timofea leave, and a part of her wanted to reach out, to tell him that—

She stepped away from Anton. "Timofea, wait. My camera—I want a picture."

Timofea stopped, turned, his face dark. He shook his head. "I–I'll need your camera, Oksana." He stepped closer, his voice lowered. "What if someone should find it? Link you to your family?"

She stared at him, a cold horror rooting through her. She had pictures of Alexei, of Maria and Tatiana on that film. But. . .no. . .she put a hand to her chest, shaking her head. "No, Timofea, please don't—"

"Olga." Anton's gentle voice cut through her agony. "You will always have them. In your heart. Let it go, *maya doragaya*. I, too, left behind my memories, my journal, at the monastery chapel. It can only incriminate us should anyone search us. Believe me, it is a new beginning for us, and we'll trust in God's enduring love and promises to create new memories."

She closed her eyes and felt his hands on her shoulders, steadying her. It took all her courage to allow Timofea to take the camera from her bag. "May God keep you and bless you," he said as he edged out.

Anton drew her farther into the compartment and held her in his strong arms. The whistle blew, and they felt the train jerk.

Anton stepped back from her, searching her eyes a moment before he lowered himself to kiss her. Sweetly. With a bittersweet taste that pushed tears to her eyes. "I know this isn't the life of a princess you'd hoped for. But I hope to make you happy, someday."

She leaned away from him, caught in the peace of being with him, finally. Her husband. The man who loved her in sickness and health. In richness and poverty. . . . She smiled. They had each other. And they had God's promises to Anton and, someday, to all his generations.

She ran her hand along his stubbled cheek, already feeling healing taking root in her heart. "I'm not a princess anymore, Anton."

He closed the compartment door behind them, locked it, then gathered her again into his arms. He smiled, his gaze sweet despite the sadness, and lowered his forehead to hers. "Yes, you are, Olga," he said softly a moment before he kissed her. "You'll always be a princess to me."

The day seemed too beautiful to serve as the backdrop to so much sorrow. Birds sang, the fresh smells of summer ladened the breeze, and the sun warmed Timofea's face as he drove Yulia and himself back to Pechory after sending his brother monk home to the monastery. Timofea wanted to be alone with his sister. The sunshine that broke through the darkness each morning seemed a fitting analogy to faith in God's goodness in the midst of sorrow; why it was possible for those who believed in God to endure heartbreak. Only by believing in who God said He was and trusting in God's goodness and love in the midst of all the darkness would Anton and Olga—now Oksana—know their happily-ever-after.

God is good, and His love endures forever. Timofea lifted his face to the blue sky, seeing beyond the tufts of clouds to the endless beyond that God held in the cup of His hand. Anton and Olga would endure, heal, and find new happiness. He believed God's words for them. For himself. For Russia.

Even for Yulia, who sat beside him, tears running unhindered down her face. He knew she blamed herself for Olga's trauma, the loss of her child. Despite Olga's words of peace, Yulia seemed broken by her suffering, her guilt.

O God of heaven, please heal your servant Yulia. Timofea

put his arm around his sister in an unfamiliar gesture. She leaned into him as she had in their youth at the deathbed of their mother and when their father had sent her away to the palace. His heart twisted for all she'd endured alone.

"With you working at the orphanage, Yulia, we must see each other more often." His words sounded feeble.

Yulia looked at him, her brown eyes glistening. "What's to become of me, Tim? I have failed Him. I have betrayed my mistress. I have lost Boris. There is nothing left for me."

He felt bereft for her, pain rising up to fill his throat. He took her hand. "Believe in God, sister. He does have a plan for you. I know it in my heart. Trust Him."

She nodded but didn't bother to wipe her tears.

They rode in silence through Pechory toward the orphanage. The sun glinted off the golden onion domes of the monastery, and he heard the afternoon prayer bells chiming.

They pulled up to the building, and Timofea helped Yulia down from the carriage. Children played in the yard, their voices happy. "You have a life here, Yulia. For now. God will see to the rest."

He opened the gate and escorted her inside, smiling when a child ran up to him with a dandelion in her chubby grip. One of the attendants met Yulia in the yard, her wide, lined face framed by a white scarf.

"I am so glad you're back. I just transferred a new foundling from the hospital wing to the nursery, and she needs feeding. She's in your unit."

Her words nudged Timofea's heart. "See, Yulia?"

She gave him a sad smile.

The woman turned to Timofea, bowing slightly. "Your prayers were answered."

His expression must have betrayed his question.

"The foundling is the one you brought to us," she said in explanation, shaking her head. "She lived."

He felt his chest tighten, all breath leaving him. He opened his mouth, but nothing came out.

Next to him, Yulia covered her mouth, her eyes wide. "Oh no."

He closed his mouth, silenced Yulia with a look. "Can I see her?"

"Of course."

He followed Yulia and the woman into the nursery. Bundled like packages, four babies lay side by side in a long, troughlike crib. She picked up one and handed it to Yulia.

Her little mouth opened as if hoping for food, and then she broke out into a healthy wail. Yulia cradled her, shushing her gently.

"Why weren't we told? We sent word inquiring about her, and they told us she had died."

The woman's expression betrayed confusion. "I don't know. Perhaps. . . Yes, well, we had a child who died. Fever. But this is the one you brought to us. I'm sure of it." She reached over and unwrapped her swaddling. "Yes, see?" Timofea saw stitches dissecting the baby's perfect shoulder. "The wound wasn't serious, but she had so much water in her lungs, she ran a high fever, and we feared infection. We kept her in isolation until just today."

Timofea put a hand over his eyes, feeling weak.

"What shall we do?" Yulia said softly.

The Lord is good, and His love endures forever. His faithfulness continues through all generations.

Timofea turned to Yulia, feeling peace fill his chest. "I believe you have a new charge, Yulia." He reached out and ran his finger along Marina's soft skin. "Perhaps God is calling you to continue your duty to Him and all of Russia."

Yulia's eyes widened. She looked at him, then the baby. She closed her eyes and nodded. "By His strength, I will."

The attendant stared at both of them, confusion on her face.

"When it is time, when God tells me, I will find Oksana. The family will be restored. Until then, you've been given a sacred trust, my sister. Keep it in faith." He put one hand on Yulia, the other on Marina, and closed his eyes. "Bless them and keep them, Lord, under Your hand, by Your power, in Your love, in this generation and in the generations to come."

AUTHORS' NOTE

This is a story of "what if," not "as was"—not a chronicle of history but a fictional parallel to historic events. In all likelihood, the real-life grand duchess Olga Nikolaevna Romanova died with her family in the Yekaterinburg cellar of the house where they spent the last three months of their captivity. However, many rumors and theories abound concerning the purported escape plans hatched to save the tsar and his family.

The characters in this story, both those created solely in the writers' minds and those based on actual historical figures, represent the authors' flight of fancy and are never intended to cast aspersions or reflect negatively in any way on persons living or dead.

For more on the

HEIRS of ANTON

read:

Marina

Nadia

Ekaterina

also from Barbour Publishing

SUSAN K. DOWNS

Susan served as the Russian adoption program coordinator for one of America's oldest adoption agencies prior to her decision to leave the social work field and devote herself full time to writing and editing fiction. Through her adoption work, however, she developed a love for all things Russian and an unquenchable curiosity about Russian history and culture.

A series of miraculous events led Susan and her minister-husband to adopt from Korea two of their five children. The adoptions of their daughters precipitated a five-year mission assignment in South Korea, which, in turn, paved the way for Susan's work in international adoption and her Russian experiences. The Downses currently reside in Canton, Ohio. Read more about Susan's writing/editing ministry and her family at www.susankdowns.com.

SUSAN MAY WARREN

Susan and her family recently returned home after working for eight years in Khabarovsk, Far East Russia. Deeply influenced and blessed by the faith of the Russian Christians, she longed to write a story that revealed their faith during their dark years of persecution and a story of their impact on today's generation. The Heirs of Anton series is the fruition of these hopes. Now writing full time in northern Minnesota while her husband, Andrew, manages a lodge, Susan is the author of both novels and novellas. She draws upon her rich experience on both sides of the ocean to write stories that stir the Christian soul. Find out more about Susan and her writing at www.susanmaywarren.com.